Other Books by Jane Ann McLachlan

Historical Fiction:

The Sorrow Stone
The Lode Stone
The Whetstone

The Girl Who Would Be Queen
The Girl Who Tempted Fortune
The Queen Who Sold Her Crown

Science Fiction and Fantasy:

Walls of Wind
The Occasional Diamond Thief
The Salarian Desert Game
Midsummer Night Magicians

Memoir:

IMPACT: A Memoir of PTSD

Creative Writing:

Downriver Writing: The Five-Step Process for Outlining Your Novel

The Girl Who Would Be Queen

Jane Ann McLachlan

ISBN: 978-1-7774996-3-1

Cover Design by Heather from Expert Subjects
Formatting by Chris Morgan from Dragon Realm Press
www.dragonrealmpress.com

For my sister, Linda

"she is my sister: a bond that can never be broken."
~ p. 234

The Angevin Line in the Kingdom of Naples from Charles I to Joanna and Maria

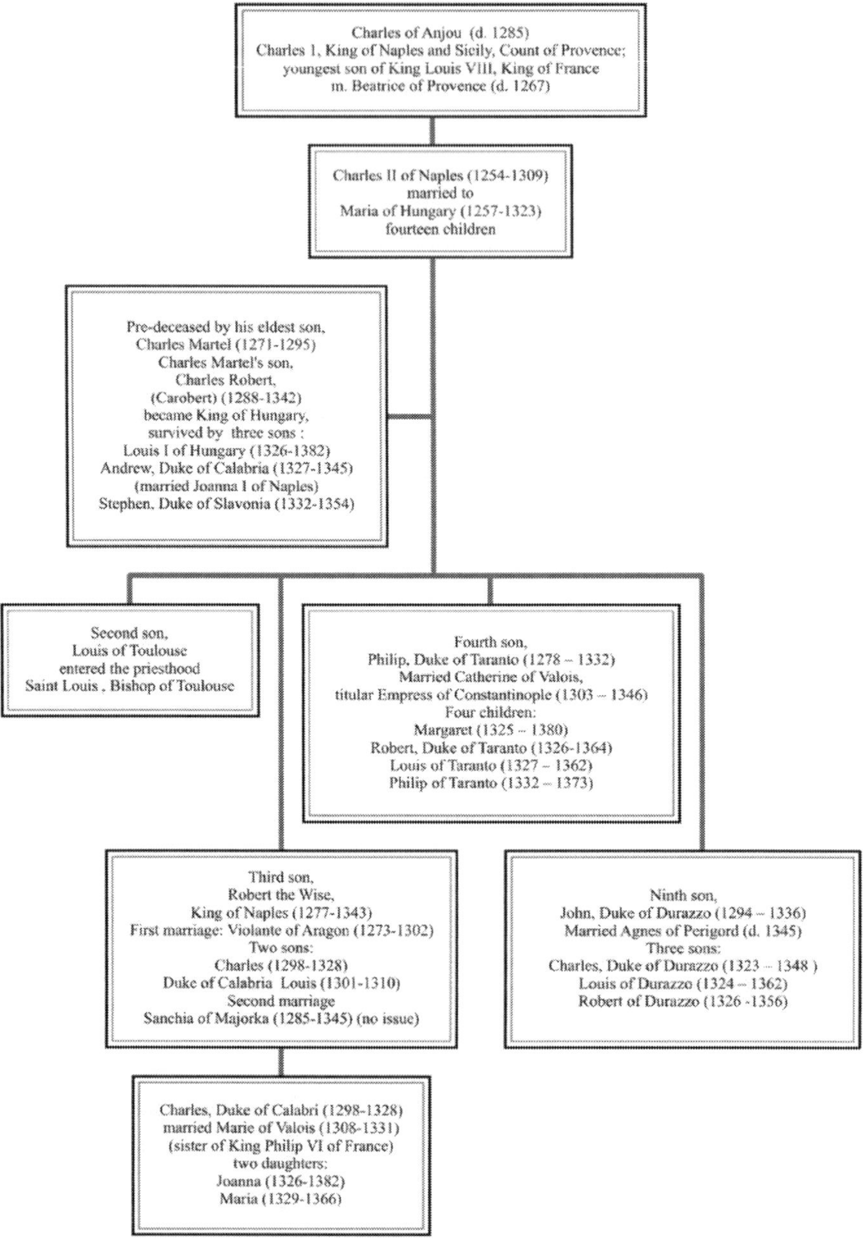

CONTENTS

Chapter 1

A Christmas Masque

Naples, 1342

"A masque!" I echo my sister's words with delight. The ladies-in-waiting gathered around us in our presence chamber—gathered around my sister Joanna, actually—laugh at my excitement, but I do not care. I love a masque! "Will there be a theme?"

The last time Joanna arranged a masque we disguised ourselves as creatures in our royal menagerie. I received the marker with 'zebra' written on it. I like the little zebras with their wide, gentle eyes and striped markings, but I had hoped to come as a parrot. They are so beautiful with their brilliant plumage, what a costume it would make! I had already learned to mimic their funny, scratchy voices, asking for treats and singing songs for us. But my sister gave that marker to our older cousin, Marguerite of Taranto, who did not even try to sound like a parrot when she spoke. Joanna herself came as a tiger. Quite by coincidence Marguerite's brother, our handsome cousin Louis of Taranto, also received the tiger marker. Their older brother Robert came in a lion mask. He expected Joanna to come as the lioness, and was furious to see her matched with Louis, which made me giggle. Robert's and Louis' competition for Joanna's attention is constant. She smiles at them both, although I know she secretly favors Louis. I hope she has thought up something equally fun for this Christmas masque.

"The theme will be…" she waits, enjoying our suspense as we hang on her words, "…the ballad of Tristan and Isolde."

I am not the only one who gasps. That is not a Christmas story at all. Yesterday, when Joanna arranged a chanteur to sing the ballad for us at the first of our December feasts, many of the older ladies frowned. I was surprised, also—delightfully surprised, for I had never heard the ballad sung, though everyone knows the tale of Tristan and Isolde, who swallowed a love potion and could not escape their forbidden love for each other.

"But Your Royal Highness…" Elisabette, the oldest of our ladies, stammers to a stop as Joanna turns to her.

"Did you not enjoy the chanteur's song, Lady Elisabette?" Joanna asks.

Don't, I think. *Don't let her ruin it!* Already I am desperate to perform this masque. How could anyone not have enjoyed the chanteur's ballad? I listened as one spellbound to the glorious tale of lovers defying everything to be together, and wept in front of everyone as the chanteur sang the final tragic verses. Grandmother Queen Sancia scowled down the table at me. She disapproves of the public display of any emotion other than piety. But Joanna's eyes were moist, too, and many of the other ladies', so I pretended not to notice my Lady Grandmother and wept happily. Is it not wonderful to think two people could love each other as much as Tristan and Isolde?

"Of course I did, Your Highness. Your entertainments are always delightful. It is only… King Robert has many nephews at court, might they not be offended to see a king's nephew betraying his sovereign uncle?"

"Tristan did not seduce Queen Isolde willingly," Lady Marguerite, sister to three of those nephews, says. "The ballad serves as a warning against the perils of potions and spells and demons' magic. Surely that is a message to us all."

I nod as solemnly as the other ladies, but the thought of my handsome young cousins wanting to seduce my Lady Grandmother makes me bite my lip to keep from giggling. Even if she were not ancient, it is no secret that she is too holy even to share her husband King Robert's bed.

"I do not think my honorable cousins will see themselves as Tristan." Joanna's face is solemn, her eyes steady but for a single quick glance at me.

I am overtaken by a fit of coughing. I cover my face, which I know is turning red, my eyes watering. Lady Marguerite fetches me a cup of small ale. I gulp it down. Joanna watches me solicitously as though she was not also fighting the urge to laugh beneath her calm expression.

Marguerite rescues me by asking Joanna to explain her idea for the masque. As my sister describes the tableaux we will portray of the pivotal scenes, while the chanteur sings our parts, my excitement mounts. I can picture it already, how charming we will look, how tragic it will be. I want to leap up and down, and hug myself… but I am a woman of thirteen, it would be unseemly and childish to do so. Still, the urge is so strong I consider going into our bedchamber where I can hop on one foot and twirl with excitement and no one will sigh or call me giddy. But I might miss something. So I sit still and only imagine myself jumping with glee as I listen to Joanna's plans. She will write the tableaux, and we will all have parts—oh! I do want to jump!—and the masks will be large, covering our whole faces, so no one will know who we are. I am breathless with excitement as my sister explains the different parts. Joanna's entertainments are more fun than anything at the grand court in Paris, I am certain of it!

"Who will play Queen Isolde?" Lady Marguerite asks. She is my friend, even though she is older than me. I look hard at her, willing her to suggest a name—my name. She pretends not to notice.

There is a long silence. None of the married ladies wants to play the part of an adulteress in front of her husband, despite Joanna's assurance that no one will know who we are beneath our masks. The unmarried ladies do not want to frighten away suitors with a convincing performance, either.

Prince Louis of Hungary will never know. He is so far away, and besides, he is already contracted to marry me whatever I do. King Louis of Hungary, I correct myself, crowned four months ago after the death of his father, King Carobert. I have been waiting in fear that he would send for me and I would miss the feasts and songs of the Twelve Holy Days of Christmas at our brilliant Neapolitan court, but no summons has come. Even if it arrived tomorrow, I could not be ready now until spring. I smile with satisfaction.

I do not trust Louis' brother, Andrew, but Duke Andrew will be drunk long before we throw off our masks. He will not care anyway, he never pays attention to the entertainments Joanna goes to such trouble to arrange. I open my mouth to volunteer, having waited as long as I dare in order to avoid looking over-eager.

"I will play Isolde, then," Joanna says smoothly, before I can speak. "I understand your loyal reluctance to take the part of the queen, in my court." She smiles around at all of us. Is it my imagination or do her eyes linger on me?

"It is only a masque," I mutter, as though I have been caught out. Trust Joanna to turn the issue from adultery to allegiance. We have all sworn our fealty to her as heir to the throne of Naples; Grandfather had everyone do so as soon as we came to Castle Nuovo, three full years before her marriage to Andrew when she was seven and he was six. I was too young to swear fealty then, but that does not matter. I know my duty to my future queen, even if she is my sister. I have been taught it all my life. Still, I cannot help admiring her subtlety. Now she is taking the part because it is a queen's role. Everyone around me is nodding and smiling, as though she has waved her hand and changed the story. They see her as Isolde the Queen, not Isolde the adulteress.

I wish I could do that. I wish I could make people see me as I want to be seen. But I never think of the right thing to say until it is too late.

Joanna does it naturally. She is the heir to the throne. Always. She wears it like her skin. She is seen as the future queen because that is who she is, at every moment, whatever she is doing or saying; she is always the heir to the throne of Naples.

I will be a queen when I marry. When I marry Louis of Hungary, Joanna will not be greater than I. Our grandparents, King Robert and Queen Sancia, will notice me when I am Queen Maria, and not only when they catch me doing something they do not approve of. That will not matter, then; a queen can do what she wants!

"Marguerite of Taranto and Sancia of Cabannis will be Queen Isolde's ladies-in-waiting," Joanna says. "You will carry letters and tokens between Tristan and Isolde, arranging their trysts." They smile at her, making me wonder if they have already carried similar notes in our court. Elisabette is to be Isolde's disapproving nursemaid. Elisabette frowns. "Perfect!" Joanna cries, as if the old sourface was actually acting the part. One by one, all the best parts are taken, and none of them given to me. I look down at my lap, biting my bottom lip.

When I marry King Louis of Hungary, Joanna will only be married to Duke Andrew, my husband's younger brother. Louis will send for me soon, now that he has come to his throne. I am his assurance that whatever happens to Joanna or Andrew, the kingdoms of Hungary and Naples will be united again under the rule of a grandson of his father, King Carobert of Hungary.

Louis' father called our grandfather, King Robert the Wise, a usurper. King Carobert believed he should have inherited both kingdoms as eldest son of the eldest son of Charles II. But King Charles II gave the Kingdom of Naples to his third son, Robert the Wise, our Lord Grandfather, and gave Hungary to his seven-year-old grandson, Carobert, the only son of his deceased eldest son, Charles Martel. Naples was too important a kingdom to entrust to a child. The trouble began when Carobert grew up and pressed his claim to Naples as well as Hungary. It almost caused a war, both sides arming for battle—I shiver, imagining for a moment the possibility of soldiers fighting in the streets outside our castle!

To forestall that war, King Robert agreed to marry his heir, Joanna, to King Carobert's second son, Andrew, and promised me to King Carobert's heir, his eldest son Louis, thus giving Carobert a son on each throne, Naples and Hungary, and King Robert a granddaughter on each throne. Joanna explained all this to me, for she remembers it; she was seven at the time, but I was only four. "We will be equals when we both marry," she told me grandly.

Equals. I have not even been given a part in the masque. She will never see me as her equal. Even when we are both queens, Joanna will be Queen of Naples, the most renowned court in Europe, outside of Paris. Our royal Grandfather cares about Naples. He is training Joanna to be his heir. My Lord Grandfather does not care at all whether I will be a good queen of Hungary. My only task is to produce an heir if Joanna does not, and thus fulfill the contract that keeps Hungary waiting patiently for Naples, a drooling wolf at our door.

Hungary is a barbaric, uncivilized land, but it is very rich. Well then, I will make it my duty as its queen to introduce learning and culture when I am there, and courtly entertainments. In Hungary, I will be the one giving out the roles in a masque, and keeping the best one for myself. I will be a patron to artists and sculptors and poets. What will my grandparents, who expect so little of me, think of that? I will be known as the queen who brought civilization to Hungary!

"Would you be in charge of costumes, Maria?" my sister asks, scattering my reflections. I look at her, not quite certain I have heard her right. Perhaps it was part of my daydream? But she is looking at me, waiting for an answer.

"Will I have access to the royal wardrobe?"

She nods. "Of course."

I can barely believe it. The royal wardrobe, with its silks and satins covered in jewels and seed pearls, its cloth of gold and silver, its golden, bejeweled belts and girdles. It holds almost as great a portion of the kingdom's wealth as the royal jewels. And I will be in charge of deciding which of its treasures we will—I will—use for our masque! Everyone will have to come to me for their costumes. I will choose colors to suit their roles: dark for those playing the solemn parts, light for those who are innocent, multi-colored for the figures of jest. And when I know who will stand beside whom I will match their outfits subtly, to create a pleasing tableau, and set a mood. Some of the roles may need more than one costume, light and dark shades of the same color...

"Maria?"

"Yes!" I grin at my sister, who knows that I can do this better than anyone. I have an eye for such things. My wonderful sister smiles back at me.

Later, when our ladies have undressed us and gone to their beds, and the boy is building up the fire in our bedchamber, Philippa comes in. Our maids are brushing our hair and our bed has already been turned down, ready for us.

"Mother," Joanna greets her with a smile. I smile without speaking. Joanna may call Philippa 'Mother' if she wants, but I will not. Our royal grandparents gave her the title of our 'surrogate mother' after our real mother—a royal princess, sister of the French King—died when we were barely out of our babyhood.

I blush even now to think how long I called Philippa 'mother'. Two years ago my cousin Robert of Taranto, newly returned to Naples, overheard me say "Yes, Mother," when she called my name. He laughed out loud.

"I thought you were a princess," he said. "But now I learn you are the daughter of a washer-woman, who was herself the daughter of a fisherman."

I was confused by his words but not by his tone or his arrogant laughter. "Our Lord was a fisherman," I replied smartly, changing Lord Robert's sneer into a glare as our other cousins laughed at him, now.

Afterwards, my cousin Charles of Durazzo, who is three full years older than Robert and yet never laughs at me or treats me like a child, explained to me Philippa's background—a village girl chosen by my real grandmother, King Robert's first wife, to wet-nurse her son, who grew up to be my father, when she discovered herself pregnant on campaign with the King.

It is not Philippa's background that upsets me; it is that she let me think she was a grand lady in our court. She acted a part, and I believed it, and made myself foolish doing so.

Joanna shakes her hair loose from her maid's brush and rises to embrace Philippa. I have to force myself not to do the same. Robert does not sneer at Joanna when she calls Philippa 'Mother', oh no. Joanna is the same age as Robert and she is the heir to the throne. Joanna may call a cat 'Mother' and everyone will find it charming, proof of her affectionate heart and humility. Everything is so much easier for Joanna!

Philippa is not my mother, I remind myself. But she has been my nursemaid since I was two. Aside from my sister, she is the only one who loves me. I love her, I cannot deny it, and I cannot stop myself from wanting her affection.

Philippa makes sure that all is ready and sees us into our bed. She strokes my hair back from my forehead before she leaves, as she has always done, and I close my eyes, grateful for the caress. I think she understands. I hope she does. I hope she still thinks of me as her child, even though I cannot—

"Maria." Joanna's whisper breaks the silence in our room.

I open my eyes and roll over. The oil lamps have been tamped off, but the fire still throws enough light for me to see my sister's face. She is grinning. "I have a part for you in the masque," she whispers.

I feel my heart skip. But the parts for ladies have all been given. Unless she has changed her mind. Does she not want to play the part of Isolde after all?

"What is it?" I whisper, hardly daring to hope.

"The most important part."

My breath catches in my throat. I am going to play the beautiful, tragic Queen Isolde! I cannot speak for happiness.

"Without it there is no masque. You must do it," she whispers urgently, mistaking my silence.

"Yes!" I whisper. "Of course, Joanna, I would love—"

"I want you to be the sorceress who sells me the love potion."

Chapter 2

The Sorceress

I do not tell anyone about my part. We have agreed to keep it secret, but I insisted that the sorceress will be rich and young and very beautiful.

"A powerful sorceress can make herself look however she wants to others," Joanna agreed, which is not the same thing at all, but I am mollified by the word "powerful".

The sorceress must wear a dark color, it cannot be helped. I choose a beautiful dark red, my favorite color, which will show off my fair skin and complement my yellow hair when we pull off our masks. It is covered in seed pearls, one of the most glorious gowns in the royal wardrobe. Our grandmother Queen Sancia will complain of the extravagance of refitting such an expensive gown to wear to a masque; the money would be better given to her precious Franciscan friars. I am going to say it was Joanna's idea. Joanna will back me, because I have agreed to play an unwanted part. Then our grandfather King Robert will nod and agree that royalty must put on a good show.

I do not tell the seamstress who works on my gown who it is for. She must refit it without a model, but I have her bring the sides in and tighten the lacing so it will follow a very slender woman's figure.

"My Lady," she objects, timid and stammering, "It will not fit any lady who wishes to wear it." She would like to say that it will not adequately hide a woman's curves, for she is old and obviously not in favor of the newest fashion.

"It is for the masque," I tell her, and instruct her to use the pearls from the discarded cloth for the girdle that will rest low on my hips. Then I shock her further by ordering the neck cut low to expose the top of the breasts. I may be skinny, but I am already beginning to show a woman's curves, and I will be wearing the latest fashion from King Philip VI's court in Paris. This sorceress will bewitch them all!

Joanna chooses a light blue dress for the first set, when Tristan is bringing her, a virgin bride, to Ireland, and a light purple gown for when she is queen. She would have chosen richer colors, but I explain my theme of light shades for the innocent and darker for the villains. She gives me a look—we are both fair and look better in bright colors—but I quickly add that the light blue represents innocence and purity, lest any think Isolde chose her fateful passion. Joanna nods and lets the gown be fit on her for its alterations. When she stands before the dressmaker, I know it does not matter if my gown is the more flattering color or the more stylish cut; Joanna will still outshine me. She is a great beauty, whatever she wears. Fortunately, the perfect oval of her face and that thick yellow hair that shines like gold in the sun will all be hidden behind her mask.

I have all the dresses altered to the new style, but none so daringly as mine.

On the night of the masque, when I put on my beautiful gown assisted only by my maid—whom I have threatened to send away forever from Castle Nuovo and the court of Naples if she ever breathes a word of who is in it—I almost decide not to wear it. It is so tight everyone who looks at me will see… well, they will see me as though I were… well, they will know exactly what I look like. Exactly. And they will still know it, the next time they see me. When I slip the girdle down over my hips it, too, fits snugly, the pearls flashing against the dark red in a way that will draw all eyes down there… I giggle self-consciously. Then I catch my maid's expression and giggle even more, and cannot stop, until I am nearly hysterical and she looks truly alarmed.

"Shall I call one of your ladies, Princess?" she asks.

"No!" I fall into a chair, gasping for control and wiping the tears from my eyes. It is as much nerves as humor that has set me off. How can I wear this gown? I am not so daring as I thought I would be. But what choice do I have? I have only this one gown in the new style. I could wear one of my older gowns, which everyone will recognize and which will look loose and dowdy beside all the stylish costumes I have had refitted for the others. I stand up resolutely. I would rather be too daring than look like one of my Lady Aunts. "Bring the snood," I tell my maid.

To further ensure our anonymity I have had gold satin snoods made for everyone participating in the masque. (Not real cloth of gold, our royal grandparents would never condone that, even for Joanna; it is only gold-colored satin, which is quite expensive enough.) They have been designed not only to hold the lower hair, but to reach right up to the forehead.

"There must not be a single hair showing outside your snood," I told everyone, and Joanna agreed at once, so how could the others object?

They still do not know I am to participate. Margherita is very concerned. She has commiserated with me so often it was almost more than I could do not to tell her. Now, as I stand in my alarmingly tight wine-red gown while my maid gathers my hair and tucks it into the gold snood, I am exceedingly glad I did not tell. I decide not to remove my mask even at the end. I will slip away before the masque is finished, and change into my blue gown, even if it is not in the current fashion, and return to the dance as myself before the others unmask themselves. In fact, I will send a note to my Lady Grandmother, telling her that I am lying down with a sick headache and will come later, when it has passed.

We have agreed to perform the masque in silence, a mummer's play. The chanteur, who has stayed to entertain us all through the season of Yuletide, will sing the appropriate verses for each tableau. Even during the dances between the tableaux, we are forbidden to talk, for our voices would give away our identities.

My maid hands me my mask. I hold it against my face as she ties it securely behind my head. She hands me a glass. I look into it anxiously. The mask is beautiful. I have had the artist paint all the women's faces identical, and do the same for the men, except that he has painted brown hair for the wicked characters and yellow for the good ones. I search the glass for any trace of myself. Will my eyes, peering through the holes, give me away? Joanna and I have always been told we have our father's eyes, but we are not the only blue-eyed ladies in the Neapolitan court. I had the holes in the masks cut small, so it will be difficult to determine the shape of the eyes behind it, and I am satisfied. I smile behind the flawless painted face I see in the looking glass. For once I will be exactly as beautiful as my sister, save for the painted brown hair. That cannot be helped. I will not undo the effect of my tableaux for the sake of vanity. I hand the glass back to my maid. She curtsies, her mouth turned down in disapproval.

"Tell no one who is in this costume," I remind her as I write a quick note. "Take this to Queen Sancia. Tell her maid I have a headache, but it is nothing serious. Then come back and wait in this room for my return. Do not let anyone into my bedchamber while I am at the masque." She curtsies again, looking even more sour.

Joanna can get her maids to do anything, and do it eagerly. They are well-dressed, too, unlike this one. I sigh. I do not have a very big allowance.

"If you do this for me without telling anyone, I will give you my yellow dress after Christmas." I have had it for three years, but there is still enough material in the hem to let it down again. Nevertheless, necessity calls. My maid's expression instantly changes to delight. Well, surprise, then delight.

I throw a light cloak over my gown and leave the room.

Yesterday, Joanna and I marked off a section of the great hall for the play. We had curtains hung in front, so they could be dramatically pulled back when the lords and ladies in their costumes were all arranged in their tableaux. Between sets, the curtains will be drawn and everyone will join the feasting and dancing.

I time my arrival for just before the first of the two tableaux that include the sorceress, waiting in an alcove in the hall until the one before mine is completed and the curtains drawn closed again. Then I slip into the room and hide behind the curtains while everyone dances. I am still wearing my cloak—an old, ugly thing, I do not know why it is still in the wardrobe, with a hood that covers my head and shadows my face—when the music ends and the others assemble: Joanna as Isolde, with her two ladies-in-waiting. I move to the side, where I will be the last one revealed as the curtains open. Marguerite of Taranto and Sancia of Cabannis look at me curiously.

It goes almost as I imagined. The curtains are pulled back, revealing Isolde and her ladies. Then I step forward and throw off my cape, holding out the little vial, supposedly filled with the love potion. A gasp goes through the hall as my costume is revealed. A feminine gasp. I do not look at the men, but they, apparently, are not affronted. Joanna, already reaching for the vial, blinks behind her mask, where only I can see it.

At the corner of my eye I see Grandmother Sancia half-rise in her chair. I hold my breath, terrified she will disrupt the tableau, or worse, order me to reveal myself for shame. We stand frozen, my heart pounding as the chanteur, oblivious, sings the verses of our tableau. I breathe again when I see, at the corner of my eye, King Robert lightly touch Queen Sancia's arm, bidding her sit again. He is proud of his fashionable, cosmopolitan court. How proud would he be if he knew it was his granddaughter thus revealed, I wonder? That makes me want to giggle. I am nearly bursting with it as I wait for the chanteur to finish the verses of our tableau.

The verses end, the curtain is pulled across again, and everyone applauds, if a little less enthusiastically than for the previous tableaux. Even then I cannot laugh, for everyone knows my giggle. I feign a coughing fit.

Joanna whispers, loud enough for only the four of us behind the curtain to hear: "It is no surprise, Lady Sorceress, that you are coughing, exposed as you are to every draft."

The musicians announce the next dance and play a prelude, giving those who wish to dance time to find partners. Marguerite and Sancia of Cabannis leave, laughing. I do not know if Joanna deliberately spoke down to me as though I was one of the paid performers in order to hide my identity, but I know she is not pleased with me. I will likely have to wait till I get to Hungary before I have access to a royal wardrobe again.

Joanna gives me a last look, her expression unreadable behind her mask, before she turns to join the dance. After a moment, I follow her.

No one asks me to dance. I have never, since I was old enough to attend feasts and dances, been left without a partner. If they knew I was Princess Maria, I would have a dozen courtiers asking me to dance. I stand through the first one, tapping my foot as a little hint, but no one comes forward.

The music ends, the dancers part, and there is a brief pause before the next dance begins. The room is cheery with laughter and conversation, I can see the other ladies in the masque using glances and gestures to flirt gaily behind their masks with the younger dukes and lords, protected by their anonymity. But no one comes near me. I stand in a little bubble of silence.

Who do they think I am? A maid, perhaps, or an actress hired to play a role no lady would take? But a maid or an actress would never be given such an expensive gown. No one will imagine, not even for a moment, that it is me, little Princess Maria, not so little now. I have completely fooled them. But I do wish someone would ask me to dance!

Then I see my cousin Andrew, the Duke of Calabria, crossing the room. Andrew does not care what others think of him, which is a good thing for him as no one thinks much of him here. He is Joanna's husband in name, and will be in fact when our Lord Grandfather deems he has proved himself man enough to consummate the vows they made as children. Why is he coming toward me? Even if he does not know who I am, he must know I am not Joanna.

Andrew stops before me. He is not wearing a mask. He declared he would not participate in Joanna's entertainments years ago when he did not like what he was asked to do, and has not been invited to join one since. I can clearly see the interest in his eyes when he looks at me in my low-cut red gown. No one has ever looked at me like that. I feel my face flushing and am glad the mask hides it. It is gratifying to be considered a woman at last, not a child, but I do not entirely like his expression, although I could not say why it disturbs me. When he holds out his hand to dance with me, I am surprised, for he has never paid me any attention before. I would rather not dance with Andrew, but the music is beginning again, and I will be forced to stand here, shunned, if I do not accept, so I curtsy and offer my hand to him.

Andrew does not speak to me. Everyone has been told that the players will not speak until the last tableau has been completed and they unmask themselves. But it is more likely he simply has nothing to say; he seldom speaks to anyone other than his men. He dances adequately, however, which comes as a pleasant surprise, and the music makes me happy, light on my feet. If I were dancing with anyone else I would want to laugh with pleasure. But that would give me away, and after the reaction my costume has had, I am more than ever determined no one shall find out who is (barely) inside it.

When the music ends I curtsy and return behind the curtain for my second tableau, the one where Isolde tries in vain to return the potion, having decided she does not want to deal in magic. As the curtain opens I raise my hands, blocking her. I turn my head aside when she falls to her knees, her hands clasped in supplication, while the chanteur sings the fateful verses.

There is very little applause when our tableau is finished. No one likes the wicked sorceress; her beauty is tarnished by her deeds. They do not blame Isolde, which is exactly the effect we planned, but I had not realized how it would feel to be a villain, to be the one blamed when in truth I am only there by circumstance, offering not a temptation to sin but a gift of love. It is Isolde, not I, who will turn it into a wicked thing by drinking the potion with Tristan instead of her husband the King. My intentions were virtuous. I shake my head as she pleads. I am the sorceress in the story, not Maria, and the woman who stands before me, whether she is a peasant or a queen, freely chose her path. I am sorry to deny her, but one cannot take back one's choices.

When the curtain closes again I feel dizzy, as though I had left my body and become someone else, and am just now returning. I am Maria again, not a sorceress. It was ridiculous to stand there justifying in my mind a creature who does not exist.

Joanna's last words before she left our little curtained area, were a hissed whisper to go and change, now my part is done. Normally I do not care to take orders from my sister, but this time I am eager to go to my rooms and return as myself. My blue gown may not be cut in the new style, but I am surprisingly eager to put it on.

Duke Andrew appears beside me at the doorway. The mask cuts off much of my peripheral vision and his sudden appearance makes me start. He bows mockingly—at least it seems so to me.

"Shall I walk with you, Lady Sorceress?" He does not wait for me to respond, but holds out his arm for me to rest my fingers on. I do so nervously. Will he recognize my hand? But he barely glances at it as he guides me through the door; he is busy looking at my low-cut bodice. One of his men, the one who is always with him, follows us closely, as though I was a real sorceress and might harm the duke. I straighten, shoulders back and head high, and let my cape hang open rather than pull it close as I want to, so he will not know I am nervous. I have seen Andrew taunting servants when they let him see their fear.

We walk through several rooms in silence, away from the grand hall. I cannot go to my own rooms now, so I let him take the lead. The farther we go, the fewer people we see and the fewer wall sconces are lit, until we are quite alone, walking in semi-darkness, and I am becoming alarmed.

He leads me toward a dark alcove. I stop, pulling my hand from his arm, but he pushes me against the stone wall. For a moment I am too surprised to protest. Andrew leans against me, pinning me to the wall, and reaches down my bodice to cup my breast. Horrified, I try to push him away, but he is stronger than I am. He catches my wrists easily in one hand. I struggle against him, truly frightened now.

"Stop!" My voice comes out high with terror, unrecognizable. Not that I care any longer; I want him to recognize me, he will stop at once when he does.

Andrew pushes his hand under my mask and wraps it around my mouth. "I like you better silent," he growls. I cannot breathe, his hand is so wide it covers my nose as well. He will suffocate me here, not knowing who I am! I struggle desperately against him, but he has my arms pinned, all I can do is kick my slippered foot against his muscle-hardened leg. Behind him, his man coughs discreetly.

Andrew shifts, his hand moving so my nostrils are uncovered. I slump against the wall, sucking in the precious air in great gasps. His elbow still has my right arm pinned to the wall, his body against mine. I feel his left hand fumbling, and realize with terror that he is loosening the drawstring of his hose!

He shoves my head hard against the wall. "Why are you struggling? You wanted this, you came with me willingly enough. Do not pretend to a false modesty now, not in that gown. Be still, whore, you are getting what you asked for!"

The fight goes out of me. I stand, pinned against the wall, stunned. I did not know, I did not understand, I want to cry. But even if his hand were not pressed firmly against my mouth, I could not protest. Why did I come with him away from everyone, unchaperoned and alone? What did I think? Is he right about me—?

Andrew flattens himself against me, I can feel his hard manhood, throbbing against my stomach through the tight fabric. He releases my mouth, his hands under my arms to lift me, and I am so terrified it overcomes my guilt, I do not care if everyone comes and finds me like this and I am shamed forever. I close my eyes and scream!

I feel his arm rise and cringe, thinking he means to hit me, but instead he tears my mask off. It catches in my hair. He rips it off anyway, my scream choking off into sobs as he pulls it away, a handful of my hair ripping out with it. For an instant I see fear in his eyes, then a look of rage so fierce it stops my sobs. I stand before him, unable to move for terror, waiting for him to murder me.

"What is this? Are you mocking me? Who set you up to this?" He looks around wildly.

"We are quite alone, my Lord," his man says quietly.

Andrew turns on him a look that makes me shiver. "If you tell anyone, I will kill you," he says, his voice low and hard. He looks back at me, and I am not certain which of us he is addressing. He must see the terror in my eyes, the tears still damp on my cheeks, because he smiles then, an ugly twist of his thick lips. I flush, hot with shame, as though I am naked before him, caught in a mortal sin. He ties the drawstring of his hose, casual, no longer concerned we may be caught.

"You look unwell, Princess," he says mockingly. "Perhaps you are disappointed?"

I look away. "King Robert will have you hanged for this." My voice trembles, lacking conviction.

"Oh, but this is our secret, Cousin Maria. We must keep you fit to be married to my brother." He laughs as though the thought of having something on his brother pleases him. I am humiliated, but also relieved: No one will know. Andrew laughs again, a cruel sound. I cannot look up. I cannot bear to see him looking at me, to see the scorn in his eyes, the knowledge that I will gladly keep a secret with him.

"Do not be disappointed, Princess Maria. Perhaps your sister will die, and you will learn what you have missed this night."

I think I will be ill. If Joanna dies without issue, I must marry Andrew; it is in the treaty keeping Naples and Hungary from war. I clench my teeth to keep from vomiting.

"Straighten yourself up, Princess." He hands me back my cape. "I will walk you to your rooms. I know a back way. No one will see us."

Trust Andrew to know the back ways through the castle, the secret, cowardly routes. I take the cape, shaming myself further by my willingness to creep back to my rooms after him.

When we are nearly there I remember my maid will be waiting inside. I reach under my mask and wipe my eyes and cheeks dry, and stiffen my shoulders, trying to stop their trembling.

"Ah, the Princess returns," Andrew says. He leans toward me. "I know what you are now," he whispers. "You had better treat me nicely if you want me to keep your secret!"

I do not turn to watch him go. It is not true. I did not want this! I did not understand. But who will believe me? They will remember I went with him willingly. No one will ever know about this, I promise myself. I will forget this evening completely. It will be as if it never happened. Wrapping my cape more tightly about me, I march toward the door to my presence chamber, and enter it without a glance at the guard who holds it open for me.

Chapter 3

A Broken Vow

Naples, 1343

"Princess Joanna! Princess Maria! You must awaken."

I open my eyes groggily. Philippa stands at the foot of our bed, I can see her outline through the linen curtains. Beside me Joanna sits up. I peer through the bed-curtains: a servant is hastily lighting the silver wall-lamps in our bedchamber. The sweet smell of olive oil fills the room.

"It is still night," I protest, closing my eyes again. Grandmother Sancia cannot expect us to pray before dawn, even if our grandfather King Robert is ill. He has been ill before and always recovered. I am too sleepy to pray in the middle of the night. We are not Holy Sisters, we are royal sisters. I smile to myself at my wit, repeating the phrase in my head.

The bed creaks as Joanna climbs out of it. "Maria," she says. And to Philippa, "What is it, Mother?"

It is still night. I scrunch my eyes closed, feeling the pucker between my eyebrows and in defiance I deepen it. If Philippa notices I can blame it on a bad dream. She will know better, but she will have to pretend to accept that. She may instruct us but she has never gone so far as to punish us, and she will not speak to our Lady Grandmother about such a little thing now.

"His Majesty the King requests your presence."

I open my eyes. Philippa is looking at Joanna, whose question she has answered, but I know she is well aware of my rebellion, and also aware that she has neatly foiled it.

I sit up. "Both of us?"

Although I would never mention it, I am a little jealous of all the time my sister spends with our grandfather, even if it is boring. He has her sit beside him when he is hearing supplicants or signing laws, and he takes the time to discuss his decisions with her. Joanna is interested in such things, but I should be learning them too. I am going to be a queen as well, even if I will only be a queen consort and not a reigning queen when I marry. But I would be just as happy not to learn to be a queen in the middle of the night.

"Both of you," Philippa says.

Joanna glances at me. She has already washed her face in the bowl of rose water presented by her maid and is waiting to be dressed. Before she can say 'Maria' again, I slide out of my side of the bed, my back toward them both, and cup my hands in the cold water scented with rose petals which my maid is holding out to me.

I feel my cheeks flush and pat the cold water over my face to hide it, glancing across the room at Philippa. She has the disconcerting tendency of knowing what I am thinking, especially when it is a thought I would prefer not known. She is focused on my sister now, but I wonder if it is that tendency that helped her rise from her humble origin to being a royal adviser, even to being honored as surrogate mother of the royal princesses.

I pat my face dry and raise my arms so my maid can remove my nightdress and put on my shift and gown. Turning my head I see that Joanna is already dressed in her rich purple gown with fleur-de-lis stitched on it in golden thread. This is a formal audience, then. Now I am impatient to be dressed, but even so my dalliance has cost me, for no sooner is my hair combed ready to plait and pin up than Joanna rises from her dressing table and announces she is ready. Philippa leads her out of our room and I must follow with my hair down like a child.

He may be dying, I realize, and everyone will be there. I am nearly fourteen, a woman grown, and they will all see me enter looking like this, behind my sister, whose hair is elegantly done up and whose neck and fingers are jeweled and who is the fairest flower of Naples to all who see her. I hurry to catch up, not wanting to trail behind like a shadow to her sun. If Joanna would act human just once, and not always be thinking of her duty, there would have been time for me to have my hair done, also. I frown at her back, ahead of me.

Then I remember her laughing in the garden with me the day before, and I am ashamed. Of course we would not be wakened in the night for no reason. I should have realized that at once, as Joanna did.

If we have been wakened to go to him, he must be dying.

And everyone will see me with my hair down.

The hordes of courtiers I expect to see in the presence room outside King Robert's bed-chamber do not appear. Instead I hear his voice even before we enter his chamber. He is angry, but instead of the low and terrifying thunder that always reminds me of the lion in our menagerie—the one that took its keeper's hand as well as the fresh meat he was pushing through the bars of its cage—my royal Grandfather's voice has become the high-pitched whine of illness and old age.

The door opens and a man tumbles out like a leaf tossed in a gale. He is fat and short and dark, with a face as covered in hair as the back of his head. He wears the Hungarian livery of Joanna's husband, Andrew. We pause to let him pass. He peers at us through his greasy black hair, eyes wide with terror, and rushes away without remembering to bow. In another it might be insolence but in a Hungarian it is simply ignorance and stupidity. I take a quick breath and straighten my back, preparing myself in case Duke Andrew is inside the room. I have avoided him since the night of the masque, but if I must stand near him now, at least he will not see me afraid.

"…lying, vow-breaking, scheming, untrustworthy…" Grandfather's voice, thin and treble but nevertheless rising to the task of conveying a royal rage, can be heard clearly through the open door. I am glad now to be able to follow Philippa and my sister, third in line before the breaking storm.

Grandmother Sancia is already there, standing tight-lipped and composed beside Grandfather's bed. It is no secret that this is probably the closest she has been to it in all their years of marriage.

"…they have broken their word to His Holiness the Pope…"

My Grandmother's face pales: can there be a greater sin?

"…they have broken their vow before God…"

Grandmother Sancia clasps her hands together, but it is too late now to send a prayer in advance to prepare God to hear this awful declaration.

"…and they have broken their treaty with me, with the house of Angevin!" Grandfather finishes with a roar, albeit a high-pitched one.

Joanna's face pales. I try to look suitably horrified but it would help if I knew who has done what.

Grandfather turns his head and sees us. "Maria," he says.

I jump and look around, as though there might be another Maria in the room. Immediately I feel stupid, because I have already seen that there are only the four of us in here, as well as Grandfather's physician and a manservant who looks like he wishes even more than I that he were someplace else. To cover my nervousness I drop into a deep curtsy and say, "Your Majesty." It comes out part whisper, part croak.

He beckons me closer. I have to stop myself from looking at Joanna because I cannot believe he has seen her and still wants me.

"Come here, little Maria."

I step forward, ahead of my sister, and start to curtsy again but he catches my hand and stops me. I straighten beside him. And now I do want to look at Joanna to make sure she is taking this in, how he is holding my hand and looking into my face, not hers, but I hold my head up and return his gaze steadily, like the queen I will one day be.

Whatever you want, you must act like you already have it, Joanna told me once. I thought at the time she meant the gown she was being fitted for, or a new ornament for her neck, but today I understand her comment as I stand like the Queen of Hungary in front of my dying grandfather.

He looks down at my hand, soft and white and small against his wrinkled palm. I start to remove it but he closes his hand, completely engulfing mine. "They have broken our contract," his voice is angry again, "your cousin Louis and his Lady Mother Queen Elizabeth. They have spurned you."

I only have one cousin Louis who could be linked to me. I have been waiting in fear and anticipation for his summons, secretly excited to think that I would beat Joanna onto a throne. With Louis' silence and Grandfather's illness that ambition is dying, but now, with Grandfather holding my hand, I think: He has sent for me. I will be crowned before her after all!

Before I can sort out why the thought does not make me entirely happy, my grandfather's expression, and his words, *spurned you,* register. I pull my hand back as though the insult came from him. "Spurned me?"

"She has married him," my Lord Grandfather's eyes burn with rage. He has to stop for a coughing fit before he can continue. "She has married him to Princess Margaret of Bohemia. She chose Bohemia over Naples." He says this last less in anger than in sheer disbelief.

"They already have Naples," Joanna says, referring to her marriage to Andrew. Her voice is controlled but tight; she is as angry as our grandfather. Not on my behalf, of course; on behalf of the Angevins.

"Margaret?" I ask, stupid with shock. I will not be queen? I have lived my whole life expecting to be Queen of Hungary, and now I will not be. "Margaret of Bohemia? But she is a child. She is…" I think. "…Seven years old. And she is not the heir to Bohemia, she is only the daughter of the heir!" My voice rises into a wail. I cannot help it. A child half my age has skipped her way onto my throne.

I am not an heir, either, an ugly little voice inside my head whispers. I am just the sister of the heir. In that moment I hate my sister as much as I love her. She was not spurned. She is a prize worth having. I feel my eyes fill and blink back the tears. Who will I marry? Who will want me now that I have been so publicly shamed?

My Lady Grandmother is watching me. A royal princess does not weep in public, and never weeps for herself. I raise my chin a little. Now I will not have to go to Hungary and live among barbarians, I tell myself firmly. They have lost me. I will never come and civilize them, and certainly little Margaret of Bohemia will not be equal to the task. They will remain barbarians forever! I feel a little avenged, but it is poor consolation for losing a crown.

King Robert's expression of furious disbelief disappears when he glances at me. For a moment, so brief I think I might be mistaken, a look of tenderness crosses his face. Almost immediately it is gone, replaced once more by fury.

"Bring Raymond at once!" he shouts to his man, who jumps to relay his command. "And Andrew, that sniveling, useless little pup!"

Chapter 4

A Dangerous Will

We wait in silence for our Royal Seneschal, Raymond the Ethiopian, to arrive. Grandmother Sancia looks about to say something, but the King begins to cough again. His physician approaches his bed and offers a potion that smells so vile I am sure it will poison him, but after he has taken a swallow the coughing stops. Most likely so they will not give him more of it, I think to myself. He lies back against his pillow and closes his eyes. Grandmother Sancia folds her hands and begins to pray, her lips moving soundlessly in the quiet room.

I notice all these things as from a distance. It cannot be possible that all of this is happening. There is a signed treaty between Hungary and Naples, and my marriage is part of that contract. Grandfather will do something; he clearly has a plan. Meanwhile I am grateful for the silence. Conversation would make this real, and it is not real. All I want to do is wait in silence until King Robert has made things right.

Joanna would like to say something, I expect. I expect she is itching to be Queen and not need anyone's permission to speak. She must be beside herself to know what our Grandfather the King intends to do. The still intentness of her body beside me pierces the silence I would draw around myself. This is real. Joanna knows it is real. She is not praying, as though this bitter cup could be removed from us. She is preparing herself. Whatever our Lord Grandfather does, she will inherit it. And soon, by the looks of it.

Who will I marry now that the contract which bound me to Louis is broken? I grit my teeth. Whoever he is, he had better sit on a throne! What countries have unmarried princes waiting to inherit their father's crown? For the first time, I admit to myself that I did not want to marry Andrew's brother and travel far away from the beautiful Neapolitan court to live the rest of my life among barbarians. What if Louis is like Andrew? I shudder before I can stop myself.

Last week I learned that Andrew's man—the one who was with him that night—was killed in a street brawl. *If you tell anyone, I will kill you,* I still hear Andrew's voice saying. And now his man will never tell anyone. But that was his favorite companion, the man he trusted most… Surely I am wrong?

What if Louis is like Andrew?

Perhaps it is not a tragedy that King Robert will have to find me another husband.

Raymond stops just inside the door and bows, waiting there for the King to be informed that he has arrived. When the King motions him forward he crosses the room in that way he has that makes any room look too small to contain him. Tall and powerful, even in the clothes of a courtier he looks like he should be on a battlefield, where he has proven himself many times. No one can question his value and devotion to our royal house, but he is not well-liked. Even I know it, not that anyone would confide that to me, the granddaughter of the only king in Christendom who would elevate an African slave to such a lofty position, no matter how capable and intelligent he is.

I peek through my lashes at Philippa. I have never seen her acknowledge Raymond when they are together at court, but when he is present she is no longer a ladies' maid, or a royal adviser, or even the surrogate mother of the heirs to the throne; she is Raymond's wife. She may not stand near him, she seldom even looks at him, but there is a subtle change in her voice, and the way she stands, the way she holds her head and moves her arms and even how she glances sideways at him is confession enough. Looking at her, I think, what do I care if my husband wears a crown as long as I can feel that way about him?

I narrow my eyes and try to see Raymond as she does: the intelligence in his large brown eyes, the toned, muscular body of a fearless soldier, the controlled movements of a man used to commanding others in battle, the confident way he holds his head in the presence of royalty, the ready expression on his face, as capable in the intrigues of court as on the battle field. I blink, and see him now as others do: his black face, thick-lipped and broad-nosed with flaring nostrils, incongruously sitting atop the elegant embroidered silk tunic of a courtier. A black monkey wearing men's clothes, he has been called—never in our royal family's presence, but I have heard the rumors, spread by jealous and inferior men. I scorn them, as my Grandfather does. He respects Raymond's manly abilities. But still... I glance again at Philippa; is it possible love can make you so blind? I will never let it do that to me. My husband must be truly handsome and honorable for me to find him so.

The door opens again. Joanna and Philippa do not look around, but I cannot resist a quick glance, moving my head as little as possible so no one will notice. Andrew has entered. He stands uncertainly just inside the door, short and dark and wide-eyed. His facial hair is just beginning to grow, so most of his face is still clean, but soon he will be as hairy as his men. Why do they deliberately want to look like animals? I shiver. He *is* an animal. No one else may know it, but I do.

The King's face darkens. "You know what your brother has done," he says, without looking at Andrew, as though this relative-by-marriage is not even worth a glance. "Come in and witness my response."

Andrew creeps forward. When he reaches the foot of the bed I can see he is trembling. My fear of him changes to scorn. He is a year older than I am, a grown man only eighteen months younger than Joanna. He is arrogant and cruel in front of women and servants, yet as soon as he is in the presence of a king—a dying king, at that—he trembles like the coward he is. His brother Louis is already a proven soldier, and a formidable one. But I will not think of Louis; he is not worth a thought after what he has done. Beside me, Joanna acts as though she is not even aware of Andrew, and I am not certain it is an act.

Raymond stands by the bed with his stylus and a scroll, ready to take down the King's words. The King turns back to him and Joanna draws a little breath. It focuses me, that little breath that no one could hear but me, standing so close beside her. What is she afraid of? Should I be afraid as well? It occurs to me that there are worse husbands than King Louis of Hungary, including none at all. I do not want to be a spurned and unmarried princess, subject to my sister all my life.

King Robert opens his eyes. He looks at Joanna, and begins to dictate his last will and testament. Joanna is named his sole heir and successor to all his empire: Queen of Naples, Countess of Provence, Sovereign of Sicily, titular Queen of Jerusalem, and overlord of Piedmont and Forcalquier.

Some of these titles are as thin as the scroll they are written on: Jerusalem, for example, and Sicily, which our grandfather has been trying to regain all his life. Even so, the list as he recites it for Raymond to copy down is impressive. I will never have so great an empire. Briefly I regret losing Louis, for his empire is even larger, and very much richer since the discovery of gold. They may be barbarians, but they are very rich barbarians.

"If Joanna dies childless," King Robert continues…

I hold my breath. Will I have to wait, and marry Andrew? Never! I could not bear it now!

"…the entire inheritance goes directly to Maria."

I let out my breath in a whoosh. Grandmother Sancia's face twitches with disapproval. Philippa does not move, but I will hear from her for my indiscreet reaction later. Nevertheless, the entire inheritance! And no mention of marrying Duke Andrew! King Robert has bypassed Andrew completely. It will all be mine!

Joanna shifts beside me; I feel it like a little shock. Only if she dies. In that moment I hate Naples as much as I love it, because I love my sister and I cannot have both. Then I think, surely my Lord Grandfather does not intend me to wait? Will I not be able to marry until my sister dies? What if she lives until I am too old to marry? And in that moment, I hate her as much as I love her, for every prince will spurn me as long as she lives.

King Robert continues without noticing my temporary distraction. "Should the contracted marriage of my younger granddaughter Maria to Louis of Hungary not take place—" he pauses to glare at Andrew, who actually cringes. Cringes before a dying old man. Well, so he should, I think, indignant again because of course the marriage cannot take place now, we all know it, my grandfather is only reminding everyone whose fault that is.

"—Maria is to wed the heir to the French throne or, if he is not available, a younger brother."

This time I gasp out loud, and do not even care about my Lady Grandmother and Philippa disapproving. Queen of France! I shall move to Paris, a city even more elegant and cultured than Naples. And why not? My mother was sister to King Philip VI, my great-great-grandfather was the younger brother of Louis IX. I have the royal blood of France in my veins already!

"What do you think of that?" King Robert says, turning to our Grandmother Sancia.

"I think she will never marry," my Grandmother says.

I do not intend to narrow my eyes. I am not aware I have done so. Joanna moves beside me, as though merely shifting her weight from one leg to the other. I am annoyed because she is blocking my sight of our royal grandparents, and then I understand. When she shifts back my face is as clear as a sunny day, but underneath I am thinking hard. Grandmother Sancia is only saying out loud what I thought a moment ago. If I do not want to wait for my sister to die, what prince will want to? And that is if she and Andrew have no issue; if they do, there will be nothing to wait for.

King Robert looks at me. Thanks to my sister I am able to return to him a clear and obedient gaze.

He glances again at Grandmother Sancia, nods to himself, and turns back to Raymond. I listen in disbelief and delight as he dictates a provision for me of lands and castles to a value of ten thousand florins, as well as a dowry of thirty thousand florins, to be paid when I marry.

I am giddy at the thought of such a dowry. I breathe deeply, praying my legs will not give way. No one will consider me worthless now. I may not be as clever as Joanna, or as pious, but I am still worth something as a princess of Naples. With a rush of affection I realize my grandfather does intend me to marry, and marry well, to forge a valued alliance for Naples. I am no longer a bone to be thrown to the Hungarian dogs in recompense for my Uncle Carobert not inheriting Naples as he should have; I am a spoke in the Angevin wheel moving us forward. I raise my chin proudly—not enough to be noticed and accused of arrogance by my pious grandmother, but enough to claim my place.

My grandfather the King continues to recite his will. Joanna will rely on a council headed by our Grandmother Sancia until she reaches her majority at age twenty-five; neither of us may sign legal contracts until we reach our majority; we are to submit to the authority of the Holy Pope and are commended to his protection; and on and on. I listen closely, trying to discern what it means for me, although most of it is about Joanna. Unless she dies, I remind myself. But still the details are tiring, so I decide to ask Joanna about it later, and try to imagine what the French princes look like. I am sure they will be tall and blond and handsome, and they will be civilized already.

When he is finished, the King sends for a judge and a notary and each of us, Joanna and Andrew and I in turn, place our hand on the Holy Gospel and swear in King Robert's presence that we will never do anything in opposition to the intent of this will. My sister is very pale and her hand trembles as she makes her oath, but I place my hand firmly upon the Holy Book and speak as the notary directs me in a clear voice. When it is Andrew's turn he mumbles the words with a sullen face, barely touching the Holy Gospel. But he dares not object—he has sworn his allegiance to King Robert, and he is bound to that oath.

Before we are allowed to leave the room, King Robert looks at Andrew. There is such contempt in his expression I wonder how Andrew can endure it, but to his credit he looks back steadily. The King looks even more disgusted at this show of false bravado, and everyone in the room knows why. He closes his eyes.

"Two days after my death," he speaks slowly, as though the words pain him, "the Duke of Calabria will be knighted—"

No one moves or says anything. Even Raymond's busy scribbling stops. I do not think anyone in the room even dares breathe. I try to imagine our court celebrating a knighthood while the King's body is lying in state awaiting burial and the city is officially in mourning. Impossible! The entire civilized world will be as shocked as we are in this room.

Andrew's knighthood ceremony had been planned for Easter, to celebrate his return from leading a campaign against Sicily—the campaign that was planned a year ago and which Andrew has postponed three times now. Grandfather has given up on him, I think. And then I realize the extent of our grandfather's disgust, for Sicily is all he cares about. He has been trying to reclaim it all his life. My father was born on one such expedition, for my grandmother—my real grandmother who died before I was born, as brave a queen as ever lived—accompanied him. And when King Robert grew too old to lead a battle himself, he sent others: my cousin Charles of Durazzo and then Charles of Artois, my grandfather's bastard son, each of them no older than Andrew when they proved themselves men, for they fought bravely regardless of the outcome.

"—And on that evening the Duke will appear at the door of the Duchess' rooms and know her carnally."

Somehow I manage not to gasp, and equally difficult, not to look at my sister. The King opens his eyes to glare at Andrew, who swallows—I can see his Adam's apple bobbing without moving my head. I almost giggle. Is it the King's glare or the thought of approaching Joanna's bed that terrifies Andrew? He is saved when the sound of scratching brings the King's focus back to Raymond, who is busily recording this last directive. I cannot help, I truly cannot keep myself, from glancing ever so little sideways.

Joanna stands still and straight, her head held high. Her face is pale, but her cheeks bear no sign of the blush I expect to see. Instead I am again shocked, because looking at her proud, stiff face I see the tiniest movement of her lips, so small only I who have lived beside this face every day and slept beside it every night of my life, would notice. She is staring directly at King Robert, the corners of her mouth moving unbelievably into the barest suggestion of a smile. The King turns his head and their eyes meet in that way they have of perfectly understanding each other.

What? I wonder. I risk a glance at Andrew. His face is as pale as Joanna's, but there is no hint of a smile on his lips; they are pressed together in a tight line that belies the bland expression in his eyes. Then I understand. There will be no ceremony for Andrew's knighting. It must be done, but it will not be celebrated. No court in Christendom would expect us to celebrate while the King lies unburied. Nor will Andrew be knighted by a king; King Robert has found an irrefutable excuse to avoid that distasteful task. Joanna will have to knight him—she will be the only royal above him in rank. Knighted by a woman, by his own wife! Andrew is not being honored with a knighthood; he is being prepared to do the only task he is good for, the task of a daughter, not a son. He is breeding stock. While Joanna is being given, in his presence, the task she has been raised for, the task of a son, not a daughter. She is to rule King Robert's empire.

I make a little choking sound. Not quite a laugh, my Grandmother would scold me and even my Grandfather, much as he despises Andrew, would disapprove. But Andrew hears. I feel him stiffen, his face flushing red, and I am glad. Who could blame me after what he did?

Joanna is silent as we walk back to our rooms. I sneak little glances at her, trying to fathom her silence. There is nothing she wants more in all the world than to be Queen of Naples, and now she can rule it without Andrew's interference. And without his help? A woman ruling a kingdom on her own? With no man to rule her? I do not doubt my sister's strength and intelligence, but she is a woman, with all the frailties of her sex. And if she does not know it, nor our Lord Grandfather admit it, still every one of their subjects will.

"Andrew will lead your army and help you make your decisions," I say helpfully.

Joanna snorts. "God forbid it."

I am shocked. Not as shocked as I would be if I did not hate and despise Andrew, but surely she cannot imagine ruling Naples on her own.

"King Robert has forbidden it, at any rate," she adds. Her lips twist upward but her eyes are not smiling.

There is no dissuading my sister when she has determined on a course. "I will stand by you when I am Queen of France," I promise her. At least I will have a King to govern and protect me. "You do not forget my inheritance, do you, my Lady Sister?"

She does not answer at once. Can she be jealous that my kingdom will be greater than hers? I am secretly pleased at the thought of her envying me for once.

"I hope you will have the opportunity to inherit it."

I feel my cheeks flame. "I will marry better than you, and claim it soon enough," I retort in a low voice so that Philippa, walking ahead, will not hear us quarrel. Will she dare refuse me my inheritance?

"You had better do it soon," she says. "For when our cousin King Louis and his mother—Andrew's mother—learn that Duke Andrew will never be crowned king, not even as my consort…"

She does not finish. She does not need to. I am well aware that Louis of Hungary, like his father, King Carobert, would welcome an excuse to press his claim on our kingdom. Louis delights in warfare as much as his younger brother Andrew shrinks from it. But would he… would he really invade us? I try anxiously to remember the details of our tutor's lessons concerning the treaty between our two kingdoms.

Louis' and Andrew's grandfather, Charles Martel, was our grandfather's oldest brother. He should by rights have inherited the

Kingdom of Naples as well as Hungary. Instead, Charles Martel died before his father, King Charles II. He left behind one son, Carobert. But Charles II feared his grandson, Carobert, was too young to hold the important Kingdom of Naples. He sent seven-year-old Carobert to claim his inheritance as King of Hungary, expecting Carobert to be killed in the attempt, the Hungarians being lawless villains. Then King Charles II passed the Kingdom of Naples over to his third son, our grandfather, Robert the Wise, blatantly disregarding the law of succession. Against all odds, Carobert succeeded, and when he had brought Hungary under his firm control, he turned his attention to the rest of his father's rightful inheritance. In order to avoid a war with the huge army of Hungary, our grandfather agreed to marry his heirs to King Carobert's sons, joining the kingdoms once again. They signed a treaty, and we have lived in peace since Joanna married Andrew. So why is Joanna worried?

"Louis of Hungary chose not to marry me." Our marriage was part of the treaty, but Louis must know my Lord Grandfather would marry me to someone else. How furious Grandfather was on my behalf! I smile. So furious he made Andrew swear never to…

Joanna's husband Andrew will never be crowned King of Naples, not even as royal consort. A Hungarian will never sit on our throne. At least, not until one of us has a son, and what if it is my son, who will now not have a single drop of Hungarian blood?

My initial pride in working out my sister's meaning—she is often deliberately obscure, just to annoy me—is immediately overwhelmed by fear. Will the Hungarians see this as excuse enough to break the treaty?

Ignoring the fact that they have already broken it, I think, scowling. But to the Hungarians, it is one thing to spurn a princess, and another entirely to spurn a prince.

Now I understand why our Lord Grandfather wants the marriage legally consummated before his last testament is read. But will that be enough? Will Louis invade us anyway? King Robert will be dead when

King Louis finds out, I remind myself, my fear growing, and only Joanna, a sixteen-year-old girl, sitting on the throne…

"What will you do?" I whisper, horrified. How could I not have realized there would be repercussions if Andrew is shamed so publicly? How could our grandfather not realize it?

She turns to me, her expression so fierce I step back. "I will keep the oath I made this night," she says, "whatever it requires of me. Before God, I will be sole ruler of my kingdom!"

Chapter 5

A Tryst

"My Lady Sister," I murmur, dipping my head as Joanna passes me.

I should have said, Your Majesty, and curtsied low enough to touch the floor with my hand, bowing my head until she spoke to me, for she is now my Queen. But so much has happened, so suddenly, I have not had time to decide how I feel about any of it. Joanna does not notice anyway; she brushes past without even acknowledging me. Turning to watch her retreating back, I do know how I feel: I am glad I did not curtsy.

Immediately I am ashamed. Joanna is distracted by grief and worry. *I love my sister,* I tell myself firmly, *and I have promised her my allegiance.* As if there could ever be a relationship as simple as that between the two of us.

Then another thought occurs to me, and now I do regret my lack of courtly manners. I am nearly fourteen, a woman raised in the elegant and renowned Neapolitan court, not some crude barbarian like our Hungarian cousin, Andrew. I know proper behavior. I look around quickly, in case someone saw my slip and is already comparing my manners to his, but the room is empty. Relieved, I continue toward my Grandmother Sancia's chapel. No doubt she is waiting.

As I near the entrance to her rooms I see a figure leaning against the wall, looking away from me. He turns, and I recognize my cousin,

Charles of Durazzo. "Princess Maria," he says, bowing his head. When he raises it he is smiling.

"Lord Charles." I return his smile. Even if he had not smiled, I would have. I cannot help but smile when I see him, try as I might to hide it. Why is he here? Is he waiting to see my Lady Grandmother, so early in the morning? He must know she will be praying in her chapel at this hour.

"You are going to your prayers," he observes. "We have all lost a great king, but you have also lost a grandfather. Although you are a beautiful sight in the pure white of mourning, I would never wish to see you sad."

I blush and lower my eyes. I feel my heart's pulse in my throat, and I am afraid he will see in my eyes how far from sadness I am at this moment. "You are kind, Cousin," I murmur, and feel my blush increasing. I dare not look up until I can compose myself.

"It is not only kindness, Maria," he says, boldly dropping my title, creating an intimacy between us, as though we have an understanding…

I glance up quickly to see the same suggestion of intimacy in his smile, a warm invitation in his dark eyes. My breath catches. I am hot all over now, not only in my cheeks. I lower my eyes again at once, before he sees too much and laughs at me.

"What else could it be?" I manage, wincing at how silly, how childish I must sound. Am I trying to flirt with him? I look up to make sure he is not laughing.

He is not. He is looking at me more earnestly than he has ever done. "Surely you must know, my sweet Maria. Surely you will let me hope for more than kindness between us?"

My mouth falls open. With a little gasp, I press my lips together and look down quickly. He must hear my heart pounding, so loud in the silence after his words. I clasp my hands together to hide their trembling, my knees are so weak I can barely stand. I am not accustomed to this. It is Joanna the courtiers flirt with. *My sweet Maria,* he said. I cannot think what to say, I can barely remember to breathe.

In a burst of daring I look up again and tell him, "Anyone can hope."

And then I blush even more at my boldness, and stammer that my Lady Grandmother is waiting, and hurry toward her chamber, almost running, without even saying goodbye.

At the door to Grandmother Sancia's rooms, waiting for her guard to open it to me, I glance back. Charles is gone. Was he only here to speak to me? Can that be why he came? For me?

The guard clears his throat. I struggle to collect myself, and hurry through the door toward Grandmother Sancia's private chapel. The chapel door is already open for me. I am quite late.

My Lady Grandmother is kneeling before the altar when I enter. I drop into a deep curtsy, which does nothing at all to appease her.

"You have kept us waiting," she says, without turning to look at me. I walk forward and kneel beside her as I have done every morning for as long as I can remember. I only half-listen to the prayers and exhortations of my grandmother's Franciscan monk; just enough to provide the expected responses and genuflections.

My sweet Maria, I hear him saying still. And: *Surely you will let me hope for more than kindness between us?* I have to stop myself from grinning foolishly.

Beside me, my Lady Grandmother stiffens. I do not think she can hear my thoughts, but I am not certain she does not know them, nevertheless. I force his face—his dark, inscrutable eyes, his full, passionate lips, his straight aristocratic nose, his charming, heart-stopping smile—I force his face out of my thoughts, firmly. This is no time to think of my cousin Charles.

Our grandfather will be laid in state at Santa Chiara this morning. Joanna was probably on her way to confirm the arrangements for the ceremony. I concentrate on the Franciscan monk murmuring his prayers in Latin.

I was not yet born when our father died, and only two when our mother followed him into the afterlife. I do not remember her at all. My earliest memory is clinging to Joanna's hand when we left our parent's castle and came to live with our grandparents at Castle Nuovo.

"You are like your mother," Grandmother Sancia says when I have said or done something she considers frivolous or vain.

"Like her mother," Grandfather the King used to say when I could not follow a philosophical point he and Joanna were debating.

"You are as beautiful and sweet as your mother was," Charles told me two Christmases ago, when I attended my first dance.

Does Joanna remember our parents? She will not talk of them. Her loyalty is all transferred to Philippa, a servant, and Grandmother Sancia, who sees to our religious training but shows us no affection whatsoever, and most of all to our grandfather, King Robert the Wise, for Joanna was his darling.

Will I ever be someone's darling?

Was Charles only flirting? I feel a pang in my chest. *Sweet Maria.* Do not let him have been merely flirting, I pray earnestly.

The chapel is silent. I blink, looking up through my lashes. Grandmother and the Franciscan are both looking at me with stern disapproval. They *do* know my thoughts!

No, they cannot. Only God, and maybe Philippa, can know my thoughts, and that is bad enough. My grandmother and the monk are only suspicious.

Looking down again I let my shoulders tremble and open my eyes wide, willing them to fill with water. In a moment I feel the moisture collect, and blink it onto my cheeks, allowing myself a little sob. Just one. Too great a display of emotion will annoy my Lady Grandmother as much as my lack of attention to the monk's words has. I think of King Robert, dead this morning, and the dowry he bequeathed me, and the fact that only my sixteen-year-old sister and her cowardly, untrustworthy husband stand between us and a Hungarian army that might even now be rushing to destroy Naples…! My eyes water in earnest.

Shielding my face in my hand—not too much, enough to claim modesty but not so much as to hide my tears—I rise and stammer an apology for not following the Franciscan's discourse, but I have been praying for my Grandfather the King's soul. "And for his children, the people of Naples, who have lost his strong protection," I add for good measure, since a queen always thinks of her subjects and I will be Queen when I marry the French prince. That is my destiny, even though it will break my poor cousin Charles' heart. The thought causes me to shed fresh tears.

Unable to chastise me now, Grandmother Sancia curtly dismisses me to collect myself and prepare for the ceremony of King Robert's interment.

Back in my rooms I look at once for Margherita di Ceccano, my friend as well as one of my ladies-in-waiting. She is the niece of a Cardinal; her mother and my Lady Aunt Agnes, Charles' mother, are close friends because of their mutual connections in Avignon. Margherita was raised here like a sister to Charles. She looks up as I come in.

I sit down beside her and take up my sewing, but I am too excited to sew. We have often whispered about the courtiers, which ones we think are handsome, and who is flirting with whom. I have confided to her more than once how much I like Charles, and she has talked to me about one of the young counts. But now that I have something to tell her, something new and much more exciting than anything we have whispered about before, there are no words that sound right.

"I met Duke Charles in the hall on my way to my Lady Grandmother's chambers," I finally say, keeping my voice low. Can I tell her he was waiting for me? Would it sound foolish? Was he?

"He must have risen very early," she murmurs. "I wonder what could have brought him there at just that time?" She smiles knowingly.

She has guessed! And now it does not sound foolish at all. "Do you think he was waiting for me?" I whisper, my voice catching with delight, eager to hear someone else say it.

"I have told you often that he likes you," she says. Her eyes crinkle, sharing my happiness. "What did he say?"

"He said…" already I feel myself blushing. I stare down at my sewing, hoping no one will notice. "He said he hopes there might be more than kindness between us." I whisper all in a rush.

"Ohhh," Margherita sighs. It is most satisfying to hear her sigh like that over something said to me.

I cannot hold the rest back after that. I lean in close and whisper in her ear, "I told him, 'anyone may hope.'" She giggles with me at my wit and daring. We have never been the ones flirting, always the ones listening to others' witticisms, ladies and lords of the court who are older and bolder than we are. It is a heady thing to join their ranks at last. Should I tell her he called me 'my dearest Maria'? I am wondering if I want to share that, or keep it just to myself a while longer, when the door to my receiving room opens and the guard announces, "Her Majesty the Queen!"

I am surprised to see Joanna enter my chambers. We all rise to curtsy, but she is in a hurry and comes to me at once. She leads me into an alcove where we can talk privately, and slips a note into my hands.

"You will see Louis today when we lay King Robert in state," she whispers as she hands me the note.

"I cannot! Everyone will be looking." I try to push it back to her but she has withdrawn her hand. I cannot return her note without it being obvious to others in the room, even though we are standing with our backs to them.

"They will not be looking at you."

Charles will. I hope he will. If he does, I do not want Charles of Durazzo to see me coquettishly slipping a note to Louis of Taranto! I have seen how Charles looks at Joanna as she flirts with the young men at court, especially our handsome cousins of Taranto. *Anyone can hope,* I told Charles. I meant him; he knew I meant him. But if he sees me give a note to Louis, he will think I really meant "anyone." I could not bear to lose his good opinion now! Surely there will be a better time than tomorrow to give Joanna's note to Louis.

"Can it wait?" I need not say how unseemly it is to be thinking of our handsome cousins today. Joanna flushes slightly, but I do too, as guilty as she.

"Tomorrow Andrew will be knighted, and tomorrow night… No, it cannot wait." Her face is impassive, but I do not need an expression to tell me how she feels. I would want to see someone handsome and fond of me before I bedded someone like Andrew—God forbid!—and Louis is one of the most handsome men in the Neapolitan court. He and his brother Robert won every joust at the Christmas tournament. Duke Andrew was furious—he led his men galloping through the narrow streets, heedless of the people scattering before them to avoid being trampled by their horses. I do not want to think of Andrew now, or imagine him watching me slip a note to a courtier. I have avoided Duke Andrew since the night of the masque, but I can remember the scorn in his eyes. If he sees me passing notes to lords on the day of my Grandfather King's interment... I look up at Joanna, ready to refuse.

"Please, Maria," she whispers. Is that a tear on her cheek? Does she love Louis? Does he feel about her as Charles does about me, and call her, 'my sweet'? Does she feel like giggling, and blushing, and all shivery inside when he glances at her, as Charles makes me feel?

I look at her doubtfully. Have I ever seen my sister blush? Even if I dared ask her such questions, Joanna would not answer. Joanna is married to Andrew of Hungary, cowardly, stupid, ugly, brutal, cruel Andrew. I feel a surge of pity for my sister. I cannot tell her I understand, or that I am sorry for her, without disclosing what Andrew did; and she would know, as I do, that I deserved it for wearing that dress. I could not bear my sister's scorn—Andrew's is bad enough—so I do not say anything as I close my fingers around her note.

But if I am seen passing a note to Louis when I should be mourning my Lord Grandfather, the King? Joanna will never claim the note if I am caught; she could not. I would not say it was hers, anyway. We do not tell each other's secrets. So if I am caught, it will be bad.

"If King Robert were alive you would not do this," I tell her.

"If King Robert were alive I would not need to."

I look at her, and see in her frightened eyes that she is not thinking of Louis of Taranto now; she is thinking of the other Louis. I shiver. King Robert's testament will be read aloud after his interment. Louis of Hungary will soon learn that his brother will not be crowned.

"Naples must have a Hungarian heir to the throne," my sister says. I think I hear her voice tremble. She has been Queen for one day and already she looks older than her sixteen years. Her face is drawn and pale. If our grandfather was alive he would never permit Andrew to go to her bed before he had proved himself a man. My sister would know at least that she had a soldier in her bed, a man worthy and capable of fathering a son.

"Give it to Lady Marguerite," I whisper, looking over my shoulder to where Louis' sister is sitting among our ladies-in-waiting.

"I trust only you." She says this quietly, neither pleading nor insisting. It is simply the truth, and I accept it because underneath everything there is between us, she is still the big sister who held my hand when I stopped at the entrance to Castle Nuovo, afraid to enter this imposing new home. And I am still the little sister who held her hand when she cried herself to sleep that night for parents I was already beginning to forget.

I trust only her.

"Tomorrow night there must be blood on your sheets," I say, tucking the letter into my sleeve. I feel very worldly saying this, although I do not know why everyone says there should be blood on bridal sheets. I am not a child; I have seen my grandfather's stallion with a mare, but I did not see any blood.

"Of course there will be blood." And then, smiling, as she turns to leave: "I heard about your tears this morning."

It is a good thing we trust each other, for we can never fool each other.

Chapter 6

A Walk in the Garden

"I would speak with you, Princess Maria."

I turn. Charles is standing behind me. He has leaned in close to whisper in my ear so no one else can hear. Or perhaps to make the curl of hair that always escapes my plaits tickle my cheek with his breath, so he can see me shiver. I glance around quickly at the ladies-in-waiting sitting about my presence chamber. Their attention is focused on the minstrel playing for them, and on their sewing. A few are chatting with the young noblemen who have joined us. None of them are looking at us. This does not fool me, I have lived in a royal court all my life. Every one of them is aware that Charles and I are talking where we cannot be heard.

"You are speaking to me now," I murmur. I feel his breath on my skin, as soft as a caress.

"Alone."

Who would imagine a single word could sound so delicious?

"Why, what have you to say, cousin?" I ask, hoping he does not hear the catch in my breath. I am so awkward at this.

He makes a noise and I see he is impatient with courtly teasing. I fear I have displeased him, but then he smiles and leaning very close, he whispers, "Surely you have some idea, dearest princess Maria."

If I move, just a little, his lips will brush my cheek. I stand very still, trying not to move, desperately wanting to.

I have been raised in the flirtatious Neapolitan court, and yet I cannot speak. Is this courtly flattery, or does he mean something more? Has he realized at last that I am no longer a child? Even so, he will not dare say anything beyond a pretty compliment; he knows that I am not for him. And yet, how I hope he will. Oh, I wish he were my French prince!

Joanna has beaten me onto a throne, she has beaten me into a marriage bed, whether it is a happy one or not, and in the month since King Robert died she has done very little toward arranging my engagement. The last time I asked her about it, she told me sharply that a letter had been sent, and she is too busy with matters of state and hearing petitions from her subjects and supervising the building of King Robert's tomb in Santa Chiara to do more.

Why should I not talk to my cousin Charles? He has not forgotten me for affairs of state.

"I will walk in the garden," I announce. "Please do not disturb yourselves. The Duke of Durazzo will accompany me." They are too surprised to move as I sail across the room with Charles following meekly as though he has been commanded. What can they say? Charles has been my friend since I was a child, I have grown up with him. Why should we not walk in the garden together? Margherita smiles at me as I pass her, and I have to bite my lip not to giggle.

I can smell the sea from the gardens, a clean, salty smell that mingles with the sweet perfume of the roses, gilliflowers, and jasmine. The natural music of falling water from the fountains covers our conversation as we walk, my hand resting lightly on Charles' arm. He points out lavender as clear as my eyes, rose petals as fair and translucent as my skin, a pink bud just opening that reminds him of my lips. I cannot speak, I am so intoxicated with his voice. He has never spoken to me this way, yet his words sound familiar, for I have dreamed of hearing such things said to me. By the time we reach the center of the garden and I sink onto the bench I am so dizzy with delight I fear I will swoon. Charles rests his boot on the marble seat beside me and leans upon his knee toward me, very close, so that we need not speak too loud.

"You must know now why I have asked you to come here with me," he says.

I shake my head, unable to imagine what more he might say, but eager to hear it. Unless he is saying goodbye. Unless he has brought me here to tell me Joanna is sending him away somewhere to… to increase her kingdom, when I have none at all, and only one friend, one true friend, my cousin Charles, who cares about me.

"You are not leaving?" I whisper.

He looks at me, considering my question. Charles always listens to me and gives me a serious answer, even when I have said something foolish. I wait, holding my breath.

"I might have to," he says.

"No! You cannot! You must not."

He tips his head. "Do you want to know why?"

"No!" There is no reason I will accept. I will have to, though, if Joanna orders it, or if his mother is sending him— My heart stops beating. I gasp, and sway on the bench. Charles cups my elbow, steadying me, but I shake off his hand. "You are going to marry." I can barely get the words out; my tongue feels thick and clumsy, my whole body, so light and joyous a moment ago, now feels heavy and dull.

"I am," he says solemnly. "If she is willing."

He is going to marry an old woman, then, a widow, perhaps even older than him; a young bride would have no say. She will be an heiress. His mother, Agnes of Perigord, would never permit him to marry for love. That makes me feel a little better, as I search my memory for a well-connected duchess whose husband has recently died. Someone my calculating Lady Aunt would choose for her eldest son, for I have no doubt she is behind this.

"Who is it?" I ask, coming up with no one I would consider good enough for Charles.

"I cannot tell you before I ask her."

I nod. He is a man of honor, his answer is what I would expect. And what does it matter? Whoever she is, he will be hers. She will never refuse him, no one could. I am heartbroken. I will never recover. Even if Prince Jean, heir to the throne of France, is as handsome as Louis of Taranto and as devoted to me when we marry as Philippa is to Raymond, I will never love Prince Jean as I love Charles. I will never again love anyone as I love Charles.

"Do you… do you want to marry her?" I cannot look at him as I ask it. Please, I think, although I know it is selfish, please say no.

"With all my heart."

It takes me a few moments. I cannot help that, but then I make myself look up at him even though my eyes are full of tears, for I am a princess and one day I will be a queen, and he has always been my true friend. "I am happy for you," I say. My voice quivers only a little, surely not enough for him to notice.

"Are you Maria? My dear little cousin Maria? Are you happy that I will marry? And will you be happy to marry?"

I cannot say yes. He is looking straight into my eyes and we have always been honest with each other. I should tell him yes, but how can I ever be happy with anyone else? I have always loved Charles best of my cousins, but I did not know how much I loved him until these last few weeks, when I began to hope he loved me back. I do not want to marry a French prince now, no matter how handsome he is, so how can I say yes? He will see in my eyes that I am lying. Would Tristan have believed Isolde if she told him she was happy, married to the King?

"No," I say. Then I know I should have tried to say yes, because my admission is more than I can bear. I start to weep. I cover my face with my hands and twist sideways on the seat, away from him. I wish he would go away and not see me like this. But this may be the last time I am alone with him, so how can I wish him to leave? I do not know what I wish, until I feel his hands on my arms, raising me up.

"Would you be happy to marry me, Maria?" he asks.

"Yes," I sob. "She will be happy, she cannot help but be."

I hear him laugh, a low chuckle, and I feel his arms move across my back, encircling me, and it feels so delicious, so wonderful, that I stop crying and stand still. I am afraid to move, afraid to make a sound, for fear he will remember himself and let me go. He bends his head and I feel his breath in my hair, I feel his hands warm and strong against my back.

"Would you be happy to marry me, Maria?" he asks again.

He is mocking me. He knows I am meant for the French prince, and he is to marry a… an old widow! He is laughing at me. I put my hands against his chest and push him!

He sighs and lets me go. "Maria, I am asking if you will marry me."

I stare at him. What does he mean? He is about to marry…I am to marry… He cannot have said what I thought I heard. But he did, I see it in his face. And he is not smiling or laughing as though he were teasing me.

"How can I marry you? I am to marry the French prince."

"Are you? Because I have not heard of any contract. I would not ask you if I knew you were already promised." He looks at me as though I have questioned his honor.

"I know Charles, I know that," I say quickly, and then I am quiet, thinking, he is right. Joanna has not arranged a marriage for me. Our grandfather did not say I *must* marry a prince of France, only that I should. I am still free. And if I am free, why should I not marry who I want? The idea is so impossible, so astounding, I feel it swirling inside my head as though I am drunk on it. Then I remember: "What about your wealthy widow?" and a worse thought: "What about your mother?"

"Wealthy widow?" he asks. "You mean my mother? I would not call her that to her face, dear cousin. And she is… fond of you, Maria. She approves of our match." I must look as confused as I feel, for he adds, "she has already sent a missive to the Pope asking his permission for me to marry whomever I choose."

I stare at him open-mouthed, till I catch my breath with a gasp. Papal approval to marry whomever he wants? "He will never grant it."

"I think he will. My uncle, the Cardinal Talleyrand de Perigord, has agreed to be our advocate. Pope Clement VI will not have forgotten the Cardinal who secured his election."

"You are serious." My legs tremble. I sink down onto the seat. My heart is pounding; I feel the pulse of it in every part of my body. Marry Charles! I could stay in Naples if I married Charles!

I will never be a queen if I marry Charles. But what about Isolde? She was ready to trade her King husband for Tristan. Love is more important than a crown.

Charles sits on the bench beside me and takes my hand. I feel myself falling into his gray eyes so close to mine. "I am only a duke now," he says, "but I am twenty and a proven soldier. With your resources as well as my own, I will win us a kingdom. And you will be my queen."

"Joanna—"

"—Will approve, in time. Do not ask her now. She is preoccupied with other concerns. She cannot approve it anyway, she must ask her council, and they will take forever to decide. You will be too old to marry before they decide."

I look at him, alarmed.

"We will ask their approval after we have announced our engagement. Then they will have to hurry."

I feel myself smile. I am so stunned with the unexpectedness of it all, it is like someone else is smiling, until Charles stands and pulls me to my feet and draws me close to him. "Would you be happy to marry me, Maria?" he asks a third time.

I fall against his strong chest, weak with joy, and cry, "Yes!"

Chapter 7

A Secret Revealed

"Her Majesty Queen Joanna invites you to dine with her tonight."

I look up from my sewing, startled. A messenger in the Queen's livery stands before me. Was he announced? I glance around my presence chamber. My ladies-in-waiting immediately resume their work, several of them hiding smiles.

I have been dreaming of Charles while I bent over the chemise I am embroidering, oblivious of the goings-on in my own presence chamber. Apparently everyone knows it—at least they know my mind is elsewhere. I have to stop this before they try to guess where my thoughts go when I leave them. If they have not guessed already?

"I am honored to take my dinner with Her Majesty." It is nothing, I tell myself. We used to dine together all the time. She cannot possibly know about Charles.

Will I be able to keep this secret from her? It is much harder to keep a happy secret than a bitter one. A terrible secret changes you on the inside, twisting your gut and visiting you in dark dreams or moments of sudden shame which you hide instinctively, wanting no one to know. But a happy secret affects you on the outside, lighting up your face in the daylight, making you smile at nothing when everyone can see you, leaping to your lips and begging to be shared. I have only kept Charles' declaration a secret this week because Joanna is too busy to see me except at our prayers, when Grandmother Sancia is present. Even if she wanted to, Joanna could not talk to me then; our grandmother expects our thoughts to be on God. If God is love, then I am thinking of Him.

When I am ushered into her privy chamber, Joanna is sitting alone in a chair by the fire. I approach her and curtsy, low enough to show respect for her crown but not too low—she is my sister, after all. It is only a matter of time and fortune before I am her equal in rank as well as birth. She bows her head, acknowledging me, then grins. I cannot help but giggle, for she has caught my intent and turned it into a joke between us. She gestures to the chair beside her and I sit, feeling for the first time since Grandfather died that we are two sisters with our heads together, sharing jokes and secrets between only us. And now I have a secret I cannot share, I remind myself, before I fall helplessly under the spell of our carefree past. And she must have much that she cannot share with me. I look at her more closely. Her face is pale. Even the rosy fire cannot draw blossoms onto her cheeks; instead it forms shadows under her cheekbones that make her face look gaunt and lined—yes, lined, like someone twice her age.

"You look tired, sister." I take her hand impetuously. Who has she to talk to, to share her worries, to love her as Charles loves me? Andrew? He is probably the cause of half her weariness.

I heard yesterday that Andrew and his men killed a man—not a nobleman, thank God, but an honest subject, nevertheless—for objecting when they took his daughter. The news gave me a terrible nightmare—somehow it got turned into Andrew killing my father. I woke up weeping and had a sick headache all morning. "It is Andrew, is it not?" I exclaim.

"How am I to keep order? How am I to restore peace?" She turns her face toward the fire, but not before I see the moisture glistening in her eyes. I jump up and clasp her hands in mine. There is nothing I can say. The Queen cannot have her husband arrested for causing disorder in her city.

"Is it not enough to have noblemen fighting noblemen all over our kingdom, and bands of robbers attacking the merchants bringing goods into and out of our city?" Her voice is low and tight with anger. "There are robbers and highwaymen on every road; many of them were honest men before these warring lords laid waste to their homes and their livelihood and butchered their families. They even dare to bring their quarrel into Naples itself, ignoring our Lord Grandfather's express decree banning the carrying of weapons in our city! And now my own husband…" she closes her eyes. I see the tears between her damp lashes, but when she opens her eyes they shine not with sorrow but with fury "…that stupid, stupid boy! Now he imagines that he is friends with the Count of Minerbino and the Gatti family. And I cannot tell him not to bear weapons, I cannot order my husband's guard to leave their weapons behind when they accompany him about the city!"

"Friends with the Paladin?" I gasp, using the count's feared nickname. Without thinking I drop her hands and step back in horror. "Is he joining the vendetta?" Surely he cannot. It is inconceivable! What will happen if Andrew becomes part of the entrenched warfare between the Marra family and the Gatti family? Will the Marra family extend their cycle of vengeance even to us?

"He is no part of the vendetta," Joanna says, her voice full of scorn. "He is too stupid even to understand it. He has merely been convinced that Minerbino is his friend, that the Gatti accept him as one of them. I cannot convince him they are just using him. He tells me I am jealous that he has friends in Naples, that he is welcomed by nobles here, if not by the arrogant Angevins."

"By thieves and murderers? By lawbreakers?" But why am I shocked? He has found his own kind. I know that better than anyone.

"That is exactly what I told him, but he will not hear it. He says King Robert put the Minerbino brothers in jail so he would have an excuse to confiscate their lands and sell them, and put the money into the royal coffers."

"Does he want us to let them murder each other in our streets, along with anyone who happens by and gets in the way? Is he wicked enough to want that?"

"Foolish, not wicked. And it is worse." She takes a breath to steady her voice. "My councilors tells me Andrew is only repeating what he hears. That the people themselves say King Robert did not care to enforce his laws. That he allowed his nobles to run wild, to destroy towns and cities in their skirmishes, so that he could step in afterwards and fine them."

I sink back into my chair. "It is not true!" I stammer. "They loved our Lord Grandfather. They cheered him when he rode out, they cheered us all when we progressed to Santa Chiara on Holy Days." I remember the smiling crowds, calling out "King Robert the Wise!" and "Queen Sancia the Pious!" and "Princess Joanna, Princess Maria! Huzzah!" as we threw them coins and waved and smiled, everyone smiling. But underneath the smiles…?

"Can a king believe he is loved when actually he is despised?"

"Apparently."

I look at her bleakly. I want to ask: What do they say of us? But I am afraid. I am not sure I want to know.

Joanna relents: "They also called him wise and just. He was not despised. They just wanted more. No matter how much I do, they will always want more," she adds, her voice low, as though to herself.

I do not know what to say to this. I have a sudden memory of our Lord Grandfather roaring to our Lady Grandmother, something about his laws being openly ignored. His voice frightened me, I was not used to his passions yet, and I began to cry. He glared at me a moment, then he said, "That is right, Princess Maria. Weep. Weep when justice is flouted!"

"They are wrong," I say softly, a little surprised, because mostly I believe others' opinions. But they are wrong about my grandfather; he cared very much about his laws. I feel such relief I look up, smiling. Joanna did not hear me, does not notice my smile. She has not found her way out of her despondency yet.

"My council tells me the people say I cannot rule. They say if a king cannot impose order, how can a mere girl?" She turns her face back to the fire.

"Your council says this?"

I see her stiffen. She has not brought me here to doubt her also. "But you are the heir," I add quickly. I realize even as I say it how foolish I sound. There are many eager Angevin heirs, not only the one King Robert named, including King Louis of Hungary. No one wants another Hungarian prince here in Naples. No one cheers for Andrew when he rides out. When he rides with his circle of men down the narrow streets like a black wave from the ocean washing over everyone in their path, no one cries "Hail Prince Andrew, Duke of Salerno!" They want a Neapolitan heir, a golden Angevin heir, but a strong one, a male heir, not a woman ruling on her own, and a minor at that.

Joanna is clever and able, I tell myself, trying to still the voice inside my head that agrees with them. It is not natural for a woman to rule men. We cannot help but be swayed by our feminine fancies and fears. It is as hard to imagine a woman holding a scepter on her own as to envision her leading men into battle. Charles might rule, he is the eldest grandson of King Robert's brother John. Especially if he is wedded to a princess named in King Robert's will as one of his true heirs. I push the thought from my mind at once. I have sworn my allegiance to the crown and King Robert placed that crown on Joanna's head.

"What will you do?"

Joanna looks at me sharply. "I made a vow to King Robert on his deathbed, and so did you." Her jaw tightens. "I will keep that vow, and so will you. And so will Andrew, by God."

"Of course," I say at once. "Of course we will." But I am not certain she will be able to, and she must see it. Her face, in the glow of the fire, hardens. "I will prove them wrong," she says, in a voice I barely recognize. "I will restore order and respect for the law. Naples is renowned for its laws, because of our grandfather. Her citizens, even the nobility, will learn to obey them, or face my justice. I will be the Queen Naples deserves, the Queen our noble grandfather believed I would be." She looks at me, defiant. Awed by her vision, I nod.

"Naples will have peace and prosperity under my reign. And…and I will regain Sicily!"

I blink. "Sicily?" She expects to conquer Sicily when neither King Robert nor his father, King Charles II, nor anyone they have commissioned to lead their armies has been able to? The spell of her vision is broken. She is just a girl who would be queen, no different from me. Except that she has a weak, despicable boy who cannot be trusted with a crown beside her, and I will have a man who deserves to be king, who will win a new kingdom for himself and rule it with me.

"You do not have to believe me now," she says, a little grandly, I think. "I will show you, and everyone."

"You are already Queen, Joanna." And awkwardly, because it is all I can think to say, I add: "Your people love you."

It is true. Whether they believe in her as a strong and capable ruler or not, they love her. She has ever been theirs, not only their beautiful princess, for I am that also, but the princess who loves them. Even as a child Joanna delighted in throwing handfuls of coins to the poor as she rode through the city, and sewing shirts for those who had none, and washing the feet of beggars with our Lady Grandmother Sancia before the feast of Maundy Thursday during Holy Week. I could never eat after washing those dirty feet. I would sit at the feast and the fire-roasted meat would look like blackened feet, the figs like dirty toes. This Easter I will be affianced to Charles, the intended Countess of Durazzo, I think to myself. I will not have to wash anyone's feet if I do not choose to!

"Maria, have you ever thought…"

I look at Joanna, staring moodily into the fire. "Thought what?"

"That we owe allegiance, too? We who are crowned," she says slowly.

"To God," I agree at once.

"Yes of course, to God. But I was thinking… of an earthly allegiance."

"You mean our family. Our line." I say it a little guiltily because I was raised to understand my duty, and that does not include marrying whom I will. "You mean the house of Angevin," I compromise, because Charles is an Angevin, too. Where is she going with this? Does she know? Is she testing me?

"No, above that. Do we owe allegiance to… say, our kingdom?"

"You do not have to school me, Joanna. I know I owe my allegiance to you as Queen of Naples."

Joanna sighs. "But what do we owe to Naples?"

"To Naples? The people owe their allegiance to you."

"And am I not honor-bound to serve them? To serve 'even the least of them' as our Lord commanded?"

I am silent, thinking: I will have to wash their feet again. I do not want to say anything that will commit me to it.

"I will restore justice and wealth and prosperity to the Kingdom of Naples." Joanna sits straight in her chair, her head held high. "I will hold its good above all other allegiances. I vow this before God to my Kingdom, and to my people, and I hold my sister, the Princess Maria, as my witness!"

I start a little, and look around, but no one else is here. Then I feel foolish, for she was speaking to God; and then I am afraid, because a vow to God is a dangerous thing, a threat to one's immortal soul if broken, and it is an impossible vow, and she has made me part of it. I wish I had stopped her, but it is too late now.

Joanna looks into the fire as though she can already see her future unfolding there exactly as she has sworn it will. As though she is hearing God's answer. I shiver, squinting into the fire, but all I see are flames. I glance sideways, a little afraid of her, half-convinced she can see what others cannot. What does she mean, a vow to the kingdom? A vow to land? How can one make a vow to land? The King—the Queen, in this case—is the head of the kingdom. Is she making a vow of allegiance to herself? I have never heard of such a thing.

"You frighten me," I tell her, frowning, for I may frown in private at my sister.

"Good. Then you will remember what I have sworn."

I shake my head. "How can I remember what I do not understand?"

"Never mind now," she says. "If I can frighten you, who knows my every secret from childhood, then perhaps I will be able to frighten my council into supporting my decisions."

"Our Lady Grandmother is the head of your council. Nothing frightens her," I say automatically. She nods in wry agreement.

"Well then, I will be forced to progress more slowly. Meanwhile, let us eat. I have had our meal set up here so we can talk in private as we used to."

"I have missed that," I say, glad to get away from the topic of vows and secrets, although in truth I have thought of no one but Charles this past week. I turn toward the little table, laid prettily with silver dishes and cups and a jug of mulled wine, so she will not see my face and read the lie in it. We sit in the chairs and serve ourselves cold venison and rich dark bread still warm from the oven, with quince jam from the royal orchard, and cheese and figs and walnuts and marchpane. She has remembered my love of marchpane. Joanna waits until I realize that, in the absence of servants, I must pour our wine.

She nibbles on a piece of bread spread with quince jam, while I eat my meal. She has lost weight, I notice. When we were children she could not eat after Philippa had scolded her, never mind a reprimand from our Grandfather the King or Grandmother Sancia. As a consequence Philippa, who ate with us in our nursery, always spoke more harshly to me when we had been caught in a childish escapade, and corrected Joanna gently. I resented the unfairness of it, I still do, but in the end it made no difference; Joanna always suffered for days, while I shrugged off the correction and remembered only the fun.

"I have learned something that concerns you, Maria."

My throat closes on the piece of venison I have just swallowed. I cough and reach for my cup of wine. What does she know? And how? I try to look unconcerned, even interested in what she has to say as I struggle to swallow, not to choke up my food like someone caught in a crime.

It is a crime, I realize in horror. It is treason for a princess to marry without the express permission of the crown as well as the Pope. I did not think of that. We had not got to planning marriage yet, he only asked me if I would be happy. 'Would' is not 'will'. Is 'would' still treason?

"I know you are friendly with our cousin Charles of Durazzo, so perhaps this is not a surprise," Joanna continues.

She knows! Someone has guessed and told her. I search her face. She does not seem angry, only concerned. Perhaps she thinks it is a lie? There are always rumors at court, this lady-in-waiting was seen with this or that courtier. Did someone see Charles and me in the garden with his arms around me? I take another hasty swallow of my wine.

"Do you know what I am talking about, Maria?"

"No?" My voice trembles, turning the denial into a question. Do I know or do I not, she will wonder. So do I.

Joanna looks at me. I put my wine cup down carefully and smile at her, drawing her attention from my shaking hand. "What have you heard?" My voice breaks on the last word. I press my fingers to my lips as though it was an unmaidenly burp, not a croak of fear.

She takes a breath, as though it pains her to say it. I brace myself.

"Our cousin Charles has received a bull from Pope Clement VI, granting him permission to marry whomever he chooses. Our Lady Grandmother told me." Sancia's word on this is sound, Joanna will know. Our grandmother, who likes very few people, likes Charles' mother, Agnes of Perigord. At least she prefers her to the haughty Catherine, Duchess of Taranto and titular Empress of Constantinople. Their mutual dislike of our Lady Aunt Catherine is enough for Grandmother Sancia and Agnes of Perigord to put their heads together regularly.

Joanna is waiting for me to say something.

I am waiting for her to say more.

"I am sorry if this hurts you, Maria. I know you are fond of Charles. But he was bound to marry, and you will also marry soon, God willing."

This is worse than if she knew. What can I say, where can I look? If I tell her it is me he wants to marry, I am confessing to treason. Worse,

I am accusing Charles of treason. But if I deny knowing anything, I will be lying to her face, and she will always remember it. I have not told her of my tryst with Charles, but I have not lied to her, either. Not yet. I open my mouth, but no words come out.

Joanna misinterprets my inability to speak. She reaches across the table and touches my hand. "I am sorry, Maria," she says, her voice full of compassion. "I understand what it is to love someone you cannot have."

"Why? Why can I not have Charles?" I cry, pulling my hand away.

She looks astonished. She was thinking of herself and Louis of Taranto, comparing their situation to mine. But she has been married since she was six, and she is the Queen. I am only a princess, and I am still free. I have not been promised yet to anyone.

Joanna straightens in her chair, pulling her own hand back. "You knew of the bull," she says.

"I…I know his mother requested permission for him to marry. He told me a few days ago. And that… and that he had not yet asked anyone." Not quite the truth, but not quite a lie, either, and no more than she already knows.

"That was cruel of him," Joanna says quietly. "To taunt you with that, knowing he cannot have you, knowing you are to marry Prince Jean or his brother."

I want to protest Charles' kindness, to tell her he is incapable of cruelty, but her second statement catches me. "Have they replied? Has the French King made an offer of marriage? Oh God, have you accepted?" I leap up, ignoring my chair as it teeters behind me on the verge of falling before it settles again.

Joanna watches me. "What is this, Maria? Do you imagine that you could marry Charles of Durazzo?" And more sharply, "Has he been courting you?"

"No!" I cry, regaining my wits for Charles' sake. "Only he told me that he will marry, he must marry, and…" I catch myself again. "And *I* want it to be me!"

Joanna sits still and straight in her chair. She does not speak, but lets the silence speak for her. I have been shouting. Shouting at the Queen of Naples! I drop into a curtsy. "Forgive me, Your Majesty," I murmur. I start to sit again and straighten quickly, waiting for her permission.

She nods her head slightly. When I sit down she gestures me to continue eating.

"I will throw a feast for you," she announces after we have sat a short while in awkward silence. "You will enjoy that, will not you, Maria? All the grand noblemen will pay tribute to you and compliment your beauty. You may have a new gown, and dance before the court."

I keep my head bowed over my plate. I am not a child to be enticed from what I want with a sop. Even though the feast does sound exciting, and I would like a new gown.

"The ambassador to France will be there, he will see how you are admired. I will remind him to speak to Prince Jean about you."

No offer of marriage has been made yet, then. I am still free. I push my plate aside. "I have eaten my fill, thank you, Your Highness. May I leave?"

I walk out with my head held high, but I feel her gaze on my back. I remember her weary face as she gave me leave to go. I am not really as proud as I make myself appear.

Chapter 8

A Merry Dance

My new gown is pale purple, the color of royalty, with yellow fleur-de-lis declaring our French Angevin blood, stitched in silk thread onto the skirt. No one is allowed see it, not even my ladies-in-waiting, until I walk into the hall arm-in-arm with my sister Joanna. She will be wearing her customary dark purple with gold fleur-de-lis. We will be stunning together, but all eyes will be on me, because they have not seen me in purple before. It was always Joanna who was the heir to the throne, but now she is Queen, and I am the heir.

"Let them think of that when they see you," Joanna said, for it was her idea to dress me in purple. "Let them be reminded you are heir to a throne, born to be a queen."

I would be happy if it were not that Charles has not come to court since I dined with my sister. He will not see me in my new gown. I do not want to dazzle the Ambassador from France; I want to dazzle Charles.

Nevertheless, when I look at myself in the glass, the gown is everything Joanna said it would be. I meet her at the door to the great hall and we walk in together. The hall goes silent, despite being filled to overflowing with guests. Everyone of any importance has been invited to see me honored. As we walk through the crowd of people to our seats at the head table, everyone falls back before us with admiration in their eyes, bowing and curtsying as we pass arm-in-arm.

I do not look for Charles. Joanna has banned him from court; she would not invite him to my feast. I have almost convinced myself that I do not mind, that I will enjoy this evening even without Charles, when I look around and there he is, standing with his brothers and his Lady Mother beside our Lady Grandmother Sancia. We cannot talk, but our eyes meet, his full of admiration which makes me flush with pleasure, mine full of the longing I feel for him. It is as though we have had a full conversation in that one glance before he sweeps into a low bow for Joanna and me, along with those around him. I recall myself in time to dip into a curtsy as low as my Grandmother Sancia's, since she and I are of equal rank now, while Joanna bows her head. Then we have passed. I cannot look back. I must keep my eyes forward as I progress on the Queen's arm to our seats.

We dine on pheasant and venison, mutton and capons and dove, on baked mullet and pickled herring and Spanish mackerel. Troubadours sing songs of my beauty and virtue which they have written for this evening, and the jesters compete hilariously with one another for my favor. I hand one a piece of venison for his dinner and another a piece of mackerel and they quarrel over which gift shows a greater affection on my part, with randy comments on the fertility of Pisces and the rutting nature of stags. When I offer the third jester, a dwarf, a piece of bread he tucks it against his breast as if it were my glove and mimes his preparedness to challenge the others to a tournament over it. We laugh until we are weak. I am so dizzy with delight I eat almost as sparingly as Joanna.

The musicians troop in as our plates are being cleared and begin to play while the jesters tumble out to enjoy their dinner in the kitchen. Joanna asks me to dance. I rise willingly. Joanna and I have often danced for the court, but now I must choose another partner for the Estampie. I choose Marguerite of Taranto to please my sister and my powerful Taranto relatives, and also to discredit any hint of favoring Durazzo. My Lady Aunt Catherine smiles smugly as her daughter steps forward.

Lady Marguerite is shy and pleasant, unlike her ambitious family. She has their golden good looks and fair complexion, but she has recently grown tall and moves as though she is not quite sure yet how to manage such long limbs. Dancing with her I will look as graceful as a breeze. She steps forward, looking frightened at the prospect of dancing before the entire assembly. I realize she must be thinking of the complicated leaps and twists the dance calls for and I whisper to her that I will take the lead. She smiles in gratitude.

I am very good at the Estampie. It requires strength and stamina as well as grace, and I delight in executing the jumps and twists perfectly, stamping my feet with the music. This time, however, I am barely aware of my movements. All eyes are on me, but I am aware of only one pair. Every step in this joyous dance is a message to him; every triumphant leap I take is a testament of my love for him. I am aware of him in every muscle of my body as I dip and twirl and leap for only Charles. The roar of approval which greets the end of my dance startles me. I remember for whom I am actually dancing and curtsy to my sister the Queen, who smiles at me.

For my second dance I choose Margherita di Ceccano as my partner. I have not confided to her what Charles asked me in the garden; Joanna's reaction has made me guarded for his sake. But Margherita knows how I feel about him and she guides our steps in his direction, ensuring that she is most often the one with her back toward him. I have chosen her out of friendship but also to honor the Durazzos as I did the Tarantos.

Margherita dances as well as I do, so our performance will be exquisite. But as soon as we begin I forget my vanity, forget that I am performing before the entire court of Naples. I feel his eyes on me and I respond like a cat responds to the warmth of the sun. This is a slower tune. I move as one in a dream, floating, with his presence, his appreciation, his pride bearing me up. The music that guides my steps seeps inside me, like a dream of music. I am aware of only the two of us, he and I, one of us the dream, the other the dreamer, but I do not know which is he and which is me. When the music stops I blink as one awakening, and turn instinctively to him. Margherita's hand, still holding mine, guides me to continue my turn full circle, as though it is the final step of the dance, until I face Queen Joanna, who watches me curtsy to her with a little line between her brows despite the smile on her lips.

The musicians play a rondel, opening the ball to everyone who cares to take the floor. Joanna does not rise to lead the dance. Andrew, sitting beside her, his greasy fingers still stuffing food into his mouth, would never think to invite her to dance. She has not once looked at or spoken to him this evening, nor he to her. On the few occasions they are required to attend a fete together, they are as distant as bird and fish, occupying separate realms. It is not difficult to interpret the glances passed between members of Joanna's council as they wonder how the Queen and the Duke will ever conceive a child together.

What if I am forced to marry Prince Jean of France and we are as ill-suited as they are? I know it is impossible that a French prince should turn out as dull and boorish as a Hungarian, but Andrew is my cousin, he has Angevin blood as well as Hungarian, and he was raised in Naples. Even if Prince Jean is not a villain like Andrew, even if he never tries to hurt me, we could be miserable together. A queen can be unhappy as easily as a peasant, and have no more power to improve her lot, I realize now. I torment myself with the thought until I cannot bear it. Then I get up and walk to the dance floor.

Immediately Robert, the oldest of my Taranto cousins, offers me his hand. At the corner of my eye I notice Charles guiding his partner in our direction, so that when the music starts it is only natural that they should join our circle.

Robert bows to me. I curtsy to him. We take three mincing steps forward and touch hands, palm to palm. Some ladies barely graze their partner's palm with their fingers, but I put my full palm against Robert's and smile at him. "Congratulations, Cousin, on your victory in archery," I whisper, referring to yesterday's tournament which he won. We turn sideways and slide three steps to our original places.

When we approach each other again, he murmurs, "I did not know you were fond of archery. I shall win every tournament for you, in future."

"I am flattered." I smile flirtatiously over my shoulder as I leave him. In fact I am surprised. This dress, this evening, has somehow changed me from a girl into a desirable woman, just as Joanna promised. Robert smiles back gallantly and lets his hand linger on my waist a moment before he turns me under his raised arm and sends me, laughing, to my next partner. I have mysteriously learned to flirt without blushing. When I reach Charles my real smile will be safely hidden by these foolish ones.

I must dance with two more partners before it is Charles' turn with me. I chatter with each of them. Joanna will be watching, but what can she say if I speak to everyone I dance with? We will have two brief exchanges. Is Charles preparing his lines as feverishly as I am? I do not dare ask him outright if he still means the question he put to me in the garden. But what if his heart has changed? What if Joanna has spoken to him and he has found a bride she will accept? I have to know.

Robert of Taranto, dancing beside us in our set, must not imagine we are discussing anything more serious than my comments were to him. I have no doubt he is listening even more closely than Joanna is watching. The Tarantos and the Durazzos are excessively interested in each others' doings. My cousin Robert will be very sure to hear what I say to my cousin Charles, and will repeat every word to his Lady Mother.

Lord Philip sends me twirling toward Charles. His hand, touching my waist to claim me as his partner, burns through my gown. It is all I can do not to shiver, and almost more than I can do to move apart. The music saves me, informing my steps, instinct over desire.

"I am sorry you missed the tournament," I murmur. And then, as we move apart, I am tormented by the fear that he might not know I mean that I am sorry about his absence at court, and will think I am telling him he has lost. I smile intently, flirtatiously, just as I did to Robert, willing him to take my real meaning. I can barely breathe as I take the three small steps toward him. Our palms meet.

His hand against mine is strong, sure, and warm. I imagine it touching me beneath my gown and this time I cannot help myself shivering. It is so slight I am sure only he will notice the tremble in my palm.

He smiles down at me. "It is only the first round," he says. Robert will think he is referring to the fact that there will be several more tournaments before this year's overall victor is declared. My smile widens. "I admire perseverance, Cousin," I tell him. His eyes meet mine. We are in accord! I am so filled with joy I fear it must spill out, like an overfull jug. My eyes, my smile, my very skin glows with happiness. When it is time for me to sidestep back, I cannot take my hand from his. I want to feel his touch on my skin forever. Even the music cannot make me move. We are one; it would be like tearing a part of myself away, to separate my palm from his.

With a slight bow of his head and a knowing smile, Charles lowers his hand. I take a little breath against the loss and close my hand, holding onto the warmth of his palm where it touched mine. I do not have to feign the longing gaze I send over my shoulder as I slip away.

We have one more opportunity to speak as I cross in front of him, but all the sentences I formed in my mind disappear. I can only think: He has not given up! He wants me still!

When I feel the skirt of my gown brushing against him, I long to lean back, to step into his arms. How delicious his arms felt around me in the garden; I have dreamed of it every night since. I feel him lean forward—the very air is charged with his nearness—

"My Lady Mother is very taken with… your gown," he murmurs. "She mentioned it to your Lady Grandmother, who most graciously agreed with her. I do hope you will have occasion to wear it again soon."

He takes my hand and turns me under his arm, and sends me, giddy with joy, back to Robert.

Chapter 9

An Engagement

"It does not matter what you want, Maria. It does not matter what either of us want. We marry to form alliances." Joanna regards me coldly from her chair as I stand before her in her privy room. I do not bow my head, but meet her gaze evenly, insulted that she should tell me what every royal child knows by the age of two.

"I am as devoted to the Angevins as you are, Your Majesty."

"Then marry accordingly."

It is almost more than I can do, not to accuse her of jealousy. I take a deep breath. "What will another French marriage accomplish? We are already allied with the French King as Angevins, as well as through our mother and our Lady Aunt. What difference will one more marriage make?"

"Our Lady Mother is dead, and our Lady Aunt Catherine, sister to Philip VI of France…"

She does not say it outright but we both know our ambitious Lady Aunt Catherine is not our ally; she wants one of her sons to wear Joanna's crown.

"King Robert's choice was not arbitrary," she continues in a more sympathetic voice, the voice of my sister, not my Queen. "He knew I would need a voice in the ear of France to balance our Lady Aunt's. I need you there, Maria. I trust only you."

"I trust only you," I say quietly. "So keep me here where I can support you, sister. Do not send me away."

Joanna hesitates, but then I see her face change: the sister fades and the Queen returns. "I must have you settled. You are the heir to this throne, and wealthy in your own right. Every nobleman with ambition has one eye on you and the other on who else might try to claim you. They will not fight the King of France or his son, but they would fall on each other for your hand, and the victor will turn against me, while the losers turn against both of us. I need their support. I dare not make more enemies than I already have. If I give you to Charles, I tip the balance between Durazzo and Taranto, and who knows what might fall off the scales onto my head? I cannot take that risk, not even for you, Maria. Do not ask me again."

The door opens. Joanna looks up, amazed that anyone would enter her privy chamber without her permission. Our Lady Grandmother Sancia walks in, the only person in Naples who would do so.

"And if there were a weight upon the scale? A weight so heavy and holy none would dare attempt to dislodge it?"

I stare at her with my mouth open as she walks across the room not even pretending that she has not been listening at the Queen's door. Joanna's face is still and expressionless, a certain sign that she is furious.

"If you do not wish to be overheard, Granddaughter, you must learn to keep your voice low," Sancia says mildly. Joanna's face goes even more still. Our Grandmother ignores this sign, though surely she knows Joanna well enough to recognize it. She taught it to her herself.

"My Lady Grandmother," Joanna says, inclining her head as though our Grandmother has already curtsied to her.

"I am too old to bend my knees to you in private," Grandmother Sancia tells her.

"Please be seated, Lady Grandmother." Joanna barely gets the words out before our grandmother creaks down onto a chair. "You might as well sit also, sister."

I choose a seat to the side, glad to step away from my position between them. My Grandmother Sancia's arrival fills me with hope. Charles told me she approved of our match. We sit in awkward silence. I am beginning to think Joanna will not grant Our Lady Grandmother permission to speak, when at last she says, "Have you something to say to me, Lady Grandmother?"

"Dowager Queen," Sancia reminds her. "I have come to tell you I approve of this match. And more than that, to tell you that Clement VI approves of it."

"His Holiness merely approved my cousin Charles marrying."

"He knows exactly who the young Duke of Durazzo plans to marry."

"Plans to?" Joanna's voice is icy.

Grandmother Sancia waits just long enough to let Joanna hear the tone of voice she has used to the Dowager Queen of Naples before she begins her attack.

"Would you go against your Holy Father, Grandchild? Are you already so filled with the vanity of your position that His Holiness' consent strikes you as being of less importance than your own? Are you so certain of your ability to rule that you are ready after one month to toss aside my advice? I, the head of your council?"

"They will never agree to it," Joanna says, cowed but not yet beaten.

Grandmother Sancia looks at her steadily. I am so anxious, so caught between hope and despair, and so glad that for once that measuring look is not trained on me, that I begin to hiccup, covering my mouth to hide it. Joanna does not wilt, as I always do, but she has lost. No one can stand firm against Our Lady Grandmother when she wears that look.

"The question," Grandmother Sancia says, "is how to go about it." She arches one eyebrow at Joanna.

Joanna shoots me a look intended to be as devastating as Grandmother Sancia's, but she has not been practicing it as long. I give her a very small smile, conciliatory, not gloating. I am very pleased with that smile, until I spoil the effect by hiccupping.

"It cannot come from me. I cannot be seen to award her to Charles."

"Let it come from me, then," Grandmother Sancia decides. "You are still a minor and I am the head of your council. I will throw the engagement party."

"Here? At Castle Nuovo?"

Engagement party? I hiccup loudly and clap my hand over my mouth. They both ignore me.

"Where else?"

Joanna swallows her objections, although I can see they are very nearly choking her. She turns to me. "You had better be happy, sister, for I fear I will pay dearly for this."

I am, indeed, deliriously happy.

The formal celebration of my engagement to the Duke of Durazzo is set for March twenty-six, a bare three weeks away. The day after the announcement has been made public, our Lady Aunt Catherine sweeps into my sister's presence chamber with a face that would turn the Medusa to stone. Our ladies-in-waiting scramble to their feet to curtsy, eying the door. Joanna nods for them to leave. I rise also, hoping to escape with them, but Joanna stops me with a piercing glance.

Catherine, Empress of Constantinople, Duchess of Taranto, sister to the King of France, paces across my sister's presence chamber with the same appearance of barely controlled violence as the lioness in our menagerie. "Please be seated, Lady Aunt," Joanna says calmly when we three are alone.

"I think I will stand, Your Highness," Aunt Catherine says, stopping before Joanna. She looks at me, then back to my sister. "I do not know the intent of this… engagement. I do not know whose idea it was, or why you have agreed to it. I do not know and I do not care. My sons are closer to the throne than Agnes of Durazzo's son, and have more to offer in lands and riches through an alliance, as you well know. And yet you pass us over in favor of Durazzo?"

There is a pause, as though Joanna is considering her arguments. I hold my breath and desperately try not to even think of hiccupping.

"I cannot end what I did not begin, Lady Aunt Catherine. I confess, this engagement is not of my choosing. As you know, I had hoped for a union with France." Joanna does not so much as glance at me but I feel the lash and maintain my impassive expression with difficulty.

"I will not stand for this insult, this slight to my family. The engagement must be ended at once!"

"I would happily oblige you, but as you know, I am a minor and must follow the advice I am given." Joanna spreads her hands wide, palms up, in a gesture of resignation. "The Duke of Durazzo has a bull from Pope Clement VI, permitting him to marry whom he will, and he has chosen the royal princess Maria. Our Holy Father has sanctioned this engagement, and my Lady Grandmother, the head of the council appointed to advise me, has approved it. Would you care to speak with her, Lady Catherine?"

"I have already done so!" My aunt's hands clench at her side. She is so angry she is unaware that she has just told the Queen of Naples she appealed to the Dowager Queen to overthrow a royal engagement before speaking to the Queen herself.

"When I say that I will not stand for it," she continues through gritted teeth, "I am not using a figure of speech. This is an insult to my brother the King of France, to whose son you have already offered the princess' hand. And it is an insult to my sons, who are more worthy of her hand than Durazzo. You insult us at your peril."

I am greatly tempted to defend Charles' worth. He led an expedition to regain Sicily for us. What did her sons do for the Kingdom of Naples? They were off reclaiming Achaia for their own family! I remember the curl of my Cousin Robert's sneer. As if I would willingly marry him!

"No insult is meant to King Philip or to yourself, my Lady Aunt."

"Then end this absurd engagement. What can you possibly hope to gain from it?"

"It is a marriage of love," I say.

Joanne gives me a single glance.

Lady Catherine looks at me as though a servant has spoken back to her. I am an object to her, a thing that might prove valuable in the future if she can possess it. A thing she does not want another to possess. Right now her glance is withering, as though I have just proved myself less valuable than she imagined. She turns back to Joanna.

"She may have been fooled by his pretty love-talk, but I hope you are not. I trust you know exactly what is happening here."

Before I can open my mouth, Joanna sends me a warning look. I press my lips tight together. Why am I here if I cannot defend myself and Charles from my aunt's insinuations? Joanna does not defend me either, which makes it doubly unfair that I may not speak.

She spreads her hands again. "I cannot hope to gain anything from it," she says with an air of resignation. "But neither will anyone else. Please be assured, my Lady Aunt, that this is not a slight to you or your sons. Indeed, I intend to be generous to your sons, whose virtues I well know, when I reach my majority."

Lady Catherine pauses. She glances at me as though measuring my worth against future favors. "I still object," she says proudly. "I will write to my brother to tell him of my objection."

"Of course," Joanna says smoothly. "I understand how you feel." She pointedly frowns at me as though to prove this whole thing is not of her making.

Which it is not, I think, with a pang of guilt. It is my fault entirely; I led Charles into the garden and let him see my distress at the thought of him marrying someone else. I befriended him and confided in him and encouraged him to hope that he had a chance to win my hand. I am fully to blame for him falling in love with me. Instead of regret I feel a smile tugging at my lips and must repress it.

"At any rate," Joanna is saying, "it is only an engagement. Perhaps King Philip will speak to His Holiness. Perhaps they will both write to my Lady Grandmother and my council. Anything can happen between an engagement and a marriage, Lady Catherine."

She does not look at me as she says this but I am sure my sister is as aware of my alarm as I am aware of my Lady Aunt's grim smile as she curtsies and leaves the room.

"What do you mean, 'anything can happen'?" I cry as soon as the door has closed.

"You forget yourself, Princess Maria," Joanna says coldly. When I bow my head in apology, she adds, "You need not ask me what I meant. It was you who taught me to expect the unexpected."

When I have no answer, she leans toward me. "Do you even understand what I am trying to do, Maria?"

"To keep us safe," I murmur, looking down, ashamed. I never meant to burden my already-burdened sister; I never meant to endanger her rule.

"Safe?" Her voice is weary, but as she speaks it strengthens. "I am trying for more than safe, sister. Under my rule, Naples will be the jewel of Europe, a center for learning and art, for law and justice, for faith and piety. Naples, the city Petrarch chose for his public examination for the honor of being named Poet Laureate of Rome. He would be examined nowhere else and by none other than our learned Grandfather, King Robert the Wise. Our university is renowned throughout the civilized world, and our library is the envy of European scholars everywhere. Our reign is blessed by His Holiness the Pope and by the pious Franciscans who make their home here. It is my duty to maintain all this and more, to increase Naples' prestige and prosperity.

"But first, as you point out, we must be safe, and for that, I must have our cousins' support. This love-match, this marriage as fanciful and misguided as a troubadour's song, could well bring everything tumbling down upon our heads. "

"No! I swear not!" I cry. "I promise you, Charles will be your right arm. Charles will defend Naples with his life, he will keep your kingdom safe!" I fall to my knees before her, my sister and my Queen, and I am certain, absolutely certain, that with our help, she will do all she has vowed to do. "I swear to you, on Charles' life, that we will be true!"

Joanna looks down at me. I cannot read her expression—sorrow? Regret? Resignation?—she takes my hands, and draws me up. "So be it," she says.

Charles does not return to court. Nor does Joanna send bolts of cloth and seamstresses to my rooms to measure me for my marriage trousseau. Instead, Sancia of Cabannis, Philippa's granddaughter, comes. She curtsies low to me, but I am so surprised to see her I acknowledge her curtsy and welcome her into my presence chamber with a single bow of my head. Having greeted me, she goes to an alcove apart from my ladies-in-waiting, and sits down with her sewing.

When we were young we played together, Joanna and Sancia of Cabannis and I. She was our favorite playmate, quick-witted and imaginative as well as cheerful and sweet-natured. She is one of Joanna's ladies-in-waiting now, and they are still fast friends, but I have avoided her ever since I stopped calling Philippa 'mother'. She must be here with a message from Joanna. She would not come of her own accord, unsure of a welcome, but I am so happy in the expectation of my engagement that I can afford to listen. When I am ready to.

I leave her to sit in my alcove if she wishes and walk over to the games table. Three of my ladies are playing at dice. I am about to marry a man I love; surely my stars must be aligned—so I sit down to play.

It is true that I am very good at hazards. I win more often than not, when I play in my presence chamber, and I do love winning. Today, however, I wonder if the winning is too easy. Would I win so often if I were not a princess, for all my skill? I push the little pile of coins in front of me back into the center of the table, telling my ladies to divide it and continue playing without me. "It would be unlucky for me to win at dice as well as love," I tell them magnanimously as I leave the game.

Bolstered by my own virtue, I cross the room and sit in the alcove beside Sancia. She rises quickly to curtsy, but I wave her back to her seat.

"What message has Her Majesty sent you with, Sancia?" I ask, not bothering to use a false honorific. Sancia of Cabannis, granddaughter of a peasant and a slave, is not a lady even if she is one of my sister's ladies-in-waiting. I speak to her pleasantly, though, and smile to show I bear her no ill-will.

"Her Grace did not send me. I have come on my own, because we were once friends." She looks down into her lap, biting her lower lip as though she is wondering if it was a mistake.

That single act—biting her bottom lip—transforms her. She was always unsure of herself at court. Our cousins treated her with casual mockery, sometimes so obviously that Joanna would come to her defense, telling them they were only lords when they behaved as such. I remember, too, that habit of catching the side of her lower lip when I, who was younger, would say or do something that made Joanna and my older cousins laugh. Sancia never laughed. No matter how foolish my question she would answer it solemnly in her quiet voice, and if she did not know the answer a single glace from her and Joanna would stop laughing to explain to me. Their laughter was not malicious; I am a royal princess. But Sancia was better than not mean; she was kind. I taught those hands she is clasping in her lap to play hazards. I am sure now that she already knew, but she let me teach her, she made little mistakes that I would catch. I would giggle and tell her, "No, not like that," and she would nod and thank me.

Impulsively I grasp her hands. "You have always been my friend, Sancia," I tell her, ashamed now of having let my cousins' example influence me. "I am the one who has not been a good friend."

She does not shame me by accepting my apology, but simply says, "I am glad of your friendship, Princess Maria," as though no apology was needed between us.

"Have you come to congratulate me?"

Her smile fades. She bows her head as though unwilling to see my joy. "I want only your happiness, Princess," she murmurs.

"Then be glad for me." My voice comes out more sharply than I intend.

She does not look up with a smile and a good wish, as I want. I had forgotten how stubborn she can be, in her quiet way, when she believes she is right. She waits for me to give her leave to speak.

I consider not doing so. I seriously consider just getting up and leaving her. But then I am curious, and besides, a royal princess should listen even to advice she does not want to hear.

"You may speak," I tell her graciously.

She catches the side of her lower lip in her teeth, and I have the unpleasant feeling of not knowing whether she is holding back fear or laughter. The expression is gone almost at once.

"Your Royal Highness, Princess Maria—"

I blink at her excess. *Is* she mocking me? But this is Sancia. Ah! It is a prepared speech she is delivering. I feel a momentary sympathy for her uncertainty. It must be difficult to live surrounded by your betters.

"—I beg you to reconsider your… present course. Your cousin, Lord Charles, Duke of Durazzo—"

Yes, yes. I know his titles. Will she dare abuse him to me?

"—I fear marriage to him will not… be all that you hope."

"Do you have any reason for your concern?" I am proud of my response. It is a restrained and queenly response.

"The Duke is an ambitious man, your Grace."

I wait, but she says nothing more. She is looking down at her lap again, unable or afraid to meet my eyes after what she has implied.

"I am ambitious also." Does she know he promised to win us a kingdom? How would she learn that?

"Marriage to a French prince would be a great ambition."

"I do not love a prince of France."

"Love is a changing thing, Princess. Family is a steadfast thing."

"Are you implying that I will not be steadfast, Sancia?"

"Marriage to a prince of France would keep you aligned with your family's interests. With your sister, the Queen's."

"And marriage to the Duke of Durazzo will not?"

"The Duke is an ambitious man."

I take her meaning now, and rise quickly, furious. It is all I can do not to slap her. Did Joanna send her? I will not protest my loyalty again, certainly not before Sancia of Cabannis. *Once is for honor; twice is a liar,* as they say. Sancia scrambles up hastily, and this time I let her curtsy, watching to make sure her hand brushes the floor before I turn and leave her.

Chapter 10

A Scandal

My sister does not walk into the great hall arm-in-arm with me at the feast to celebrate my engagement. I enter ahead of her, with my Lady Grandmother, to receive the bows and curtsies, the broad smiles of those associated with the Durazzo family, and the cool congratulations of everyone else.

Queen Joanna enters last. She crosses the great hall, acknowledging the obeisance of her subjects as she passes, but not once does she glance at me. She bows her head to Grandmother Sancia, who is waiting at the head table for Joanna to sit before anyone else may be seated. Standing at the table on the other side of the dowager queen, I cover my shock with a deep curtsy to my sister. I have never known Joanna not to curtsy in public to our grandmother. She has always revered Sancia, and chastised me if I offered even a hint of criticism for our cold, pious grandmother. Not that she has to; as Queen Regnant, Joanna owes exactly the gesture she has given to the dowager queen. But Joanna never gives only what is owed; she is as generous with her heart as with her coin. Only, apparently, not this evening.

Joanna's attempt to reconcile with our Lady Aunt Catherine has failed. Neither my aunt nor her sons nor even Lady Marguerite, who would benefit from being seen by the young lords here, have come to observe my engagement to Charles. I am just as glad they are absent. Their offended pride would spoil the feast, but I know Joanna is anxious about making enemies where she used to have friends, so early in her reign.

Well, there is nothing I can do about that. Charles says it will all work out, and I believe him.

Charles must feel my gaze; he turns his head and smiles at me, his warm gray eyes taking me in from my head to my waist as I sit beside him. I shiver at the look in his eyes, and feel myself blush. I cannot wait till the dance, when we can touch hands and move together through the steps of the music. I am giddy just thinking of it.

"I am glad you wore your purple gown," Charles says, his voice as languid and suggestive as his eyes.

"You told me to." I smile, reminding him of our veiled messages on the day of the feast to honor me.

"Will you always do as I say?"

"Always, my Lord." I feel myself blushing again.

"Then we will have a happy marriage, Maria."

After the feast, before the tables are cleared for the dance, Charles and I rise to our feet as the room quiets. We announce our names and our intentions before the entire assembly. Charles gifts me with a silver bracelet on which our names have been engraved twined together. As he slips it over my hand his fingers linger on my wrist as though he would like to possess me right here. I feel weak and willing and hot, and I cannot speak but look at him with my heart in my eyes as I hand him the blue sleeve which I have unlaced from my favorite mi-parti surcote. I have chosen the blue side rather than the red, which I prefer, because blue is the color of purity. I am not entirely pure; Andrew has put his vile hands where only my husband should ever touch me, but Charles will never know that. I am chaste, which is pure enough.

"I hope to unlace the rest of this gown myself, soon," he murmurs as he accepts my sleeve, causing me to blush furiously.

The priest who has been Joanna's and my confessor since we came to live in Castle Nuovo, steps forward to place my hand in Charles', the symbol of our promised union. Before he can do so, Joanna waves him back.

"Leave that until her marriage," she says.

A ripple of indrawn breaths and murmurs, quickly subdued, goes through the great hall. The Queen will not have her royal sister's engagement blessed and confirmed by a priest. A chill goes down my spine: a foreboding. I cannot look at Joanna to measure her expression, everyone in the hall is watching us, but I glance at Charles. His eyes are cold, furious at the insult, although his brow is clear, his smile tightly in place. I take a little breath and smile back at him, full and loving, as a wife-to-be would smile at her intended husband, to show him that I support him, that I will always support him. And then I turn and smile at everyone, all the lords and ladies of our kingdom, as though this has all been planned. I incline my head to the priest as if he has blessed our engagement, smiling my merry smile that shows my dimples. I smile gaily, blessed or not, because I am a royal princess and I am going to marry the man I love, who loves me also, and that is blessing enough.

"Would you walk outside with me before the warmth of the day has gone?" Margherita asks.

I look at her in surprise. My other ladies-in-waiting have left to dress for dinner, having first dressed and prepared me.

"I am in my best shoes," I say, looking down at my beautiful red pointed leather shoes. They are maybe not my best, I choose them so often they are beginning to lose a little of their stiffness, but they are my favorite. I raise my white kirtle and the red surcote over it just enough to display them, but Margherita has already admired them many times. She did not want me to wear the white kirtle, or the red surcote.

"The blue will match your eyes," she said, and I was tempted. I imagine she is tired of mourning the King after two months, but Joanna still wears the white of mourning and I have been doing what I can to placate her since my engagement feast two days ago. The sense of foreboding has not left me, but neither has my determination to be Charles's wife, whether it suits Joanna or not. I nearly agreed with Margherita about the red, and was about to have the blue surcote she brought from my wardrobe pulled over my head, but then I thought of my red shoes. I do not have blue shoes and would have to wear my dull brown ones if I chose the blue surcote.

Margherita is wearing a blue surcote—did she want us to wear the same color as we sometimes used to do when we were children? We have always been close, and now she is my only confidante, the only one who is genuinely happy about my engagement. I feel a pang of regret that I did not realize her intent and may have seemed to disdain her sentiment. Also, to be truthful, I feel slightly superior for I will soon be a married woman and beyond such girlhood fancies as matching-colored surcotes. So even though I glance out the window and shiver at the gray sky, I agree to walk outside with her before dinner, and let her fetch my cloak.

I pause on the steps. The wind is picking up. Dusk is approaching more quickly than I thought. The city is not safe at night for two women alone.

"We can walk in the courtyard," I suggest, but she begs me so prettily to walk outside the gates and into the west gardens, that I cannot refuse. I will not show myself afraid if she is not, and we will not go far. "Only to the garden," I tell her. "It is nearly time for dinner."

It is even darker beyond the torches that hang from the castle gates. The wind picks up so we have to raise our voices to hear each other. I would as soon not talk; our chatter just announces our presence. I remind myself that I am a princess, no one would dare harm me in the castle gardens.

We cross the narrow street and enter the garden. When I look back, I can no longer see the guards at the castle gate, we have passed out of their sight. Ahead, the gardens are even darker than the streets, textured with shadows, shadow on shadow disappearing into the night. I shiver and stop, gripped with a premonition of danger. I open my mouth, about to insist we go back, but Margherita has also stopped. She stands still, contemplative, as though she is waiting for someone, or considering how to tell me something. She holds her face averted, not meeting my eye.

"What is it Lady Margherita?" I ask. She does not answer.

"Do you have a lover?" I say this with a little thrill of delight; it will be more pleasant to talk to her of Charles, listing his qualities and accomplishments as I have been doing, if she has someone, too.

She still does not answer. Perhaps she has not heard me. The wind is louder here, moaning through the trees. Before I can ask her again, someone grabs me from behind. Rough gloved hands pull my arms behind my back. I open my mouth to scream for the guards, and a kerchief is stuffed into my mouth!

I struggle to free myself, to spit out the cloth, to tell them there is no advantage in this, I do not have my purse on me. But they have not looked for it. They have not reached for my belt where it would be hanging. It is not coins they are after! Dear God, who are they? How dare they touch me, do they not know who I am?

Andrew's men! Have they come to silence me as they silenced his guard?

A second kerchief covers my face, blinding me as it is tied securely behind my head. I struggle desperately, wild with panic, trying to scream my name. Where is Margherita, what have they done to her?

I am lifted off the ground. I kick out viciously and hear a satisfying grunt before strong arms secure my feet. They carry me—me, the Princess Maria, heir to the throne!—through the garden at a brisk pace. I struggle, wrapped in my cloak, but they are strong armsmen, I do not even slow them down. One of them chuckles under his breath, not a sinister sound, but as if he is amused by my resistance.

They would have killed me by now if that was their intent. My fear turns to fury. Joanna will have them hanged, drawn and quartered for this!

Where is Margherita? Why can I not hear her being carried beside me? I hope it is only the wind, muffling the sounds of her struggle as it muffles our captors' footsteps. I lie stiff and furious in their arms, the touch of their base hands loathsome to me, trying to make out where they are taking us.

I catch the heavy scent of roses and lavender, so we are still in the garden. The wind has the salty scent of the sea in it, blowing in from the Mediterranean. My cheeks are wet with exertion—maybe a few tears, but they are tears of anger, I will not let these foul men think they frighten me!—and thus made sensitive to the wind's direction. They are carrying me west, through the middle of the garden. Their steps are slowing, they must be nearly at the far side. What is on the other side of this garden?

Then I know. Of course I know, but I cannot believe it. Why would Andrew's men be taking me to—

Because they are not Andrew's men. Of course they are not Andrew's men. I want to laugh, but it is only relief, I am still too angry to find this amusing. Now I know why Margherita did not scream, why I did not hear her struggling beside me when they came upon us. Up ahead I hear the whinny and snuffle of horses, and the stamping of their hooves on the ground.

"Do not be afraid, we would not harm you, Princess," a gruff voice murmurs in my ear as I am set back on my feet and my hands untied. As soon as I am freed I whip my hand up, smacking the insolent fool's face before he can back up. I hear someone laugh.

My eyes are still covered so I cannot run, and my mouth is bound to silence, but I stand there proudly, making sure they know I am not in the least afraid of them.

"We must mount our horses, Princess," another voice says. "I would rather you ride pillion, but I cannot risk your life, so you must give me your word to sit quietly in the saddle."

I nod my head once, regally. They would never dare toss me across the saddle onto my stomach and tie me in place—but I do not want to test that. They have already gone too far to back down now. We canter over the hard ground, hidden in the darkness. I can hear the sea below us, the waves, whipped by the wind, slapping hard against the rocks. If I had not already known I would know now where we are going.

We stop, but they do not lift me down from the horse. "Open!" one of them calls. A large gate creaks open. We trot through, and it closes with a solid clang. Only then do they lower me carefully to my feet and remove the kerchiefs from my eyes and mouth. I am standing inside the entrance to Castle Durazzo, rubbing the bruises on my arms as they approach me. Margherita stands beside me with her head bowed, unable to meet my eyes.

"How dare you?" I ask Agnes of Perigord, glaring at her, and at Charles, too, as they curtsy and bow in front of me.

Charles snaps his fingers for his men to leave and they hurry to obey, their faces averted. As if I could punish them without convicting Charles as well.

"My poor darling." Charles takes my hands. "Were you very afraid?"

"Not at all." It is only a partial lie. "I was planning their executions."

"I am so sorry, Princess Maria—"

My Lady Aunt silences Margherita with a look and motions her to go inside.

"Princess Maria, I am afraid it was necessary to inconvenience you this way," she says, turning back to me. "If you were sincere in accepting my son's marriage offer."

I have always been a little afraid of both my Lady Aunts, but no one has ever accused me of faithlessness. I straighten my back and do not answer.

"Lady Mother," Charles interjects, "let me explain this night's business to our guest. But first, my dear Princess Maria, you are cold and damp. Come inside and sit by the fire with me."

I should be angry with him still. This was not well done, it is an outrage. My grandfather King Robert would have had him thrown in jail, his men drawn and quartered; Joanna might do so also… The thought of my Charles, with his sweet smile, in jail gives me pause. Why has he risked so much? He must be desperate for me! It is my fault he has done this, his wits have been addled by love. I let him escort me past his mother and into their family castle.

A servant brings us mulled wine. I hold the hot cup in my hands to warm them as Charles tells me Lady Catherine has appealed to her brother the King of France to intervene on their behalf with the Pope in Avignon.

"But he has written you a bull to marry," I protest.

"He wrote it very carefully," Charles says. "Clement VI is not a man to refuse a king in the interests of a duke. And can we take that chance? Can we risk our marriage on the hope that the Pope and the Queen will stand firm against the King of France and all our Taranto relatives? I could not bear to lose you." He takes my wine cup from my hands and leans close to me. I am afraid he will kiss me, here in the hall in front of his mother. I part my lips, in case he might.

"Would you be happy to marry me, Maria?" His voice catches on the familiar words of his own proposal; he is afraid I will refuse him this time.

"Yes," I say. "Yes, Charles." I lean a little toward him.

He sighs, and appears to come to himself, drawing back just a little. "I am a man whose life has been reprieved," he says.

Behind us, my Lady Aunt gives a small snort.

I close my lips and straighten, but Charles smiles at me, as if we two understand something that she could not possibly know. He is not at all ashamed of being heard whispering love words to me. "Will you marry me now, Maria?"

"What now?" I look around, confused.

"Now, in our private chapel. I have a priest waiting. Everything is ready."

"Now?" I repeat, stupidly.

"Before it is too late. Before Lady Catherine can turn everyone against us."

"You brought me here to marry you? Without my sister the Queen's knowledge and consent?"

"The Queen has already consented. We are engaged, are we not? Marry me now, before she can change her mind."

I take up my wine cup and gulp the hot, spicy drink, trying hard to think. It is very hard to think with his eyes looking into mine, so close. I am a royal princess, I cannot marry in secret. Joanna will know I gave my consent; the priest would not marry us otherwise. She will never forgive me.

I trust only you, I hear her say. No, I cannot. “She will not change her mind, an engagement is binding.”

“Did she allow the priest to bless our engagement?”

“That was only to appease—” I stop. Our Lady Aunt Catherine and our Taranto cousins were not at the feast of our engagement. I look at Charles, my mouth falling open. Is my sister planning to cancel our engagement? Was she planning it from the beginning, just waiting until it would look like she had no choice?

I trust only you, I told her.

Charles rises and holds out his hand to me. I take it and let him raise me to my feet.

“You are a most beautiful bride.”

I look down in horror. “I cannot marry you! I am wearing white!” Our marriage will be plagued by grief if I marry him in the color of mourning. And red! A bold color. Yes it denotes wealth, red is a very expensive color, but it is not a color for a new wife. There is neither submissiveness, nor purity, nor love in red. I should be in green, the color of young love, or blue, the color of purity; those are the right colors for a young bride.

Margherita wanted me to wear blue tonight, I suddenly remember. She knew all along! She tried to guide me to wear the blue surcote—was she so certain I would agree to this?—but I would not listen. I never listen. Red is my color, surely, the color of a bold, headstrong, foolish girl. But I cannot be married in it! *Be still, whore, you are getting what you asked for!* I hear Andrew’s voice accusing me. Accusing, or recognizing who I really am? I close my eyes to hold back the tears. “I cannot be married in red,” I whisper.

Charles laughs at me fondly. “Maria, you are barely fourteen. I will mold you into the wife I want, whatever color you wear today. And you are very pretty in those colors." He holds out his arm to escort me into the chapel.

Everything is ready. A priest is waiting there, and all of Charles' family, and Margherita. She turns to me as I enter, her smile tentative. Without a word she comes to me and curtsies very low, and holds out a wide blue ribbon. I take it gladly, although I will not thank her, and tie it around me so that it sits on my hips. It cuts the red, dividing the color's strength, so that the blue, the symbol of maidenly purity, is stronger. Andrew was wrong about me. I am not secretly a whore. I am just a foolish fourteen-year-old princess. But Charles will take care of me. He will make me better. He has promised to make me into a wife worthy of him.

Charles waits patiently as I look around the chapel. They have forgotten nothing. Even the wedding contract has been prepared, listing all my holdings and assets including my pension and dowry, according to King Robert's final testament. It is lying on a table waiting for the ceremony. I stop when I see it, frowning a little. How long have they planned this? Was he so sure of me?

In King Robert's bedchamber I put my hand on the Holy Scriptures and swore an oath to uphold his will. I swore an oath of obedience to Joanna.

"I am breaking my vow of allegiance to my Queen," I murmur, low enough that only Charles can hear.

"You are not breaking your vow. The Queen agreed to your engagement to me, and an engagement is intended to be binding. This is its natural extension, as she well knew. Besides," he grins at me, leaning down to whisper into my ear "you have been abducted. You are my helpless prisoner until you agree to marry me."

I find it hard to breathe.

Charles motions to the best man to stand at the chapel door as it is closed behind us. He is huge. I have never seen anyone so big. I do not know whether he is the best swordsman and fighter among the Durazzo family's men-at-arms, or has been hired for this day, but I do not doubt that he will do his job and stop anyone who tries to interrupt our wedding before it is completed.

My legs shake as I walk down the aisle. I grasp Charles' arm for support, but I hold my head high, and when we reach the priest, and he asks the traditional question, am I of age, I answer proudly that I am. I have had my courses for a year now. I hesitate only a moment when he asks whether I have received consent for this marriage, then thinking firmly of Clement VI's bull and Joanna and my Grandmother Sancia agreeing to my engagement, I tell him I do.

The priest pauses a moment before he puts to me the final question, "Do you consent of your own free will to this marriage, Maria of Anjou?"

I realize in that moment that I am about to be married, that Charles and I will be man and wife forever after this, and that I really have no idea at all what that means. Am I to spend my time praying and planning the building of cathedrals, like my Grandmother Sancia? Am I to manage his household like a noblewoman? Will I some day be left widowed to raise his children, like both of my Lady Aunts? And what will happen when he comes to my bed? I have no mother to tell me how to please a husband. No one has prepared me to be married!

The room seems to move. I sway a little on my feet, trying to find my balance. Charles let go of my arm for the questions, I must answer them on my own. I want to grab onto him but I must not. The priest raises his eyebrows. Everyone is waiting.

I look desperately at Charles. He is looking straight ahead, letting the decision be mine, but his face has paled, his smile is strained. He is terrified I will break his heart. I feel a surge of tenderness. I breathe out, my heart begins to beat again, and, still looking at Charles, I say in a loud, clear voice, "Yes. I consent."

The priest smiles. I hear murmurs of approval and relief behind me, even though there are no more than a dozen people in the chapel, but all I care about is Charles, who turns his head to me with a smile so wide it splits his face.

Charles answers the same three questions confidently. When he comes to the third I am afraid for a moment, and I realize what he must have felt, and am sorry I hesitated.

The priest asks for the contract and reads aloud my assets and dowry for all present to hear. Then he gives a short sermon in Latin about the seriousness of matrimony which makes me so nervous I want to reconsider, and at the same time makes me feel proud and very adult. When he warns us against lust, exhorting us to go to our marriage bed solely for the purpose of producing children, I am horribly aware of the Duchess of Durazzo, Charles' mother, listening behind us, and I blush as red as my surcote.

Charles produces the ring, a beautiful gold band studded on top with sapphires and emeralds, blue for a pure bride and green for our young love, and slides it onto the third finger of my right hand. I admire it in delight. Then he takes out of his pouch the wedding brooch. It is cunningly made, with a tiny bride and her Lord husband standing side by side, surrounded by precious stones and pearls. He pins it to the front of my red surcote, proof, despite the bold color, of my modesty and chastity, for none but he may open it and see my breasts. I look down at it, and realize he has pinned it through my white gown, also: the symbol of our marriage clasped to the white of mourning. I feel a chill and open my mouth to tell him to move it, to pin it onto my surcote alone, but what if he misunderstands? What if he thinks I do not want to be chaste and keep myself for him alone? What if he wonders if someone else has already seen my breasts?

Before I can think what to do, the priest directs us to kneel. He leads us in prayer and pronounces us married. It is too late then to repair the damage, I can only hope nothing will come of it.

I watch the priest give Charles the kiss of peace, and then Charles bends and passes it on to me. When his lips touch mine, all my misgivings vanish. I am as hungry for the touch of his lips, for the love he has offered me, as a babe is to suckle. I have to force myself to end the kiss. We turn together to receive the congratulations of our little group of witnesses, and I have a heart as joyous, if not as carefree, as any bride ever had.

Charles takes my hand in his arm and leads me out of the chapel. I expect him to escort me into the great hall for our wedding feast, small though the company may be, but he turns toward the stairway.

"Where are we going, my Lord?" I whisper as he draws me up the steps. He does not answer, but continues. I hear the others behind me and turn and look. They are following us, every one of his family. His brothers have grins on their faces that I do not like. Louis, nearest to Charles in age, starts to call out something to us but Charles looks back and stops him with a motion. They continue to follow us, whispering jests to each other and laughing uproariously.

Even I understand where we are heading now. I stop and try to pull my hand from Charles' arm, but he holds it tight and pulls me on with him. I cannot stop long anyway, the rest of his family are right behind me. I remember being lifted against my will and carried through the garden and do not want that again, not in front of everyone. It would be immodest for me to look eager for my wedding bed, but it would be humiliating to turn and try to run, as I would like to do. Behave as a queen would behave, I remind myself over the pounding of my heart. A queen would be modest but unafraid. I raise my chin and walk as steadily as I can beside my husband.

We enter the outer chamber of Charles' rooms—at least, I assume they are his—all together as a group. "What is this, my Lord?" I whisper, trying hard not to weep in front of everyone.

Charles puts his hands on my shoulders and bends to kiss my cheek. "I will explain when I come in. It will all make sense when I explain. Go in now, and trust me, Maria. I will not hurt you." His brothers snicker when they hear this.

Charles ignores them. He gives me a little push toward the door to his bedchamber. Margherita has squeezed through the others and is waiting for me at the door, but I am afraid and confused. Are we not to have a feast, and a dance, and wine and singing and music? I look back at Charles, searching his face. He frowns and nods toward the door.

I feel a tear slide down my cheek. Before anyone can notice, I turn away, so that his brothers will not have something else to laugh at, and enter the bedchamber with Margherita. As soon as the door closes behind us, she takes my hands.

"Do not be afraid, Princess Maria," she begs. "You were so brave in the garden, so proud and royal. This is nothing to cry about now, this is only what every woman must endure."

"But I want a feast." I wipe my eyes and hiccup. "And dancing and music! I want a wedding feast!"

"You shall have them, you shall have it all. The cooks are preparing it now, I promise you." Margherita unclasps my wedding brooch and lays it on a table.

"Then why… why are we here?" I blush. Of course I know why we are here, I just do not know why we are here now.

"Charles will explain." She has already unlaced my surcote and lifts it high for me. I am so used to being dressed and undressed by my ladies-in-waiting that I duck my head and step out under her arm while I am still objecting, "I want to know now."

"We must hurry, Princess Maria." Margherita begins to unbutton my white kirtle. "They will know that you are not coming to dinner in Castle Nuovo by now. Your ladies-in-waiting will have told them you are not in your rooms." She lowers the kirtle for me to step out of. "They may already be searching the grounds." She shakes my white kirtle gently and lies it on top of my surcote over a chair. "When they do not find you…" she pauses.

"My sister the Queen will be worried. She will fear that I have been harmed, or abducted—" I stop, my mouth forming a little "o" of surprise, when I realize that she will be right. I have been abducted. "They may guess who would do it," I say slowly.

"Your Lord the Duke of Durazzo only wants to be sure that the marriage cannot be annulled." Margherita finishes unlacing my chemise and bends down to lift it from the hem.

"But it is not night-time." I raise my arms so she can lift my chemise over my head. "And I have nothing else to wear." I shiver in my nakedness.

Margherita opens a chest at the bottom of Charles' bed and takes a pretty blue nightgown out of it. "You have this," she says, giggling at my expression of surprise. She helps me into it and pins the brooch at my breast. I am pleased to see it on blue, as it should be, instead of white.

There is a loud knock at the door. Margherita pulls the bedclothes down and helps me up into the high bed. "You haven't undone my hair," I remind her. "My Lord will want to see my hair down."

She looks at me apologetically. "There is no time to let down your hair and plait it up again," she says. "We have to hurry. You will have to be careful not to…" she stops and blushes. A second, louder knock comes.

"But I do not know what to do!" I whisper urgently. "No one has told me what to do!"

She is already on her way to open the door and let them in. She looks at me in the bed and whispers, "Princess Maria, I cannot tell you. I do not know either!" She hesitates, thinking, her face as worried as mine. Then she shrugs and whispers, "The Duke of Durazzo will know." She opens the door to let him in.

Chapter 11

Unbalanced

BAM! BAM! BAM!

I start awake to the sound of shouting and pounding. I lie frozen in fear, the darkness pinning me to my bed, trembling at each new volley of fists against my chamber door. What? I cannot make a sound even to demand what is happening The bed shakes as my bedmate climbs out quickly, pushing aside the curtain. The volume of angry voices and banging on the door increases.

Do not open the door! I struggle to cry to Margherita, but I cannot move, even to speak, in my terror.

"I am coming," a male voice calls beside my bed.

Charles' voice. Charles! It is not Margherita sleeping with me! My sleep falls away. I strain to see in the pitch dark room, pulling the cover up around my chin. Why are they so angry? They have already seen the sheets.

I hear the door open. The shouting stops. "I will get her ready," Charles says, and aside, as to a servant, "Light the wall lamps." I clutch the blanket closer about my neck.

"Maria." The bed sways as he climbs back onto it. Our bed. Our marriage bed. I am a married woman. I close my eyes. I have done everything he asked of me. I am sure he was as gentle as any man can be, but no one told me it would hurt.

Charles shakes my shoulder gently. "My Lady wife, Duchess of Durazzo. You must wake up for only a little while."

I open my eyes. What can he want of me now? Surely not to be stared at by those rough, loud-spoken men?

"It seems they have found us out." Charles grins down at me until I smile back. "We have had longer than I feared, but less time than I hoped. Nevertheless, you are married, and bedded, and no man can deny it."

I blush at the memory of him holding up our blooded sheets to those waiting in his sitting room, and their raucous cheer at the sight of them, while inside the bedchamber Margherita dressed me again to go down to the feast. Neither of us mentioned that my hair was barely mussed at all.

I should never have agreed to this hushed and hurried wedding. My sister would not go back on her decision after letting our Lady Grandmother throw an engagement party for me. Charles is persuasive—too persuasive. And I am too easily persuaded. I have been cheated of a proper wedding day, of the glorious progression to Santa Chiara while the people of Naples cheered me in the streets, of a public ceremony and a sumptuous feast attended by all the nobles in the land, and a merry dance and a respectable—well, more respectable—bedding. I shut my eyes so he cannot read my thoughts in them.

"Open your eyes, little wife. We are about to have visitors."

"What, here?" I sit up quickly. "Now?"

"Your sister's men believe you are being held against your will." He traces the curve of my cheek with his finger. "Are you here against your will?" His eyes crinkle with laughter.

"I gave my consent," I tell him—and remind myself.

"That is all they need to hear," he says.

I look down, not meeting his eyes. Outside Charles' rooms we hear the jingle of spurs and stamp of heavy riding boots as the Queen's men wait impatiently outside. I feel Charles looking at me and glancing up I see him frowning. "They will hear it from me," I tell him.

"Will you not smile for me, as you used to?"

I smile. It feels more like a grimace, but it is not meant to be.

He gives a little snort, much like the sound his mother makes when she is annoyed, and glances at the door. But when he speaks, his voice is patient "What can I do to put a real smile back on your face, my little Duchess? Or do you not love me anymore? Have I been too… rough? I have tried to be gentle with you."

"I do, Charles. I do love you," I say in a rush to prevent him from being more explicit. "I am glad we are married." I say this last with some difficulty, even though it is true. I know it is true, but I am having trouble feeling it right now.

"Then what is it?"

I take a breath. I will sound foolish, but the concern on his face encourages me. "Charles can we have another feast? A real one, for me as your wife, when our marriage has been accepted? With musicians, and a dance? And can I wear a new green gown for it?"

He stares at me, and bursts out laughing. But when he sees me look away, hurt, he cups my chin in his hand and stifles his mirth. "Yes, Maria," he says. "I promise you I will throw a very big feast in your honor. Everyone you wish will be invited, and you shall wear green. Just as soon as our marriage is officially recognized."

I clap my hands and laugh with delight. Charles leans down to kiss me, and that is what the Queen's men see when they walk into our room.

Margherita stays to attend me at Castle Durazzo. I do not quite trust her as I did before, but I must accept her company. She is the only one of my ladies-in-waiting who will join me here. The others are all too scandalized by my abduction and unauthorized marriage. So they claim—I think they would simply rather stay at court.

I can hardly blame them. I have never lived so meanly. I have my own bedchamber, and the smallest privy chamber I have ever seen. It has two chairs by a fireplace and a single table. The bed in my bedchamber is as good as any I have ever slept on—ready for Charles when he comes, which he does every night. But I have no presence chamber at all, and only Margherita to wait on me, dress me, do my hair, bring me what I need.

My mother-in-law, now the Dowager Duchess, has the larger rooms that should belong to the Duchess of Durazzo. She also retains all the privileges and responsibilities that go with the title. I have no say in anything, I am not even consulted, I who have been mistress, with Joanna, of our own rooms, our own kitchen staff, our own entourage, our own court, ever since we were old enough to wear a surcote over our kirtles. I tell myself it is temporary, that I will learn what I need to know to manage this household and be the Duchess in fact, but Agnes of Perigord seems to be telling herself quite the opposite.

Meanwhile, Joanna sends me letter after letter begging, then ordering, me to come back to Castle Nuovo. I write to her that my husband wants me at his side, but she does not invite Charles to come with me. Instead she writes that I must leave him and return to my home, and she will have the marriage annulled.

Why sister, I think, reading her letter, *did you not intend to honor my engagement?*

Charles was right about her after all. I write back that I *am* at home and that I think I will stay here, because my husband wants me in his bed at night. Let her know I am a woman who is desired, unlike her, I think, furiously scratching my quill across the paper. I ask that she release to my husband my dowry of lands and monies, according to our Grandfather's will. She sends me back a curt refusal, saying if I wanted it, I should have married according to our Grandfather's will. I scrunch the letter into a ball and throw it into the fireplace in a temper. She knows full well the testament we swore on does not mention exactly who I should marry, as no marriage had been arranged at the time.

Queen Joanna writes to Pope Clement VI to complain of Charles' and his mother's conduct in abducting me, calling it an insult to our royal family. She bemoans my insolence in refusing to leave the Duke of Durazzo. She demands that His Holiness annul my marriage and order the Durazzos to return me, as though I am a plate or a silver cup.

We hear of this from my Grandmother Sancia, who remains in contact with my Lady Aunt Agnes, Charles' mother. Immediately I write to Clement VI to say I am very happy in my marriage and thank him for his bull permitting the Duke of Durazzo to marry whomever he chose. I point out that my Grandmother the Dowager Queen and my sister the Queen both celebrated my engagement to the Duke, thus consenting to it. His Holiness writes me back that he is pleased with my marriage, and counsels me to appease my sister and reconcile with her, which advice he has also given Joanna. I throw this letter into the fire also. Joanna is the false one—she never intended to let me marry Charles; that is clear now. Let her appease me!

A torrent of letters pours from Queen Joanna's writing table, from mine, from my Lady Grandmother's, my Lady Mother-in-Law's, my Lady Aunt Catherine's desks, all hammering at each other over my marriage and appealing to the Pope for justice. Even Joanna's mother-in-law in Hungary contributes her letters to the flood of protest. While we women and ecclesiastics conspire to drown each other in paper, the men take arms.

Our cousins of Taranto raise a small army, which attacks and captures one of the Durazzo family's outlying castles. Charles calls on his vassals to arm themselves in defense, and the triangle of power in the kingdom of Naples—King Robert's line, his brother Philip of Taranto's line, and their brother John of Durazzo's line—prepare in their fury and greed to tear Naples apart, while the descendants of their eldest brother, Charles Martel, wait like vultures in Hungary to finish off the war-weakened victor. It is just as Joanna predicted.

I stand at the window of my tiny sitting room and watch Charles' brother, Louis, drilling the house guard in the courtyard below. Does he really think our cousins of Taranto will attack us here? That we will have to barricade our gates and defend ourselves? I cannot imagine that it will come to that, here in Naples. I cannot believe that I, who was never important as a princess engaged to Louis of Hungary, am suddenly being fought over as the wife of Charles of Durazzo.

Below me, the guards form two lines and attack each other, their swords clanging fiercely. I step back, stifling the urge to scream, and slam the shutters closed. Margherita runs in alarmed and I fall, weeping, into her arms.

"It is all my fault! All this—I have caused this," I sob.

"No, no. You must not think that," Margherita says, but when I look up my tears cannot blind me from seeing the same guilt in her eyes, for she led me into this. We hold each other, but we find no comfort in each other's false assurances.

I think of my sister facing the prospect of civil war in the first year of her reign, because of my impulsive marriage. She must hate me for this. My anger at her falseness fades, but still I cannot go to her. Because, despite my shame, my fear, my regret, I cannot do the one thing she asks: I cannot leave Charles. We love each other.

But if it comes to war? If Charles is killed, and someone else decides to do as he did, this time without my consent?

I cannot sleep at night. I toss and whimper with nightmares of running through the dark, pursued; of being taken, a prize of battle, while my guards lie murdered around me. I rise every morning nauseous with exhaustion and throw up. I hide it from Charles, ashamed of my weakness and unwilling to burden him with it while he is fighting to hold on to his lands and estates, which I have put at risk. I do not want him to wonder if I am worth it.

In the midst of all this, Sancia of Cabannis comes to see me. She is more honest this time; she does not pretend to come out of friendship for me, but asks me to return with her for the sake of the Queen. I do not even grace that with an answer. We are no longer three children playing together, and my husband is not a toy I can toss aside when playtime is over.

"At least, please speak to Her Majesty," she begs me.

"I will speak to Her Majesty if she orders Robert of Taranto to disarm, and return my lord's holdings," I tell her. Our cousin Robert, arrogant and cruel though he is, would surely have to listen to his Queen. But even as I think it, I have my doubts. Robert listens to no one.

"Robert? Robert is in his bed with a fever, and has been this past month."

"Who is leading the Taranto army?"

"Louis is the head of the family Taranto while his brother lies ill."

"Louis?" I stare at her, dumbfounded. Hot-headed sixteen-year-old Louis of Taranto is leading the army against us? This is at my Lady Aunt Catherine's command. Matriarch of the Taranto family, she may not be able to control Robert, but she has her younger sons in hand.

"Louis is attacking us," I repeat, as it sinks in. I passed him Joanna's note at our grandfather's interment, before her marriage was consummated. Louis, Joanna's favorite, is attacking my husband?

I raise my head and stare levelly at Sancia. "Tell Joanna I will speak to her when she orders *Louis* of Taranto to disarm, and return my lord's holdings." I turn, dismissing her from my privy chamber.

"Princess—"

"Duchess!" I snap, without turning back.

"…Duchess Maria," she takes a step closer and lowers her voice. "Your sister does not want any of this, you must know that."

I whirl on her. "And how would I know that when Louis, *Louis of Taranto*, is attacking me?"

"Not you, never you. He is defending you! Your honor!" Her voice is almost a whisper.

"I am *married*!" Despite my fury, I strive to keep my voice low. If Charles learned what she has said, he would kill her. I want to slap her myself, for insinuating that my honor is sullied, that I went to Charles' bed without the sanctity of marriage.

She takes a breath and steps back. "I meant no—"

"Oh, did you not?"

Another careful breath. "Duchess Maria, the Queen cannot order Louis of Taranto to desist from defending your honor. It would amount to admitting she approves of your marriage, that she has favored the Durazzos over the Tarantos as the heirs to her throne."

She did. She attended my engagement party. But we are both aware that Joanna prevented the priest from blessing our future union.

"Better the Tarantos fight the Durazzos for my honor than that they fight for her crown," I say bitterly. Joanna warned me: the balance of power, the scales she has to keep carefully equal. And yet I feel betrayed. "She is playing both sides."

"She is the Queen. She is Naples. There is no other side."

I watch from my window as Sancia's carriage leaves, returning to the Queen's court. Despite our dispute, our mutual deceptions, I miss my sister, and I know she is missing me. But this has gone too far for that. I am married and bedded, and the whole kingdom is involved; neither of us can turn back now. Joanna will have to make do with Sancia. Sancia of Cabannis will be her friend and sister now. My sister will no longer trust me, as I no longer trust her.

Joanna's words come back to me: *I will restore justice and wealth and prosperity to Naples. I will hold her good above all other allegiances.*

I should have warned Sancia, I think, as I watch her carriage turn out of sight.

I send word to my husband that I cannot eat and retire early to bed. He comes to me anyway, as he has done every evening since our wedding, save only those nights my womanly courses prevented him. I have come to look forward to his arrival, not only because I see him so little during the day now that he is busy preparing his men to fight, but because… because I have become as loose as a strumpet, longing to be touched. There, I admit it. He only has to slide into the bed beside me for my heart to pound and the queasy feeling in my stomach to spread lower. When his hands squeeze my breasts gently, suggestively, and stroke down over my belly and lower—he does not have to part my legs, they are already open, eager for him. He runs his fingertips along the inside of my thighs, barely touching the curls of hair, until I am panting. Then, teasing me, he moves his hand up, caressing my belly, his fingers circling the little round curve of it.

"You did not come to dinner," he says. "Are you unwell?"

At the moment I feel very unwell, I feel desperately unwell, and only he can resolve it, but I am not quite brazen enough to say that. "I am well," I murmur, hoping he will not notice the catch in my voice. I run my hands down his back, feeling awkward even after three months, for I am embarrassed to ask him what I should do, and he has not made any suggestions. I would like to take his hand and push it lower again. I close my eyes, as though that can stop the impure thought.

He bends down and kisses my stomach, making me gasp. "Why did you not come to dinner, then?" His lips slide further down.

I groan. As if of their own volition, my legs spread a little wider. "It… it comes and goes," I gasp, hardly knowing what I am saying.

He raises his head. "An illness that comes and goes? Is there a fever?" His fingers very gently tickle the hairs that mound below my stomach. Yes there is a fever!

"No, no fever…"

"Is there any nausea?" he whispers. His fingers stroke the inside of my thighs, brushing my hairs, as light as a feather, sending little shocks of pleasure and excitement. "In the mornings, perhaps?"

I nod, unable to speak.

He hesitates, his fingers still.

I have never done this before, but I am desperate. I slide my hands down to his hips and pull him closer, my legs fully spread. With a groan he enters me.

Later, when we are finished, when we have caught our breath and can speak again, he tells me, "Maria, I believe you are with child."

I sit up in the bed, shocked. "With child?" I think back. It has been a while since my courses. I have only had one since coming here. And I have been here since March, three months now. I look at him in wonder. "Are you pleased, my Lord?"

He laughs and cups my belly in his hand, its roundness even more obvious when I am sitting up. "I am delighted, my little wife. But I cannot come to your bed again." He laughs at the disappointment on my face. "I did not expect this when I married you, Maria."

I blush, embarrassed. I am not acting like a royal princess, as my Lady Grandmother often told me. To my surprise he kisses me, a strong, hard kiss that leaves me panting again.

"You please me, Duchess. You please me more than I thought. And now that you are carrying my son, no one can deny our marriage.

Chapter 12

Return to Court

I wear my new green gown for my return to court. The Queen and her royal council have officially recognized my marriage, as Charles said they would. Not even the Tarantos can expect Joanna to annul my marriage when there is a child in my belly. Neither the Queen nor my Lady Grandmother has offered to feast us, and my husband and his mother, the Dowager Duchess, have not been invited to court with me. Charles has decided it would be impolitic to host a marriage feast until the Queen has forgiven them as well, but he approved the expense of my new gown, green just as he promised, with a darker green surcote to hide my expanding belly.

As Duchess of Durazzo, I am to be one of my sister's ladies-in-waiting. The irony does not escape me. I grew up in this castle sharing a court with my sister; now I return to wait in service on her. Margherita is not invited back. I am sorry for her but it is her own fault; she led me into this. If I plead for anyone's return to court, it will be for my husband's.

"Goodbye, my Lord," I say awkwardly as Charles holds out his hand to help me into the litter that will take me to the Queen's court.

"Be sure to please Her Majesty," Charles instructs me. "And let her see how happy you are. She must want you happy."

I look at him doubtfully. My sister is not happy in her own marriage, why would she want me to be? Charles is very dear, but he does not understand sisters.

"Remember you are the Duchess of Durazzo. This is your family now. You must do what you can for us," my Lady Aunt says, interrupting our leave-taking.

"I will, Lady Mother-in-Law," I reply. My aunt has been disgruntled since she learned of the considerable payment Robert of Taranto was given from the royal treasury to placate him and his mother over my marriage, especially since my husband is still waiting for my dowry. I glance at Charles. I hope he does not think he got the worse deal. At least he and my cousins have disbanded their armies.

He looks down into my anxious face and smiles—a little stiffly, I think—and hands me into the litter. "Take good care of my son," he says. "Do not over-exert yourself."

I wonder what he thinks a lady-in-waiting does that is so taxing. "I will return safely in time for my confinement," I assure him, before he pulls the curtains closed.

I am going to join Joanna at the royal castle at Somma, outside of Naples on Mount Vesuvius. We often go there in July and August to escape the heat and the illnesses that breed in the city during the hot summer days. I settle back in the litter. It is the middle of July and stifling in here. I can barely breathe. It would be faster and cooler to ride my horse in the open air, with the breeze on my face, but I cannot even suggest such a thing in my condition.

I have not admitted it to anyone—I am barely willing to admit it to myself—but I am ecstatic to leave Castle Durazzo, where I have nothing to do and no one but Margherita to talk to. I do love Charles, but he is away all day and now that I am with child, he does not come to my bedchamber, either.

How I wish we were going to our seaside castle at Baiae instead of Somma. We have always had such fun there—plays and music and picnics on the beach. Last summer Joanna and I, and all the court ladies, spent long days boating and hunting for sea-shells along the shore, and dancing to music in the evenings. Joanna invented little games and contests: which lord could compose the most charming song, which lady could sing and play it most sweetly, who might find the most strawberries or seashells, or row their little boat fastest down the river. It seems so long ago.

Joanna is Queen of a troubled kingdom now, I remind myself, and I am a married woman carrying my husband's child. We are no longer carefree maidens, and we have each deceived the other. I look out the carriage window, my gaiety subdued. There is no road that can take us back to last summer.

When I arrive and follow the servant in his royal livery to my quarters, I find I have been given a single bedchamber. I did not expect a presence room, I will not have a little court of my own here, but I assumed at least I would have a privy room and not have to sit in my bedchamber when Joanna dismisses us. At least I have my own room, which is better than most ladies-in-waiting have. It is more likely due to my condition than intended as an honor. The lack of a privy room tells me clearly enough I am to be considered a Duchess now, not a Princess of the palace. A little maid brings me a bowl of rose water, and I wash the dust of the trip from my face and hands, and join the lords and ladies in the Queen's presence chamber.

Joanna is standing at a window, looking out. Behind her I see the spires of Naples' churches in the distance.

"Your Majesty," I murmur, curtsying.

She turns.

If I thought before that she looked pale and weary, it was nothing to the face that greets me now. I stop at the bottom of my deep curtsy, staring at the lines under her eyes, the pallor of her skin, the glum expression on her face. The carefree sister I recalled on my journey here cannot be seen anywhere in this gaunt woman.

"I am glad you are here, Maria." She holds out her hand to me. I rise quickly and take it.

I do not know what to say. How can I ask what is wrong, when it is I who have wronged her? How can I offer my help when I have been so unhelpful to her? Nor will I apologize, for I cannot regret being Charles' wife. I hold her hand and tell her, "I am here with you now, Your Majesty."

She draws me to the window. We stand there together with our backs to the room. I am not sure what we are supposed to be looking at. Naples lies in the distance through a haze of summer heat that rises from the land like a pestilent cloud.

"She will arrive tomorrow. Andrew has ridden out to meet her and escort her to my castle."

I wait, but she says nothing more, so at last I have to ask, "Who?"

Joanna looks at me as though she wonders where I have been. A brief expression of scorn passes over her face, gone almost at once. I flush, but before I can defend myself—how should I know of state matters? No one speaks to me of court doings at Castle Durazzo—she says, "his mother, the Dowager Queen of Hungary."

"Queen Elizabeth of Hungary is coming here?"

"Dowager Queen. She will stay at Castle Nuovo with Andrew."

"She has not seen Andrew since he was six." I ignore her reminder that there is a new Queen of Hungary, and it is not me. Why is Elizabeth coming? Andrew has lived here since he left his home to marry my sister, and his mother has never once visited him. "Why has she come now?"

Joanna looks at me as though I am a fool. I feel like one, for of course I do know; Joanna herself predicted it the night our Grandfather wrote his will. She turns back to the room and claps her hands, calling out to the minstrel to play something lively. "Dance," she says to her ladies-in-waiting. "Dance for us." We watch them in our separate silences as they vainly attempt to amuse us.

The Dowager Queen of Hungary waits three days for an audience with the Queen of Naples. When she finally receives her mother-in-law, Joanna, dressed in her robes of state and wearing her crown, sits on a raised chair at the center of the great hall with Philippa and Raymond the Seneschal standing to one side of her and the lords of her council on the other. Grandmother Sancia, claiming she is too ill to travel, has stayed at Castle Nuovo.

I have been given a chair, a small concession to my condition, off to the side, but I stand and curtsy like everyone else as Elizabeth of Hungary sweeps down the room toward Joanna. Elizabeth does not curtsy to her daughter-in-law, but bows her head formally. Queen Joanna bows hers to the same degree, and officially welcomes her mother-in-law to the Kingdom of Naples.

"I have been made welcome by my son, the King of Naples," Elizabeth of Hungary says pointedly.

"I am sure your reunion was most tender," Joanna replies to this most hardhearted woman.

They continue in this way, each courtly, crafted sentence sharp with hidden innuendos, little arrows aimed at the other's weakness. I am not the only one in this silent assemblage who is relieved to go in to dinner before blood is drawn.

Tumblers and jesters entertain us through the many courses of dinner; the musicians and dancers enter immediately after and perform until the long evening ends. No expense has been spared in the food or in the entertainment. The Hungarians brought a fortune with them, I have learned, and my sister is determined to show that she is in no need of it. The Dowager Queen of Hungary takes her leave at the end of the evening, after securing the promise of a private sitting with Queen Joanna in two days. Then she is gone back to our city, our castle and her son.

When Elizabeth returns, Joanna sends her ladies-in-waiting away, save only me and Marguerite to serve them.

Elizabeth of Hungary is ushered into the Queen's privy room. She curtsies to Joanna, a shallow dip, and Joanna curtsies to the exact measure back. When she looks around and sees us, Elizabeth's displeasure is clear. Before she can comment, Joanna introduces us: "My sister, the Duchess of Durazzo and Lady Marguerite of Taranto." I understand then why Joanna has chosen to have us here. We three represent the three great families of Naples, descendants of King

Charles II, with Durazzo and Taranto in service to the recognized Queen of Naples. Marguerite and I curtsy low when we are introduced, and manners require Elizabeth to bow her head to us. She does so with the smallest bend she can politely offer.

Marguerite pours the wine and offers the royal queens—Joanna first—the platter of cheese and olives and sweetmeats placed on the table in advance by the kitchen servants. Joanna motions Marguerite and me to eat and drink as well, as though we were nearly equals, her allies as much as her attendants.

I am not her equal. I am a duchess in the presence of queens. I might always be a duchess. Then I remember Sancia of Cabannis speaking to me of Charles' ambition, and Charles himself promising me he will win us a kingdom. I smile and choose a sweetmeat. I will be a queen as well one day.

"This has been a difficult year for you, daughter-in-law," Elizabeth of Hungary begins.

Joanna takes a sip of her wine. "I understand your husband faced an uprising when he arrived to claim his crown. I am fortunate, for my people love me."

"I have heard they do not love each other."

Joanna looks surprised. "Have you heard anything of this sort?" she asks Marguerite of Taranto and me, the Duchess of Durazzo. We shake our heads on cue. "How strange," Joanna murmurs. She smiles at Elizabeth. "I wonder where you could have heard such a thing?"

"I am glad to find my son and daughter-in-law's kingdom at peace," Elizabeth says stiffly. "But you cannot expect to be at peace forever."

"What are you suggesting, Your Grace? Do you know of a kingdom that intends to march against us?"

"I meant only to point out that a woman cannot rule alone. You need someone to share with you the burden power brings. And if your kingdom is threatened by enemies, you need a husband who can meet them in battle."

"My Lady Mother-in-law, I already have a husband. Surely you were not suggesting I choose another?"

Elizabeth flushes, her lips pursed in frustration, but she persists. "I hope to see my son's coronation while I am here."

Joanna smiles. She nods to Marguerite to offer the platter again.

"I would be pleased to finance the festivities, and to provide funds for King Andrew to raise an army, should there ever be need."

"That is generous of you," Joanna murmurs. I recognize the way her voice sounds when her jaw is clenched, though it is so well-disguised under her smile that neither Lady Marguerite nor Dowager Queen Elizabeth would know. "But we are not in need of money."

We are very much in need of money. Our Grandfather King Robert the Wise poured half the royal treasury into his campaigns against Sicily. Joanna herself complained to me of the state of our treasury before my engagement and marriage ended our confidences.

Elizabeth of Hungary continues to press her point. Joanna responds mildly, her smile fixed in place, pretending not to understand some arguments, agreeing with others only to turn them aside from where they are leading, promising to consider everything her mother-in-law says. Elizabeth is no fool; she knows she has achieved nothing, for all Joanna's seeming agreement. She insists on talking with Joanna again when Joanna has had time to reflect on her concerns, and Joanna agrees.

My sister's agreeableness alarms me; Heaven help Naples if Andrew and his Hungarian men-at-arms had any real power. Rash, thoughtless, cowardly and cruel, I know him to be all these things. Joanna's tight control over his allowance keeps him in line. As a crowned King, under the influence of his rough men-at-arms, and of the Paladin and the Gatti family, he would be ungovernable.

I want to speak to her about this, but we are no longer on close terms. As soon as Elizabeth leaves, Joanna dismisses both me and Marguerite. My one brief conversation alone with her at the window of her presence chamber when I first arrived is not repeated.

Elizabeth returns again and again, presenting her arguments for Andrew's coronation. Each time she is met by Joanna's smiling courtesy and renewed promise to bear in mind her mother-in-law's sage advice. Never, in all these 'private' meetings to which I am invited—sometimes with Marguerite, sometimes with my Lady Aunt Catherine of Taranto and my mother-in-law, Lady Agnes of Perigord, sometimes with the head of her council, the Dowager Queen Sancia, sometimes with Philippa—does Joanna raise her voice, or lose her patience, or refuse her mother-in-law anything. There is nothing Elizabeth of Hungary can object to, and yet I know—as everyone now knows—Andrew is never going to be crowned.

The Dowager Queen eventually arrives at the same conclusion: she will never convince Joanna to share power with Andrew. She announces that she is departing.

"I will take a little tour of France and Italy before I return to my home," she tells us, as if we do not know exactly where she is going with enough gold to buy her son a crown—from anyone but Joanna.

When her mother-in-law has left, Joanna and her court return to Castle Nuovo. It is August now, the worst of the summer's heat is over. Although it is only a small distance, our travel preparations take days. The tapestries must be taken down and rolled up, the bedding dismantled, the dishes and kitchen pots, not to mention our clothes and Joanna's crown jewels, all must be carefully packed and readied for the journey. Even the food in the kitchen, fresh and salted, the spices and preserves, must all be sealed in barrels to come with us.

I am pleased to be returning to Castle Nuovo, where I will be closer to Charles and, I hope, able to meet him from time to time in the west garden. Our baby has begun to kick. I want Charles to put his arm around me, with his hand on my belly, and feel our child growing. I want to ask him about names and show him the little gowns I am sewing for our son. I am certain it will be a son. The gowns are green linen, the color of new life.

We have been back at Castle Nuovo only a few weeks when a letter arrives from Clement VI. Joanna rushes into a hastily-called meeting with her ruling council. It is late when they leave. Joanna comes out last, her face pale and drawn. She dismisses the servants and ladies from her presence chamber, asking only Sancia of Cabannis and me to stay and prepare her for bed.

She stands silent and still as marble while we unlace her, moving only to step over the folds of heavy fabric we lower to her feet. Her back is straight, chin high, nor do her shoulders sloop, yet she looks burdened down even as we remove the weight of her robes.

"Our Holy Father has written that he intends to appoint a legate to rule Naples."

Sancia, bringing Joanna's night gown, nearly drops it. Her shocked face alarms me more than Joanna's toneless statement. Sancia is the granddaughter of the two most influential advisors to King Robert; she knows what a legate will mean to Naples.

"How will we ever recover from the cost?" Sancia asks, the night gown in her arms forgotten. My first thought, that a man will finally be in control of Naples, fades as I realize this man, this legate, will feel no loyalty to Naples. A papal representative will direct as much of the kingdom's resources as possible to himself and the Church. We will be ruined! Joanna should have taken Elizabeth's money. When I am a queen, I will be more practical. But I am not foolish enough to say it.

Joanna looks at Sancia. I note that look and take satisfaction in understanding my sister better than Sancia does. We were raised by our pious Grandmother, whose dearest wish is to leave her worldly position and join the Poor Clares. Joanna is not thinking of the royal treasury as she stands like a figure robbed of its soul, letting us undress her.

"He would not do this if I were not a woman! He would not strip a rightfully-crowned seventeen-year-old *King* of his sovereign authority!"

I am right. It is her crown, not her treasury, that she will not trust to another. But a legate is temporary, she will regain her crown. And surely a legate, a man who represents the Pope…? I feel the beginnings of genuine fear. A man who feels no loyalty to Naples. A stranger in control of our kingdom, a stranger who knows nothing of our court, of our rivaling cousins, of how to maintain the delicate balance of power and enticements that Joanna has only recently restored. How will such a man, even a papal legate, keep our proud and passionate cousins from civil war?

"What will you do?" I ask, my voice catching in the tightness of my throat.

"I will send a formal objection to the Pope. He has no legal grounds to do this. We have had an agreement between the papacy and the monarchy of Naples since 1265."

Another letter, I think. This is the year of letters. I am well aware of the agreement Charles of Anjou, our great-great-grandfather, made in order to rule Naples: an annual tribute to the Pope of 7,000 ounces of gold, and Clement VI is aware of it also. He does not need a letter to remind him. I wonder that he has not become sick of letters.

Sick of letters and sick of complaints. I have not been married long, but I have learned one thing: Charles does not like to hear me complain of his mother, or to hear her complain of me. He does not complain to me of my sister, or write me letters objecting to her barring him at court, although I know it is ever on his mind. And when Louis of Taranto took my Lord's castle and laid waste to it, Charles did not write to the Pope. He called up his vassals and prepared for war. I shiver, but I know I am right. If my sister wants to be treated like a king, she must not behave like a young, inexperienced queen.

"What does your council say?" Sancia asks.

Joanna looks at her thoughtfully. She motions for the night gown. Sancia flushes and hurries to lift it over the Queen's head.

"There will indeed be a high cost for this, Sancia. The question is, who will pay?" Joanna watches Sancia's face as she laces the front of the night gown.

"You must not let them blame you," Sancia says.

"Why would my lords blame me? It is clear who is behind this. It is the work of Elizabeth of Hungary and her money. Andrew and his mother between them will ruin us all if we are not careful."

"The Dowager Queen and her retinue have already cost us enough in upkeep during their visit, and now she is costing us our sovereignty and the expense of a legate!"

I look at the two of them amazed—not at them, at myself. Only months ago I would have been taken in, gullible as a child, by their outraged remarks. But I have since watched my husband and mother-in-law as they weave their past actions—particularly concerning my engagement and wedding—into the design that best suits them. Not actually false, outright falsehoods can be disproved, but not the entire truth, either.

So I am ready, when the two of them turn to me expectantly, to add my thread to the loom. "All for Andrew who would not even lead a campaign to Sicily and does not deserve to be King," I say.

Joanna smiles.

Joanna understands her council and her lords. A few regretfully-murmured comments, certain of their insinuations not checked, and they are won over. If Andrew was not liked before, he is hated now that his mother has stirred Clement VI to ruin us with a legate. The council and the lords know who will pay, and pay dearly, for this legate's upkeep and his papal causes. No one will blame the Pope—the Holy Father is immune—but Elizabeth of Hungary and her son…

When the lords pass Andrew they spit at his feet or jostle him, knocking him against the wall. He develops a wary look in his eye, a nervous way of startling easily when he walks. He does not leave his room without his men surrounding him. He writes to his mother, who writes to Joanna, who writes back that there is nothing to it, no one dislikes Andrew, how could they?

How could they, indeed?

The year of letters continues.

Chapter 13

Economics

Joanna chooses one of her most trusted advisors, Hugo del Balzo, who she elevated to Count of Avellino shortly after King Robert died, to head the delegation that carries her formal protest to the Holy See. As September slips by with no word from Clement VI—and no legate—Joanna's spirits rise.

"He is reconsidering," she tells me with confidence. "We have persuaded him with our arguments."

If he has been persuaded at all it is by her lawyers, her council, and Hugo del Balzo with his little band of Neapolitan advisors in Avignon, not by Joanna. But if they are successful, it will be a much-needed victory for the Queen. On the other hand, if Clement VI publicly confirms, by appointing a legate, that he does not see Joanna as a capable ruler, how will she ever convince her nobles to obey her when her crown is restored?

I do not share my sister's optimism. Perhaps it is simply the weariness of my condition. I am always uncomfortable. My back aches and my breasts are sore, my bladder is always in distress and shooting pains burn my chest. I cannot believe this is the natural condition of carrying a child, even if my midwives assure me it is. Who would ever do this more than once? I am too grumpy to admit that such a thought is shocking, that pious women pray to God to bless them with fertility, but I do remind myself, severely, never to say such a thing out loud.

Furthermore I am bored. It is not fair, I tell myself, as I stand at a window looking down on the courtyard where Joanna and the other young lords and ladies of her court are mounting their horses for a morning of falconing. The royal falcons sit on their trainers' gloved hands wearing their brightly-colored hoods. I watch them turning their heads sharply left and right as though trying to find a direction in which they can see. I feel as confined as they are, trapped inside on this beautiful September morning by my expanding belly.

Sancia, who does not like to ride let alone hunt, comes to stand beside me. We watch the horses stamp their feet, eager to run, as they are led to the mounting blocks. They toss their heads, straining against the grooms' tight hold on their reigns.

Robert, Louis, and Philip, our cousins of Taranto, are among the lords joining the hunt. Louis hands Joanna up onto her horse. I watch his hands linger on her foot a little longer than necessary. When he lets go, Louis pats Joanna's horse, letting his hand brush her skirt. Joanna looks down at him, her eyes half-lidded like a purring cat, her lips curving up in a secret smile. I cannot see Louis' face, only the back of his head, and his hand against her leg.

Across the courtyard, Robert watches them, his face cold and withdrawn. Something in his eyes as he looks at his brother makes me shiver. I would not want to cross Robert of Taranto. Louis is impetuous, he has a temper and can be cruel, I have seen it when we played together as children; but Robert… Robert frightens me. Robert would cut down his Lady Mother if she got in his way. I think it a very good thing Robert was sick with fever when I married Charles, and did not recover until after Joanna recognized my marriage and paid off the Taranto family.

Sancia, standing beside me at the window, glances at me, her look a clear admission that she has seen what I have seen.

"Have they been circumspect?" I ask. I sound like my Lady Grandmother, but I am afraid for my sister. I imagine the Holy Father hearing of a scandal, when he already questions Joanna's rule. Or worse, much worse, Andrew's mother, Elizabeth of Hungary, hearing of this.

"I do not know what you mean, Princess Maria," Sancia says, looking at me steadily. I step back from the window. We are completely alone in the room, as she can see.

"Of course you do. Who else would she trust to help her, now that I am gone?"

"You—?"

"Just tell me, Sancia. I do not judge her—how could I?" I smile wryly at this allusion to my scandalous marriage. "I only want to know, is she safe?"

Sancia nods slowly. "She is now. My grandmother became suspicious of my nighttime… wandering, and caught me bringing Louis to her room. She followed us into Her Grace's bedchamber and had a talk with them."

I grin. I have been subjected to more than one of her grandmother Philippa's talks. I imagine the Queen of Naples and proud Louis of Taranto guiltily squirming like children as she chastised them. "And it has worked? One talk?" I cannot help laughing.

"Well, it has not stopped their feelings," Sancia is giggling herself. "But my Grandmother Philippa sleeps in Her Grace's privy room now, against the door to her bedchamber. That stops the rest."

I find this hysterical. "I think… I think that will keep her safe," I gasp through my giggles. We are both bent double with laughter.

Sancia wipes tears from the corners of her eyes. "It is funny now, but at the time I was afraid. Not of Grandmother Philippa—of Lord Louis. He had his hand on his sword. When my grandmother threatened to tell Her Highness the Dowager Queen Sancia—"

"Holy Mary," I whisper. I clap my hand over my mouth at once, to prevent anything worse slipping out. Grandmother Sancia! She is too holy to sleep with her own husband, everyone knows she is still a virgin after a lifetime of marriage to King Robert. Imagine her learning her married granddaughter, after all her severe religious instruction, has taken a lover! She would call Joanna harlot and disown her; she would tear the cross from Joanna's neck and the crown from her head and send her into the streets—or worse! It would be our Lady Grandmother's death, and she would not go quietly. As surely as she is bound for heaven, just as surely she would order God to send Joanna to hell, and to be quick about it!

"Just so." Sancia nods as though she has read my thoughts. "I was sure Lord Louis would kill my grandmother then and there, and probably me as well, to ensure our silence. Indeed he drew his sword from its scabbard and would have—" she looks at the hard stone floor with its covering of rushes. "And no one would have objected. I know our family is not well-liked; people say we have over-stepped ourselves."

I want to deny this, it sounds so harsh, but I know it is true. The favoritism shown Philippa and Raymond and their sons by King Robert and Dowager Queen Sancia, and continued by Queen Joanna, has created envy and hatred for them, all the more now that so many are seeing their own wealth precariously ready to disappear if the Florentine bankers fail.

"He did not hurt Philippa?" I ask anxiously. My nursemaid. My mother. Who else could I call by that name?

"Queen Joanna put out her hand and stopped him. She loves my grandmother. She will always protect us." This is said with a rush of feeling that makes me want to promise the same. I start to do so, but Sancia, not noticing, continues, "I am afraid my grandmother has made a powerful enemy in one who might otherwise have been one of our few powerful friends."

"The Tarantos have no friends. They have only allies or enemies." It is true; I do not only say it because I am still bitter over their unprovoked attack on my husband's castle and lands.

"That is the nature of men," Sancia says with a shrug. "Still, I would rather he see me as his ally."

"That is why you helped them."

"I helped them because Queen Joanna asked me, for the sake of our childhood friendship. You have done the same for her, my Lady, and would still, would you not?"

She says this with a simple sincerity that shames me. Joanna is my sister, yet I laughed about her plight, I was pleased she was thwarted. The thought of her sleeping alone, with our old nursemaid Philippa the Catanian guarding her door, amused me. Amuses me still. She has a crown; I have a man I love and who loves me, in my bed—I am carrying his child. I touch my extended belly proudly. A fertile woman who is loved is greater than a lonely, barren queen.

Why must I always judge what she has against my own fortune? Why are there always scales, whose weights must be equal, before I can be happy? Or her, for that matter. Joanna did not want me happily married, she wanted me strategically married, as she is. Married to suit her needs. Can we not simply wish each other well, as Sancia does? Is there no true friendship possible between us?

This is a hard admission and I am not prepared to make it. My sister held my hand beneath our capes when I feared to enter Castle Nuovo, and I held hers in the dark when she wept for our parents. No matter what else we are, we will always be two sisters holding each others' hand in secret. I want her to have her crown and a man she loves—did I not deliver her letter that once? She wants me to have a crown and a husband I love—she just wanted it to be Prince Jean of France.

And yet, we are not equal. And if we are not equal, should there not be some form of balance? Am I to be blamed for wanting that? Is it not merely fair and just?

"The Queen is my sister," I answer Sancia. She nods, but she is not fooled. She knows it is no answer at all.

In early October Joanna returns smiling to her presence chamber after a meeting with her council. I wonder what can have made her so happy, when all the civilized world is still reeling with the shock of economic disaster. The massive trade and banking businesses of Florence—the Bardi, Perussi, and Acciaiuoli families—have just declared bankruptcy. Every kingdom in Christendom depends upon them to buy its produce and goods and grant their loans, and none more than the Kingdom of Naples. Who will purchase and distribute the 45,000 tons of grain we produce, which is the basis of our economy, now that they are gone? Everything we do, from the building and beautifying of our castles, cathedrals and monasteries, to the prestige of our university, and the luxuries—silk, perfume, jewels, spices—that are available for purchase at our famed markets—it is all dependent upon the trade and banking of these Florentine families. Not only are our nobles affected, but all who depend upon their patronage. Artists and tradesmen have lost their livelihood, and those who are still employed are glad to make half the wages they were paid before. Everyone from the mightiest lord to the poorest peasant is suffering as this economic plague infects our kingdom, and all our neighboring kingdoms, and nothing can stop it. Joanna and her council are trying grimly to find a way to outlast it; that is the best they can hope for—to survive and one day recover.

"Clement VI will be struck by this crisis also," Joanna told me yesterday. It took me a moment to realize she was thinking of her mother-in-law's tempting hoard of gold, and what Elizabeth of Hungary wants to buy with it.

So why does Joanna come through the door with the first smile I have seen in weeks on her face? Is the crisis over? Have the Bardi, Perussi, and Acciaiuoli families—or even just one of them—reopened their banks? I smile back, eager for good news.

"The honored Poet Laureate of Rome, Francesco Petrarch, is coming to visit Naples. He wants to converse with me!" Joanna announces.

The lords and ladies-in-waiting all applaud, as if they think this is wonderful news. As if they are at all interested in Petrarch's books, or have even read them. Joanna's bright eyes and flushed face, her delighted smile and contagious excitement, are enough. They are all desperate for happiness and hope.

"Play!" Joanna claps her hands to the musicians in her presence chamber. She chooses two of her ladies-in-waiting, the ones with the prettiest voices, and commands them to sing for us.

But she is too excited to be still and listen. She walks over to where I am sitting and whispers, so as not to interrupt the music, "Do you remember his last visit? When he would have none but our Lord Grandfather examine him? When he said that King Robert the Wise was the only mortal man he would accept as judge?" She is beside herself with delight, as she was then, through the full three days of query and response. I was barely twelve but I remember the moment King Robert pronounced himself satisfied. In front of the most illustrious men in the kingdom, he took off his royal ceremonial robe and draped it over Petrarch's shoulders, asking the poet to wear it in Rome when he received his laurel crown. And Petrarch did so, proudly.

"He wants to come to talk with me!" Joanna's voice is hushed with awe. I am not sure whether she is amazed at being so honored or terrified she will not prove up to it. Probably both.

"I will have him speak at the university, and bring his new book for our scribes to copy. And ask him to recite his poetry before the court!" Her eyes are shining.

I smile brightly at her. Surely there will be more entertaining events while he is here? Is Joanna concerned about the cost?

"Can we afford to entertain him?" I ask. But I am only pretending to good husbandry. In fact, I am hoping there will be lavish feasts, with music and dancing and recitations of his love poems, and tournaments and beast-baiting, and perhaps even a masque—I am doubtful of this, I do not think Petrarch is a whimsical man, perhaps there will be no masque. Then I realize, unless he comes very soon, I shall miss every bit of it!

I will have to return to Castle Durazzo in less than two weeks. Already I am so heavy with child it is impossible to hide my condition. No one there will tell me any news of court, let alone allow me to appear publicly like this. And a month after that, I go into my confinement and I will be there for three months: six weeks before the baby is born and six weeks after, while everyone else is celebrating Petrarch's visit. I will miss all twelve days of Christmas as well—the Yule log, the singers, the mummers, everything! When I come out it will all be over. Petrarch will be gone and the celebration of Christmas finished and we will be back to drearily worrying about our finances.

"When will he arrive?" I demand.

"In one week." She looks like a woman dreaming of a lover. I want to slap her. Does she imagine a mere woman will impress the greatest mind in the world, as our grandfather did? I realize, at once, that that is exactly what she dreams of doing. Of matching—no, surmounting—every accomplishment of King Robert's. Only then will she feel the crown sitting firmly and deservedly on her head.

"Joanna…" I want to warn her, to prepare her. Petrarch will never respect her as he respected our Lord Grandfather. She may be as intelligent, educated and witty as any person alive, and a monarch as well, but to him she will always be a woman, inferior by her very nature. I am younger than my sister, and not nearly as accomplished or clever, but I understand this.

She looks at me, smiling.

There is nothing I can say. She will take it as jealousy or resentment. She thinks because I do not have her intellect, I am without understanding. She will only accept this bitter truth when she learns it on her own.

Anyway, more to the point, I *will* be resentful if she has feasts and dances and mummers while I am shut away in a dark room with Margherita and my critical mother-in-law. I bite my lip, thinking.

"Your Majesty, you should throw a great feast for him as soon as he arrives. The very week he arrives, if not the very day! Fill his first days with every kind of entertainment he might like. If you impress him in the first week, he will not notice if the fetes that follow are poorer. That way, you can honor and impress Petrarch, and then also please your royal treasurer and council with your subsequent frugality."

She laughs as if she thinks I have been very clever, and I think I have been, because she agrees at once.

The feast for Petrarch is wonderful! Ten courses are served, including every kind of meat and fowl and fish, bread so light it is nearly white, olives and sweetmeats and figs, sausage and cheeses, meat pies and pasta, all followed by grapes and pomegranates and tortes topped with marzipan or sweet fruit or custard.

Extra musicians and minstrels are hired for the event, as well as the court musicians. The dancing is only marred by the fact that I cannot join in. There are tumblers who make us gasp at their feats of agility and skill, and jugglers who recite amusing poems as well as long, breathtaking tales and of course, Petrarch's most famous poems.

Joanna was so happy making her plans she allowed me to prevail upon her to invite my husband and his brothers. Charles, seated at my side, is delighted with me and properly deferential to Queen Joanna.

I could not convince Joanna to invite our Lady Aunt, Agnes of Perigord, my mother-in-law. She is not so delighted with me, but cannot complain as Grandmother Sancia assures her that we both tried our best.

In short, everything turns out perfectly.

The next morning I return to Castle Durazzo, which is duller than ever by comparison. The gloomy mood of nobles shunned from their Majesty's court pervades the castle. I love my husband and I have delighted in his caresses, but he does not caress me now. Instead, from time to time I catch him looking at my belly with a speculative air, as though he wonders whether I will betray him with a daughter. I am sure I carry a son, but if I am wrong?

All my pride in this pregnancy is evaporating. I do not want to go through with it. What if I am torn so badly I cannot survive? What if the maternal fever takes me, as it does so many women? What if the bleeding afterward cannot be stopped? How did my father's mother die, and my own mother, both so soon after their child was born? I have never asked, and now I dare not, but my dreams bring me answers—

answers I do not want to believe. My midwife reassures me, as I am sure she has done to every mother in her care, both those who survived and those who did not.

I am too young to die! Over and over these words ring in my mind: *I am too young to die!* But of course I am not. I am lucky to have survived my own birth, and then to have survived my childhood. I have gone to Somma or Baiae every year when the summer heat brought fevers to our city; I never thought about those left in the hot, still streets to face it. I have washed their feet at Easter and then fled to the cool breezes of the seaside so that I would live to adulthood. I am not too young, but still I feel my blood pounding in my chest, my throat, my ears, pounding to the ragged beat: *I* am too *young* to *die.*

One month after my return to the Durazzo castle, my husband the Duke of Durazzo holds a small feast in my honor, after which I curtsy, and kiss him chastely, and enter my confinement clutching my cross and praying fervently that I will walk out of these rooms again.

Chapter 14

Confinement

My Lady Mother-in-law accompanies me to the rooms she has prepared for my confinement, close by her chambers. She wants to be the first to know when my child is born. I would prefer to be closer to Charles, so that he could run to me if I called for him if something went wrong, and I could see him one last time. I have not said such a silly thing aloud, they would think me a coward. Charles has his battles and so do I.

Anyway, Charles is a man and cannot come near me at this time. My womanhood is too strong during this period of childbirth, it would unman him to touch me. And I do not want that!

The door into my confinement rooms opens onto an iron screen which we walk around to enter. A priest will perform mass for me once a day, standing on the outside of this screen while I kneel on the inside where I can hear him and make my confession and receive the host, all without being seen. No man may enter these rooms or lay eyes on me during my confinement, not even a priest who should not need his manhood any more. That is a wicked thought.

I am fortunate it is late autumn, not summer, for the windows are all shuttered tightly and hung with heavy cloth to keep out any draft that might carry fever on its breath. The lamps are dim and the fires in the fireplaces are banked up regularly. There are fresh, sweet-smelling rushes on the floor, scattered with shepherd's purse and motherwort, herbs that are beneficial to childbirth. Altogether it is as dark and hot and airless as my womb, where the next heir to the Duchy of Durazzo, and possibly to the throne of Naples, waits to be born. I am certain it will be a boy. My Lord husband and my Lady Mother-in-law will accept nothing else. I close my eyes and offer another quick prayer for his, and my, safekeeping. I feel better afterwards. Surely God will hear me praying when I am not even at chapel.

In the first room there are beds for Margherita and my mid-wives, and chairs for us to sit on to do our sewing and reading and entertain ourselves as best we might while we wait. I walk through it, into the second room. Together they are not much bigger than my bedchamber beside Charles' rooms. The low birthing bed where I will sleep is in this inner room. Beside it is a cradle with a beautiful carving of a woodland scene on its headboard, made up with fine linen trimmed with lace. Inside it lies a swaddling board with bands and a cunning little cap, ready for my baby. I cannot help but smile as I lay the little pale green gowns I have sewn beside them.

"You like it, then?" my mother-in-law asks as I stroke the cradle headboard, setting it to rocking.

"I do," I tell her. "It is beautiful." We exchange the first sincere smile we have shared.

"It was your husband's cradle, and his brothers'."

"I like it all the more for that." I feel my baby kick, as though he, too, likes the cradle and gowns awaiting him. "Do you want to feel?" I ask her shyly.

She hesitates a moment, then she places her hand on my belly where her grandchild is moving.

"Does he hurt you sometimes?"

"Oh, no. He is always gentle." I smile, and almost add, *like a little fish*, which is how I have come to think of him. A little fish swimming lazily inside me.

"My sons hurt me," she says. "They were strong and robust, even in the womb. We will have to hope he takes after his father when he is born, and is not a weakling." She does not say, like his mother, but it is there in the look she gives my now-still abdomen. I turn quickly and go to the other room, where Margherita asks if I would like her to read to me, to cover the fact that everyone has heard my mother-in-law's opinion.

Fortunately, she is too busy overseeing Castle Durazzo to come to my confinement rooms often, or stay here long. She does make sure I have everything I need and that the choicest cuts of meat are sent up from the kitchen. But she will not let me have anything sweet, claiming it will make the child womanly and weak. I dream of custard and candied aniseeds and marchpane until I can almost taste them when I wake up.

When I am not dreaming of sweets, or music and dancing, or any entertainment at all besides this endless sewing and reading, and when I am not dreaming of every calamity in childbirth that my imagination can provide, and when I am not on my knees praying to Mother Mary to keep me safe from them, I think that the worst part of this confinement is not fear but boredom. Oh, I would love to ride on a hunt, kicking my horse to gallop faster. I would love to walk in a garden, to feel the sun and the wind, to dance at court, or hear the latest gossip whispered in my ear.

I wonder what is happening at Castle Nuovo. Is my sister having long conversations about literature and philosophy with Petrarch, as she hoped? Before I left she confided to me her intention of appointing him the honorary title of her domestic chaplain, just as King Robert did at the end of Petrarch's examination. I try to picture him accepting, and hope he did so gallantly, but cannot make the scene clear in my mind. There is nothing a seventeen-year-old girl can do or say that will impress the poet laureate of Rome, even if she is the Queen of Naples. He has written of her beauty, but her intelligence? He is not even looking for that in her. I know that, even if Joanna refuses to. I was very young, but I remember Petrarch's arrogance. So why has he come to Naples?

It is the first time I have asked that question. At once I am alarmed and angry, because seeing the beautiful and learned city of Naples and being honored by its Queen should be reason enough to come, as we assumed—after all, he has visited Naples before. But now that I have asked the question, I know there will be another reason. And I realize Joanna has already learned this bitter truth, as soon as Petrarch had a chance to speak privately with her.

I wish I could go to her. I wish I could stand beside her when she learns her clever mind does not impress him in a woman's body, when he reveals the true motive for his visit. I wish to God that I was not locked in this unbearable, hot, little room when my sister needs me!

It is no use to ask anyone questions about Petrarch's visit. Margherita knows less than I do, shut up in these rooms with me, and my mother-in-law, Agnes of Perigord, will tell me she knows nothing, not being at court, and look at me as though that is my fault. She will deny to my face that she has spies in Joanna's presence chamber, as though I do not already know that Margherita used to be one of them. She is afraid when I go back to court I would tell Joanna who Agnes of Perigord's eyes and ears are. She is not sure where my loyalty to my husband ends and my loyalty to my sister begins. I am not sure I know that myself, so how could she?

Margherita might be spying on *me* now, for my mother-in-law. I have nothing to hide, but the thought makes me pause. Now I would very much like to know who her spy in Joanna's court is, because that girl will be watching me as well as the Queen, when I am at court.

My baby kicks, and I forget all else. It is a gentle kick, a polite nudge. What I used to think of as a sign of gentleness, I now find worrisome. Is there something wrong with my baby? I cradle my stomach in my two hands: one below, that I might always catch and hold him safe, and one above, that he may always know he has my blessing.

Agnes of Perigord has hired a wet-nurse who will be sent for at the first sign that my baby is coming, and another nurse who will clean and swaddle and rock him. I am content to hand him over to them; I do not know anything about babies. But for now he is mine, I think, as I cradle him inside my womb. For now he is mine alone.

That night I wake to the sound of thunder. The wind rattles the shutters and shrieks through the halls and stairwells of the castle. Even the stone walls seem to be trembling, so great is the fury of the storm. I cannot sleep, but lie awake all night waiting for the castle walls to fall. Is it a sign? Is something terrible going to happen to us? To Naples? In my fear I long for my sister. Her hand in mine is all the strength I ever needed; I am lost without it. My hand in hers was the support she counted on; I know she is missing it, too.

When dawn breaks I wait impatiently for my mother-in-law's morning visit. "What is the news?" I demand before she can even ask how I am doing.

She shakes her head. Her face is pale, her eyes wide as though she has seen demons. "I have never witnessed such a terrible storm. The shore is filled with bodies, strewn like debris amidst pieces of destroyed homes and fishing boats, uprooted trees and huge boulders tossed there by the wind. Brains and bowels and broken limbs cover the sand and float on the waves breaking against the shore. Those still living lie among the dead, screaming for help, while women walk among them wailing, searching for their sons and husbands caught on their fishing boats when the storm came up." She sinks into a chair. I have never seen my Lady Aunt distraught like this. It is a shocking sight, nearly as bad as the horrific picture she paints of the seashore. I reach out toward her, whether to seek or to offer comfort, I could not say which.

She straightens in her chair. "Your foolish sister! Your immodest, unthinking sister ran out of her castle barefoot, her hair undone, in her night-robes, with all her ladies similarly undressed, and raced to the Church of the Virgin Queen to pray for her intercession on behalf of the people of Naples. The Queen of Naples! In her night gown! It is a miracle she and her ladies were not killed by the rampaging winds as they ran, and it will be an even greater miracle if they do not all die of fever, praying on their knees before the statue of the Virgin, soaking wet from the rain, for hours while the storm raged."

"But she was not killed? She is not ill?"

"No. Instead, she is a hero to the people." Agnes of Perigord, who will never be loved by those beneath her, or want to be, gnashes her teeth as she says this.

"They love her for loving them." I do not know whether to smile at my sister's faith and courage, or frown because I will never be a queen like her.

"They will not love her long if she continues to risk her life this way." She shakes her head and gets up from her chair. "Well, you may get your chance sooner than we hoped," she says, leaving.

By the time I realize what she means, she has gone. I do not want my sister's kingdom! I fume inwardly. A*nd a little insincerely*, a small voice in my head whispers. Charles promised to win us our own kingdom! *Only he did not say which one,* the small voice whispers again. I will not listen. I will not believe it. I will never agree to take the Kingdom of Naples from my sister.

Oh but I would be tempted. To be a queen, without having to leave Naples?

That would be to lose my sister.

I will not think of it. I have been awake all night and I am over-tired, or such a thought would not come to me. It is impious, especially when so many of our people lie dead on the shores of our kingdom. I go to my bed and close the bedcurtains, blocking what little lamp light there is in my rooms. I close my eyes and think of nothing but sleep…

I wake up soaking wet, and lie there in the darkened room, horrified that I have wet myself and too humiliated to call someone to clean me. Then it hits, a searing pain in my abdomen, as though I am being cut open.

"Help! Help me!" I scream. Something is terribly wrong. Another pain hits me. The baby is dying, or I am, or both of us! I gasp for breath as it recedes.

My midwife appears beside me. Her assistant pads in behind her and lights the lamps, slowly, as if the calamity I feared was not upon me! The midwife slides her arm under my shoulders as the sweet scent of burning olive oil fills the small, closed-in room. She bids me to rise.

Does she think I will not die if I stand up? Men die standing in battle all the time. But I am too terrified to do anything but obey.

By the time I am standing, the pain has begun to recede. Margherita lifts my damp shift over my head and pulls a clean, dry one onto me, while the midwife and her assistant change my bedclothes. They urge me to walk when the pain eases. When it returns they lower me back onto the bed.

The midwife places her hands on my shift to feel my abdomen. The cramp increases, gathering strength under her hands, is she pushing? Is she pushing on my stomach which is already under such pressure I fear it will burst? I try to shove her hands away but she is strong and the pain is intense and I am wrung out between them. I cannot breathe with the pain, I cannot scream, only a low moan escapes me, the air flowing out of me like my life ebbing away. Surely I am dying?

I am not aware I have spoken aloud until the midwife chides me, "No, Duchess, do not talk of dying. You are young and strong, you have nothing to fear. No one will die here today."

When the cramp is over, she holds a cup of birthing ale to my lips, sweetened to give me strength. I sip it thirstily. But then I feel the first few swallows lying heavy in my belly and I do not want any more. Another spasm of pain contracts my abdomen. I open my mouth to scream when my mother-in-law walks in, stopping my protest with a single glance.

Weak like his mother, I can hear her thinking. No one will call a Princess of Naples weak. I close my lips tightly together. It is only that I was not prepared. I did not know it would hurt this much.

Now you know, I tell myself, behind my clenched teeth and closed eyes. The pains continue, getting worse and worse, for the rest of my life. Or what feels like the rest of my life, but is only the rest of the night and half the next day. I walk when they tell me to and lie down to rest when they let me. My mother-in-law comes in every so often to ask the midwife how much longer it will be. Each time the midwife says, "It will be a while yet, my Lady," apologetically, as if we are keeping her waiting unnecessarily, as if she has more reason than I to want this to be over.

I do not make a sound, even when I come to believe it will never stop. Between the waves of pain I worry about my child. If it is this bad for me, how will he endure it? If he is weak, as my mother-in-law predicts, how will he endure it? And if he cannot, if it is too much for him, how will I endure that?

I am so certain that this is all beyond endurance—his and mine—that I am taken by surprise when he emerges, when I hear his little mewling cry as I push out the afterbirth and the ordeal is finally over for both of us. I watch wearily as the midwife cleans him and puts on his little clout. Before she hands him to the wet-nurse, who arrived sometime this morning and has been waiting for hours, I reach out my arms to hold him.

How tiny he is, how exquisite. He is two weeks early and very small, but perfect. His thin little fingers grasp my shift as though he will not be separated from me, and his head turns sideways searching for food. I am entranced by his delicate ears, his perfect, rosebud mouth, puckered as though he wants a kiss. He blinks and squints in the light, as dull as it is, and blinks again as I watch him open his eyes for the very first time. I am the first thing he sees in all the world, looking down at him when he opens his huge, dark eyes. He stares solemnly up at me. I am the only thing in his world as we stare at each other, and he is the only thing in mine.

When my mother-in-law takes him from me it feels like my heart is being torn out. I cannot take my eyes from him. I can barely breathe for wanting him back. She examines him briefly, then hands him to the wet-nurse. I hear the contented, sucking noises of his little lips against her breast, his eager little swallows, and it is worse than all the pain of birthing him to hear him take nourishment from someone else.

I was not prepared. Nobody told me it would be like this. I did not know it was possible to love anyone this much.

The Dowager Duchess says, "He will be named Louis." It is the only thing she has said to me this whole time, and I am not certain she is talking to me now.

I wanted to call him Robert, for my Grandfather. She leaves before I can tell her.

When he has eaten his fill and given a satisfied little burp, the midwife binds him tightly to his swaddling board so his legs will grow straight, and hands him to me. Only his little neck and head can be seen above the binding. I stare at the lines of his blood, fine and blue as royalty beneath his pearl-pale skin, and the nearly translucent lids of his eyes. He is as perfect and delicate as white glass, as music, as the sweetest poem Petrarch ever imagined. Louis. A name like a whisper, soft and sweet. It suits him perfectly.

I will have six weeks with him. Six weeks to hold him as often as I like, with no one to say I may not, to watch him till I fall asleep and wake to see him sleeping in his cradle beside me. We will be together in these cozy little rooms for all of Christmas, until I am churched and he is old enough to go to his nursery. I am ecstatic at the thought of it.

Charles sends a Yule log for my fireplace, and a yuletide gift for me, a necklace with emeralds, brilliant green for our son's new life. I send to him the fine linen shirt I sewed for him myself during my confinement.

Plans are made for Louis to be baptized in January at Santa Chiara, for he is the great-grandson of King Robert. I am sorry I will miss it, but I cannot come out of confinement until I have been churched, six weeks after childbirth, and Louis must be baptized and sealed to God as soon as he is strong enough. I smile to think of him being presented to the court, who will be in attendance however discredited my husband's family is. My Louis will not cry when the priest anoints him with holy water. He is a quiet baby, a peaceful child. He would sleep through his feedings if his nurse allowed him to. I will miss the baptismal feast as well, but I do not care. They will bring Louis back to me and I will order all my favorite dishes sent here to us, with marchpane and candied nuts and a fruit torte. We will have our own little feast, Louis and I and Margherita.

On Christmas day I have his nurse put him into one of the little gowns I made for him, and I sing him a Christmas carol, rocking him in my arms. He does not sleep, but fixes his wide dark eyes on me as though he is listening to every word and trying to understand their meaning. I wear my new emerald necklace, and when Louis reaches up his tiny hand I guide it into his grasp. He stares at his jeweled hand in wonder, making me laugh. The sound makes him startle—he looks at me—and his beautiful little mouth curves into his first smile. The nurse reaches to pat him, thinking it is only gas, but I know he has smiled at me. It is the nicest Christmas I have ever had.

By Twelfth Night, Louis' sleepiness has his nurse worried. "He was born early," I remind her, but she just shakes her head. I ask for the priest to give me an extra Mass and to pray with me. On this night when the three Magi visited the infant Christ, surely a prayer for an infant will be answered. The priest gives me the host through a small opening in the screen and blesses Louis when his nurse holds him up. I rise from my knees reassured.

A week later, Louis closes his eyes to sleep and does not waken.

Chapter 15

Losses

1344

I am imprisoned in these rooms, as dark and cramped and airless as a coffin, for three more weeks. The memory of my son is carved into every corner. There is where I sang to him and there is where I sat to rock him; there is where his cradle sat and there his swaddling board, and on that stool I laid out the little green gowns I sewed for him. There the midwife slept with her assistant, and there the nurse and the wet-nurse cared for him, all gone now. Only Margherita has stayed with me, the two of us sitting silently, she at her sewing, me staring down at my empty hands. I have asked her not to speak, the effort of conversation is beyond me. I have nothing to say, and no one can say anything I care to hear.

Margherita remembers him with me in silence. That is something; I am not alone with my memories. But only I loved him. My mother-in-law never cared for him—I cannot bear the sight of her now. I see her still, examining him as if he was a new foal, and not a very promising one at that. And Charles never saw him.

Louis was blessed hastily, but he was blessed. The wet-nurse called an alarm when he would not wake to feed, and the priest was sent for at once. Louis was still breathing when the priest arrived, although he would not wake. He was just waiting for the priest's blessing so he could go straight to God.

They have taken my son away to bury him, and all his baby things as well. I am left with my memories, so in fact nothing is gone, I see it all clearly everywhere I look: his gowns, his little cap, his swaddling cloths, his cradle, even his tiny clouts: there, and there, and over there, I see them still. I cannot eat, I cannot sleep, with all these memories surrounding me. And yet I would not forget. I would rather starve than forget, I would rather never sleep again than forget one minute of the time I had with him. I tried to keep his green gown and his cap, such a dear little cap, still smelling of his sweet baby scent. I tore the emerald necklace from my throat and tried to make the women take it instead, but they would not. Instead they took away everything that had ever touched him. Except me. They have left me here without him, with only Margherita, poor frightened Margherita who looks at me as though she fears I have gone mad. I am not mad. I am only lost, wandering somewhere between earth and heaven, unable to follow my baby to God, unable to resume my life and give him up.

"Do you think you are the only woman to lose a child?" Lady Agnes of Perigord demands. "You have been raised to be soft, but life is not soft. Life is not what you want, but what you must endure. A wise woman does not become attached to a child before its third year, surely you have been told that?"

I do not answer, or even look at her.

"We will force you to eat!" she cries. "I did not go to all the trouble of getting you wed to my son for you to die before your sister!"

Behind me I hear Margherita catch her breath, but I do not respond. It is of no importance to me what Agnes of Perigord says. She cannot force me to eat. Until now, I have simply not been hungry; but now I would not eat if I was famished. I am a royal princess; no servant of hers would dare to touch me without my permission, whatever orders she might try to give them.

"Eat, Maria," Charles implores me through the iron screen. "We have lost our son, but we will have more. I do not want to lose you, as well."

"You should have come before," I tell him. "You should have come while our son was alive." I do not say it in anger, or to make him feel guilty. I am too weary and listless for either of those emotions. I am only sad for him that he never knew his son, never looked on that sweet little face, and now he never will.

"I am the Duke of Durazzo. I cannot come at my wife's bidding. I have much business to attend to." I cannot see his expression through the screen, but I can hear the impatience in his voice.

He had many concerns, while I had only one: to keep our son alive. And that one thing I have failed to do. I begin to weep, quietly. Not a bid for sympathy, it is only something that happens to me now, this weeping. It comes upon me, taking me by surprise, through no intent of mine.

"I am sorry," he says.

I nod, but I do not know what it is he regrets.

He waits for me to say something, but I have forgotten he is there, so distant he seems on the other side of the screen, and when I remember, he has gone.

"Wake up, please wake up, my Lady."

I open my eyes. Margherita is standing beside my bed, her hands clasped together anxiously. How long have I been sleeping? It is so dark in here I do not know whether it is day or night, and I am always tired.

"The Queen herself has come to see you," Margherita says. "She is on her way up the stairs now. I have water for you to wash."

She stops herself in time from telling me to hurry, but it is in her voice. I sit up, because it is easier than refusing. She is beside herself, afraid, no doubt, that she will be blamed for not serving me better if I am discovered unkempt and dirty.

"Let me do your hair," she pleads.

I am still washing my face and arms. What does it matter, my hair? But I am too weary to tell her this.

"Please, Princess Maria. It will feel nice to have it brushed. You will feel better when it is freshly braided up."

I will feel better? Is it as simple as a hairdo? I remember the pride I took in my long yellow hair. I was once a girl who cared very much about her appearance. It seems a long time ago. Margherita has the brush in her hand, waiting only for my permission. It will not make me feel better, but Margherita has sat with me through my confinement, has shared Louis' short life, and stays with me now, and I have not heard a word of complaint or criticism from her. I have only seen kindness and compassion in her face, and tears for Louis. I nod to her. At the least, I can let her brush my hair and braid it up.

Joanna is announced, as though this dark tomb I live in is my court and she is entering my presence chamber. She sits on the stool beside me, ignoring the cushioned chair that has been brought in for her, and takes my hand in hers. I try to slip out of her grasp, but she will not let go, so I let her hold my hand.

"I am sorry I was not here," she says.

I nod, as I did to Charles. But Joanna is here now, inside the rooms where Louis lived. Her words do not slide through my mind and disappear. They remind me of something. Something I thought once. I wanted…

I wanted to be with her when Petrarch let her down. It seems very long ago now, and trivial, but she is here and I have to make some conversation, and that will be easier than talking about my son.

"Why did he come to Naples?" I ask.

She understands I am referring to Petrarch. We have always understood each other, even when we were at odds.

"He came on behalf of one of his patrons in Rome, Cardinal Colonna, who wants me to free the Pipini brothers."

"The Pipini brothers?" What has Petrarch to do with the Pipini brothers? Have I heard her wrong? It has been happening lately.

"Imagine a man of his intellect, stooping to plead the case of such villains!" She has warmed to her topic, now. I will not need to think what to say. I can just let her talk, as I sometimes let Margherita read to me, without troubling myself even to listen. But I am surprisingly interested. The juxtaposition of lofty Petrarch and the infamous Pepinis is too astonishing to ignore.

"What case?" I ask.

"Exactly! They have no defense. Murderers, rapists, arsonists! They were justly called "the scourge of Apulia." And treason—they defied King Robert as well as his laws. How can there be a pardon for them? Everyone knows they were guilty, they hid nothing. If I were to release them, as Petrarch asked me to do, they would just continue in their ways. I would be encouraging others to do so also, seeing there are no consequences for lawlessness."

I think back. My mind moves slowly these days. Joanna sits fuming inwardly, still holding my hand. "They were rampaging when he was last here…"

Joanna nods her head, as if I have supplied a brilliant argument on her side. "Yes, you are right! They were captured and jailed after his visit. But he saw nothing then, except his own glory. Now he sees nothing but fault with me and my kingdom. He complains the city is lawless and dangerous, that he dare not walk in the streets at night. And yet he wants me to free the worst offenders! I never thought I would say it: Petrarch is a fool!"

"You did not tell him so?"

Joanna gives a bitter little laugh. "I told him I must follow the advice of my council, who would not let me release the Pepini brothers. But Andrew…" she gives a little snort of disgust, "Andrew promised to try to have them freed, if only he were king. I would to God our grandfather had had them beheaded as he wanted, and never listened to our grandmother's pleas for mercy! Their sentence of lifelong prison is just a lifelong headache for me to inherit."

I look away. I cannot bear any more of her emotion, I have too much of my own to bear. "He is gone now," I say, to calm her.

"Yes, he has done his damage and gone."

I consider whether I want to know what damage, whether I have the strength to listen or the energy to care, or even the interest to ask. I find that I do. "What else?"

"He has complained to Clement VI that I have no control of my kingdom, that Naples has fallen to barbarity and blood-lust—"

"Blood-lust?"

"A young man died in the tournament while he was here."

I nod. It is not uncommon; tournaments are known as violent sport, that is what makes them entertaining. But now I think, *if my son had lived he might have competed*, and I find I am not unsympathetic to Petrarch's revulsion. Except that every complaint he has raised is in direct contradiction to his desire to have the Pipini brothers released.

"—and my husband's mother, the Dowager Queen Elizabeth, seized this excuse to write to Clement herself, demanding that Andrew be crowned, and that a legate be appointed. And he has agreed to appoint one!"

"A legate?" Have I heard right? My sister is to lose her right to rule? I thought she had succeeded in her objection to a legate. "A legate will be appointed?" I ask.

"Pope Clement VI has issued a bull appointing Cardinal Aimeric de Chatelus as legate, with full power to rule my kingdom."

I do not have to ask if she has objected again. She will be doing everything possible to reverse or delay this odious papal bull.

"Is there any hope?" I close my fingers around her hand, no longer simply allowing mine to be held, but holding hers back.

"There might have been. Cardinal Talleyrand might have intervened, and convinced His Holiness…"

"But?"

"Our Lady Grandmother Sancia's health is failing. She has made arrangements to be admitted to Santa Croce."

"The Clarissan convent? She is to become a Poor Clare?"

"She has always wanted to go there."

"But now? When you most need her?" Grandmother Sancia is the head of Joanna's ruling council, with decades of experience running the Kingdom of Naples with King Robert. If doubt was cast on Joanna's ability to rule before, while she had the Dowager Queen Sancia advising her, now there will be no doubt at all.

Joanna does not answer. What answer can she make? I know the outcome as well as she does. I squeeze her hand in silent understanding.

The scales have realigned themselves. I have lost my son and Joanna has lost her crown. We have each lost what we most treasured. My loss was greater, I think, looking around the dull room at all the places where Louis is absent. But I also have retained more, for I have a husband I care for, who came to beg me to eat. He does not want to lose me, even though I have failed him in a wife's greatest duty; while Joanna has only Andrew, who does not even know whether she is eating, let alone care.

My sister and I sit side-by-side in the small, dark rooms of my confinement, holding hands. It is a testament to our bond, to my need for her and her need for me, that she has come at all, has humbled herself to enter the castle of the woman she blames for my shameful abduction and secret marriage; a woman she will still not allow at her court.

"I am sorry I was not there," I tell her.

She nods, and I understand that she is sorry also, for not being here.

"Will you eat?" she holds out to me a platter of nuts and figs lying on the table. She is asking me to get well, to come to her court, to help her or at least be there with her. Like my Lord Charles, she is asking me to live—or as close as she will come to asking. A queen does not ask, but a sister does not order. Joanna is simply holding out a plate of food.

I reach out with my other hand, the one not clasped in hers, and take a fig and a piece of cheese from the platter.

Chapter 16

Jealousy

My mother-in-law is finally pleased with me. By nearly dying, I have secured her an invitation back to court. When I have been churched and strengthened myself with food and sleep and fresh air away from my confinement rooms, I also return to Castle Nuovo.

It is no secret that my sister humbled herself to ask me to return, or that Charles' family, including his mother, have been permitted back to accompany me. I hesitated before agreeing, giving my mother-in-law time to consider my value. But in truth, I would rather be here, even as my sister's lady-in-waiting. Castle Durazzo reminds me too much of Louis.

Joanna has been able to delay the arrival of the legate, but not to change the Pope's decision. Every face I see is tense, or angry, or both. No one knows what the legate will do, but every one is certain that, since the Hungarians are behind his appointment, it will not go well for the Neapolitan lords.

I stand at the window in the Queen's presence room on my second day back, idly looking out—I have been drawn to the sun ever since my dark confinement—when I see Andrew and several of his men ride into the courtyard, dark with sweat from their day's hunt. Their dogs are with them, panting from the chase.

Several young lords are talking in a corner of the courtyard. They do not move aside but make Andrew pull his horse up and go around them. When one of Andrew's dogs trots through the center of their little group, one of the young noblemen draws his sword and kills it.

I gasp at my window, shocked by the suddenness, the unexpectedness of his brutal attack on the dog. Then I gasp again as the nobleman looks up: it is Louis of Taranto. He glances at Andrew, then up at the window with the tiniest lift of his eyebrows, a flicker of scorn. For a horrified instant I think he is looking at me, then I feel a movement beside me and I realize Joanna has come to stand at the window with me.

Louis is now holding up his blood-stained sword and calling something to Andrew. There is a cruel curve to his mouth, he is laughing. Two of Andrew's men draw their swords, and at once all the noblemen in the courtyard have their swords drawn and ready—for what? I hold my breath, frozen in place, unable to believe what I am seeing.

Andrew calls out something: "halt," or "stop," or "no." I cannot make it out, but I can see the terror on his face. His men are outnumbered as more courtiers suddenly appear in the courtyard, swords at the ready, and the Hungarians are at a further disadvantage, half in their saddles, half out.

I give a strangled cry, clapping my hand to my mouth in horror. They are going to kill one another! Why doesn't Joanna stop them? Why doesn't she pound on the window—Louis knows she is here. Should I raise an alarm? Call for the castle guards? Or would I only be augmenting the odds against Andrew? No one is impartial any more.

Whatever he said, Andrew's men return their swords to their scabbards. And now more Hungarians ride into the courtyard, back from their hunt. Louis of Taranto wipes his stained sword across the dog's fur and returns it to its scabbard, watching Andrew all the while. Andrew stares back at him, his face red with fear and impotent fury. The other young lords and courtiers follow Louis' lead and sheath their swords, but slowly, as if they had been willing to murder Andrew and his small band of men, and are sorry they have been stopped.

I step back from the window, shaking. I am no better than Louis, for I was glad to see Andrew as frightened as he once frightened me. A bully deserves to be bullied. But I do not want to see him murdered!

"I cannot stop it," Joanna says.

I look at her. I am your sister, my eyes remind her, but I let her lie go unchallenged. I am more shaken by Louis' animosity, and the other lords' willingness to follow him, than by Joanna's denial.

"He was always disliked…" I swallow, trying to steady my voice. Do they want him dead? Has it gone so far? Andrew may be Hungarian by birth, but he is also a prince of the Angevin line. How could they presume to harm him, a royal prince, here in daylight, in the very courtyard of Castle Nuovo?

"And now he is hated." Joanna says. "His mother bought the Pope's decision with her gold, so now we will have a papal legate raising taxes and depleting our royal treasury to pay for his luxurious lifestyle. And Andrew will be crowned with me." She looks aside. Her hands are clenched so tightly at her sides they are white. When her breathing steadies she continues. "My noblemen are furious; they swore fealty to me when King Robert died, not to the Hungarian Andrew, and not to a papal legate. They say they will defend my sole inheritance."

Charles and my Lady Mother-in-law have also written to Clement VI, demanding that Andrew's crowning be delayed. Andrew will find no advocates among the Neapolitan lords as long as he promises to pardon the Pepini brothers when he is crowned. No one wants their brutality unleashed upon the kingdom again. In case that argument fails, Joanna has quietly reminded her council and lords that if the Pepinis are pardoned, their confiscated property and wealth must be returned to them. Most of that has long been distributed as rewards for loyalty to those who support the crown. Returning it would be a double loss, coupled with the new taxes, to Joanna's council and most of the noblemen at court.

"He is an Angevin prince," I remind my sister, as well as myself. "If they dare attack him…"

"Oh, they will never go so far," Joanna says carelessly. "It is all talk and show. He would have to give them an opportunity, an excuse, and he is too frightened to goad them so far, or to be caught alone and in secret—"

"What are you saying?" I whisper. *Alone and in secret?*

"There have been threats on his life," Joanna admits. "But it will come to nothing if I can persuade His Holiness to reverse his decision and not have Andrew crowned."

I hope she is right, but there is more to what I saw than that. It is personal between Andrew and Louis; at least it is for Louis. And Joanna is at the heart of it—Louis made sure she was watching.

"And if you cannot have Andrew's coronation reversed?"

"I will do it. I must. For the sake of my kingdom." She glances back at the window. "And for Andrew's sake as well."

I doubt that answer will reassure Andrew's mother, the Dowager Queen Elizabeth of Hungary, if she witnesses anything like what I have just seen. She is arriving tomorrow to visit her son once more before she sails back to Hungary, having spent the time since her visit last summer in Rome and Avignon, stirring up trouble for us. She is sure to be a popular guest.

It takes Elizabeth of Hungary less than a day to realize her darling son is in trouble. I do not believe she ever realizes it is mostly her fault. Or perhaps she does not care. Queen Elizabeth is a wolf-mother; her cubs are either useful to the pack or not. And Andrew will be more useful with a crown on his head.

Andrew clings to his mother. Not, of course, that he actually touches her, but wherever she goes, he is with her, like a puppy always underfoot of the bitch that whelped it. And like a puppy that knows itself to be safe under the protection of its parent, he puffs out his chest, and struts, and looks very brave so that I almost forget the terrified face I saw through the window in the courtyard.

Ridiculous as this appears in a man of nearly seventeen, I find myself, against my will, feeling some sympathy. I have just lost my little Louis—a weakling, according to my mother-in-law, but I loved him all the more for it. Elizabeth of Hungary is in turns impatient and protective of this weakling son of hers. I can imagine feeling the same. Not that Louis would have grown up anything like Andrew! Louis would have been handsome and intelligent—I could see it in his eyes as he took everything in—and gentle and kind, never a bully. These are qualities that more than offset a lack of physical strength and brute courage. Andrew has nothing to commend him. But still his mother fights for him. I cannot help but like her a little for that, even though she does nothing but harm at every turn, to Andrew and to Naples.

We see them every day. Joanna cannot scorn Andrew and keep her distance from him under the watchful eyes of her mother-in-law, so Andrew and his court now dine with us, attend the entertainments with us—tournaments, dances, music, hunts—and visit with us in Joanna's presence chamber.

I remember the feel of Andrew's hand at my throat, the horror of it. I was a child then, thirteen, a foolish maiden. Now I am a married woman under my husband's protection. Andrew would not dare to touch me. Yet still when he looks at me I know he is also thinking of that night, I remember the savage grip of his hand, and I am afraid. I endure his presence but I do not talk to him and sit as far from him as I am able.

It is glaringly obvious to his mother, as it was during her last visit, that Andrew is not invited into Joanna's privy chamber, where she meets with her ruling council and other advisors. Where she signs laws and edicts and official documents in her name alone. I sit in the presence chamber with Joanna's ladies-in-waiting on one side of the room, and Elizabeth and her attendants on the other, and call for music and dancing and readings in an attempt to distract Dowager Queen

Elizabeth's avaricious eyes from the door to that privy chamber where Joanna is making all the decisions.

Only one thing distracts her, and that is when she brings up the question of when Andrew will be crowned. Joanna is unfailingly pleasant but vague, saying she can make no decisions until the legate arrives.

"But you can propose a date," Elizabeth of Hungary persists. "The Pope has approved a double coronation."

"When the legate arrives, I will be turning my kingdom over to him. Neither Andrew nor I will rule Naples, Madam. There is no point in talking about coronations now." Joanna's smile is cool, her voice calm, no one can fault her. But the words come from her mouth sharp as a dagger, as the Dowager Queen, a woman also born to rule, knows all too well.

"Perhaps it is for the best," Marguerite of Taranto whispers to one of the other ladies-in-waiting when Joanna and Elizabeth have both left the room.

I pretend not to hear, to be listening only to the music of the lute player, wondering what she will say next.

"I wonder how Queen Joanna dares to rule Naples alone?" the other lady whispers, a new girl whose name I cannot recall.

"King Robert was dying when he made his will, naming the young Queen his sole heir. They say he was not in his right mind," Marguerite replies.

Who says this? Who dares? But I do not interrupt, wanting to know what else they will reveal.

"A man is better suited to rule than a woman. He has the greater intellect, his heart is more courageous, his will more constant. It is the will of God that women be subject to men, for a man is made in God's image, and a woman is made from man. It is not natural for a woman to rule over men."

The new lady-in-waiting, who cannot be more than twelve years old, nods solemnly in agreement with Marguerite.

"Queen Joanna is King Robert's direct heir," I say, unable to hold back any longer. "Have you not heard him referred to as King Robert the Wise? Do you know better than all those who called him such? The Queen is divinely ordained, her reign blessed and commanded by God."

The new girl looks shaken, and quickly begs my pardon, but Marguerite bends over her sewing without responding. And how can I criticize them for their comments? They only say what everyone knows to be true. I could tell them it is treason to suggest Her Highness Queen Joanna should not be the sole sovereign as King Robert named her. I could point out that the rules that govern ordinary men and women do not apply to those of royal blood. But I would only make them distrust me, not change their opinions.

How widespread is this belief?

Later, when I tell Charles what I have overheard, he is not surprised. In fact, he expects me to agree. "You are willing to be ruled by me, are you not, Maria?"

"Of course, but you are not Prince Andrew."

"Naples is not a kingdom to be ruled by a woman. It is already divided by rivalries and vendettas and alliances that do not last. Naples needs a king without mercy, to hold its noble families together, to make us great by making Naples great—through treaties with other kingdoms, king to king. It does not need a sentimental and compassionate Queen at its head. Naples will only be safe and at peace under a strong king."

"You cannot want Andrew of Hungary crowned?" I cannot keep the revulsion from my voice. Charles glances at me.

"You know yourself I wrote to my uncle, the Duke of Perigord, urging him to speak to the Pope and delay Duke Andrew's crowning. My Lady Mother sent the same request to Cardinal Talleyrand. I said, a strong king, not a lawless and foolish boy. Perhaps Queen Joanna and Prince Andrew are not the best rulers for Naples."

"Not the best—you are speaking treason! You could have your tongue split for saying that." I look around, as though such words are not safe even in our own castle.

"I am speaking to my wife, the heir to the throne, of what is best for the Kingdom of Naples. That is all."

"There is no plan—?" I would like to think that the idea horrifies me. It does, I *am* horrified. But there is a small part of my heart that leaps up at the thought of being Queen of Naples, with Charles as King. No! I stifle it immediately. "I would never agree to such a plan!"

"There is no plan," Charles says smoothly. "I am not a traitor. But tell me, which is more important to you: your sister or the good of Naples?"

"They are the same, while Queen Joanna lives."

He smiles as though he is well aware that behind my cool, firm words, my heart beats hot and unsteady. He knows I am remembering that they are not at all the same thing for Joanna.

Elizabeth of Hungary has been at our court five days when she comes storming into the Queen's presence chamber demanding to speak to Joanna at once. Joanna is in the middle of a game of hazards with Sancia and me, and Joanna is winning.

"Welcome, Lady Elizabeth," Joanna says, tossing her dice. She smiles briefly as they show another winning outcome and glances up at the Dowager Queen of Hungary.

"I am always pleased to speak to you, Madam."

"Queen Joanna, I have learned upsetting news. The lawlessness in your kingdom goes unchecked. Even your royal court is beyond your control. I have decided my son, a Prince of Hungary, is not safe here. I am taking him back to Hungary with me!"

"That is a serious allegation, Madam," Joanna rises at once to face her mother-in-law. "Come into my privy chamber and tell me what you have learned."

We all sit stunned to silence as they go into Joanna's privy chamber. If it were not so serious, I would be inclined to laugh. A grown man, a prince and a husband, being dragged home by his mother like a child late for dinner? I glance sideways at Sancia and see on her face, too, a mixture of horror and humor that almost undoes me.

Sancia moves her chair closer to mine. "She is right," she whispers to me. "Louis will kill Andrew if someone else does not do it first."

"Lord Louis will never stoop to murder his own cousin."

"Andrew is in his way. Louis wants Queen Joanna."

"And Joanna wants Louis. But that is nothing new." I look at her. Her eyes are wide and she bites her lower lip nervously. "What is it? Tell me."

"Louis has been content to influence Joanna's decisions—something Andrew cannot do. But if Andrew is making decisions, if he has power? A double coronation changes everything. Andrew will soon have two things Louis wants, and Louis will have nothing."

"Joanna will control Louis."

"Will she?"

I draw myself a little aside from Sancia. "My sister would never condone murder."

"No, of course not," Sancia agrees. "I meant the Queen does not entirely dislike Louis' jealousy." Sancia gives a little shrug. "What woman would not? Louis is strong, handsome, and passionate, and he is wild for her. She wants to believe he is honorable, as well."

"God help her—God help us all if Elizabeth of Hungary finds out any of this!"

"Oh, she will not. The Queen is too intelligent for the Dowager Queen Elizabeth."

"Is your grandmother still sleeping outside the Queen's chamber?" I ask, trying to hide my grin.

Sancia gives a snort of laughter. "Not since your Lady Grandmother went to Santa Croce. The threat is gone. But there is no need. As long as the Queen refuses to sleep with Prince Andrew, she cannot sleep with Louis, for how would she explain any… outcome? And if she invited Andrew to her bed, even she knows Louis would not bear it."

I look at the door to the privy chamber. "What do you think she is telling Andrew's Lady Mother?"

"That she loves her son so much she cannot bear to have him leave."

I look at Sancia, catch her expression, and cannot help it—we both burst into laughter.

Elizabeth of Hungary calls on the members of the ruling council, along with Catherine of Taranto and my mother-in-law, Agnes of Perigord, as the heads of the two most powerful families in the kingdom, outside of the Queen herself. Being a dowager queen, Elizabeth has more respect for dowager duchesses than young dukes. They all assure Elizabeth that her son will be safe here in Naples and should stay.

"Why not let him go?" I ask Joanna when we are alone in her bedchamber, having a meal together as we used to. "No one wants him here, least of all you. And you know he is not safe." I imagine never having to see him again, never being reminded of that night…

Joanna stops eating. She stares at me, the meat speared on her knife halfway to her mouth. Slowly she lowers it to her plate.

"Do you know, Maria, the single greatest threat to my kingdom?"

I swallow the food in my mouth. "The royal families themselves," I say, ashamed of my previous naiveté. "I did not know at the time—"

"You are wrong," she cuts me off. "Though not far wrong. The greatest threat to Naples is Hungary."

"But we have a treaty. Your marriage—"

"My marriage sealed that treaty. Andrew keeps Naples safe. If Andrew leaves, do not doubt for a moment that his brother King Louis of Hungary will bring him back at the head of a Hungarian army so huge we will fall before it like weeds before the plough. They have the power to utterly destroy us. King Louis prays daily, I am sure, for an excuse to take my kingdom by force. If anything happens to Andrew, I am dead, and Naples is forfeit."

I stare at her. "But he is not safe, there have been death threats. What if…" I cannot finish, I am so terrified at the vision she has created.

"There have been threats against his life, and some are real. Most of them I made up myself, to make certain he and his guards take care, that they keep him safe, that he is never alone."

"And now your false threats have frightened the Dowager Queen into—"

"She will not take him. I will not let her. I will keep Naples safe, even if that means keeping my foolish husband here."

"Our Lady Aunt Catherine and my Lady Mother-in-law have spoken with her."

"Together, in the same room," my sister smiles. "For the first time they are in complete agreement."

"We quarrel among ourselves, but when there is a real threat, we are united."

The smile leaves my sister's face. "Do not rely upon it. Lord Robert of Taranto and Lord Charles of Durazzo hate each other. My dukes are like wolves fighting over each other's territory, never noticing the lion until he is upon them. One day they may look up from their rivalry too late."

I push my plate away. I, too, went running recklessly after what I wanted, ignoring the consequences it would set in motion.

"But you have learned," Joanna says, guessing my thoughts. "And this time, Durazzo and Taranto have looked up and noticed the lion in time. We have convinced my Lady Mother-in-law to honor the treaty and leave her son with us."

Elizabeth of Hungary and her entourage sail home at the end of February, without Prince Andrew.

Chapter 17

Kingdom Without a Monarch

Joanna storms into her presence chamber. I follow reluctantly.

"Out!" she screams at her ladies-in-waiting and the few courtiers chatting and flirting with them while they waited for the Queen's return. "Get out!" They scramble to obey.

Joanna waves Sancia over. "Send for your grandmother." Your grandmother, I think. Not 'Mother', not even 'Philippa'; just Sancia's grandmother.

"Bring us cool rose water to wash off the dust of our journey," I murmur to one of the hastily-departing ladies. The cooler the better I think, glancing at Joanna.

"How dare he?" she fumes, as soon as the door closes and we are alone. "How dare he!"

All during the ride back from the monastery of Saint Antonio, just outside Naples, where the papal legate, Cardinal Aimeric de Chatelus, is lodged, Joanna maintained a calm exterior, her face stiff—only I could see the tension in it—a smile pasted on her lips as she waved to her people. She hurtles her travel cloak to the floor, her pent-up fury erupting into a stream of insults and oaths aimed at the pompous, infuriating Cardinal Aimeric. She is entirely justified; I am angry enough to add a few oaths of my own, but I keep silent and let her rant.

She does not even pause when Philippa arrives accompanied by two servants bearing bowls of water. They stare wide-eyed at their Queen, pacing the room and swearing, before Philippa abruptly gestures them to set down the bowls and leave. I wash the dust and the insult of our journey from my face, neck, and hands while Joanna continues to unleash her fury on our ears, pacing the room like one of the fierce feline predators in our menagerie. Finally she stops in front of the bowl of water left for her. Philippa lifts the cloth, wrings it, and wipes Joanna's face soothingly with the cool, sweetly-scented water.

"He refused you again," she says. It is a statement not a question, but so incredible it can hardly be believed. This is the third time the Queen has ridden out to offer her vow of obedience to Cardinal Aimeric.

"He has not yet received all the necessary papers from Pope Clement VI," Joanna quotes, mimicking the high nasal tone of the Cardinal's voice. With a little shriek of rage she lashes her hand across the table, sending the bowl flying across the room, scattering water and rose petals over the floor rushes until it shatters against the wall.

I stare at my sister open-mouthed. I have never seen her give in to her temper like this.

"I am still Queen, thanks to Cardinal Aimeric's stubbornness. It is mine to break," she snaps. I shut my mouth.

"Do you feel better now?" Philippa asks disapprovingly.

"Yes," Joanna surprises us both by saying. "Yes I do." She grins. "I should have tried breaking things before this." I find myself grinning, too. After a moment Philippa gives a pained smile, which makes us laugh harder.

"What happened today in the Queen's rooms?" Charles asks me, as he does every evening when we have left the grounds of Castle Nuovo for the short ride back to Castle Durazzo to sleep. "I heard she had a tantrum, and ordered everyone but you away."

"I am your wife, not your spy."

"You are my spy because you are my wife. Do not imagine Joanna has any illusions otherwise. You only see and hear what she does not care if I know."

"Then what use is anything I tell you?"

"Everything is of use. We may be called upon to rule this kingdom; we have to be prepared to seize our chance when it arrives."

I pull my horse to a stop. "You promised you would win us a kingdom, not steal my sister's. You said my wealth and yours would enable you to mount an army and—"

"Your wealth? How much of your dowry have I seen? How much am I ever likely to see from your sister?"

"She will give it to you! She said she would."

"'Say' and 'do' are different things, Duchess Maria. If I cannot have your dowry, I will have to take your inheritance."

I stare at him, my mouth open. "You would never harm the Queen. You swore an oath."

He frowns at me. His stallion, feeling his tension, prances to continue, but Charles reins it in. "I swore an oath," he agrees. "But if something happens to your sister, I must be prepared to make our claim. I cannot let our cousin Louis, close as he is to the Queen, or his brother Robert of Taranto who is closer to the throne than I, steal it from us."

"Robert is not closer to the throne than I am. I am my sister's heir."

Charles lets his horse out into a trot, forcing me to urge my mare to follow.

"What do you mean, 'if something happens to my sister'?"

He is ahead of me and does not answer, although I believe he must have heard.

Charles is an honorable man. He is only thinking ahead. This business with the legate has my sister looking pale and weary again, and summer is coming on. But Joanna is stronger than she appears; she will not succumb to the heat-borne fevers of mid-summer. Charles will have to look elsewhere for our kingdom.

"The Cardinal now insists that Queen Joanna and Duke Andrew make their vow of obedience together, in public," I tell Charles as he lifts me down from my horse in the entrance of Castle Durazzo. It will be public knowledge soon enough, but he will be pleased to know it first.

I am on the ground now but he continues to hold me, his strong hands warm on my waist. “Together? And publicly?” He laughs as though he is pleased at my sister’s humiliation.

“It is a slur on us all,” I remind him.

He nods, but his eyes still twinkle.

That night, when he comes to my bed, I tell him I may be pregnant.

He stops half-way through unlacing the front of my night gown. “Are you certain?”

I lift one shoulder in a little shrug, causing my gown to slip down my arm. “I have only missed one of my courses,” I admit.

Charles bends and kisses my bare shoulder, his fingers reaching under my gown to caress my breast. “We had best be certain, do you not agree?”

I find I agree completely.

It is very hot in the bright June sunlight as the Queen and Duke Andrew kneel before the papal legate in the presence of all their court, and vow to obey him. I think I see Joanna sway as she rises from her knees, but she straightens quickly. Although her face is drained of color, she maintains a rigid expression of calm and control. She must be furious beneath her composed appearance; when we were children, her face always went white when she was angry.

Next she will swear to Cardinal Aimeric an oath of homage to the church, and officially recognize church authority over her kingdom, but this she will do later, without Andrew, as she is the sole sovereign of the Kingdom of Naples. Surely the Cardinal will not delay again. He must begin his rule of Naples; the ruling council has already been dismissed.

It is not the Cardinal who delays. When I come to court three days later, Joanna is abed, and Sancia tells me she is very ill.

"How ill?" I look around. Sancia is the only one in Joanna's presence chamber.

"The physician is bleeding her now. She has the summer fever."

I step back. "Are you well?" My hand goes to my abdomen. I have a child to think of.

Sancia catches the movement and smiles. "I am not sick. But perhaps you should return to your husband's castle, or leave the city?"

I flush. "You have not deserted her."

"Nor will I. But I have no one else to consider. The Queen is being well cared for. My Grandmother is with her, and three physicians from the university have been called in to consult with her personal physician. She suffers from an excess of care, if anything." Sancia's smile is strained, at odds with her light tone.

"I will wait to hear what the physicians say." I sink onto a chair. Sancia sits beside me. She tells me my sister has been ill for two days now, and shows no sign of improving. I nod without answering. Philippa will care for my sister, as she has since we were babies. She will know what to do. Philippa would die herself before she would allow any harm to come to my sister.

But I could not save Louis. Philippa has no power over death. And if Philippa catches it also? I feel a moment of terror at the thought of losing both of them.

Sancia glances at me. I force myself to breathe evenly, to maintain a confident visage. I am a royal princess, not a peasant ruled by fears. The discipline calms me. My sister has been sick before, and so have I, and Philippa nursed us through it. I am foolish to worry.

At least I have Charles. I am not alone, I will always have Charles. How could I forget him, even for Joanna? When I return to Castle Durazzo he will be full of questions.

"The legate has taken charge of the kingdom, then?" I ask.

"No."

"No? Who is in charge?"

“I cannot tell you who is ruling Naples, Princess Maria. No one knows.”

“Has the ruling council been reinstated?”

“They have not. Cardinal Aimeric has not come, nor sent an answer to the Queen’s advisors. He will not do anything until the Queen has officially relinquished her authority to the Church.”

“No one is in charge?” I gasp, horrified. “What does Philippa say?”

“She is busy nursing the Queen. We are all praying for Her Majesty’s quick recovery.”

“Amen,” I say fervently. Does Charles know? He must, and his mother also. They were at court yesterday. I had one of the headaches that come on me when I am with child. Perhaps they did not want to upset me with news of my sister’s illness. Perhaps Charles meant to tell me today. They left Castle Durazzo before I was downstairs this morning; I rode over with one of my husband’s men as escort.

Whatever excuse I make for them, I am still angry. Joanna is my sister. I should have been told at once. I would have come, headache or not; just as I am determined to stay, fever or not. I clasp my hands together tightly in my lap and wait for her physician to come out of her bedchamber.

When at last he does, he strides through the presence chamber with two other physicians. They are preoccupied with their subdued conversation and do not glance around. I have to jump up and call to him.

He turns and recognizes me—he was my physician as well while I lived here—and comes over to us.

“Tell me how she is.”

“The Queen is getting worse,” he says quietly. “If you go in to see her, do not stay long. Her Majesty needs her rest. And do not touch her. We cannot risk you both.”

“I was always the healthy one,” I remind him. I never caught Joanna’s childhood ailments. But still, his comment frightens me. Does he expect to lose Joanna? I do not ask, for fear of what his answer might be. Instead I hurry into Joanna’s room.

Philippa is sitting on the far side of the bed wiping Joanna's forehead with a damp cloth. She looks up and frowns when she sees me. I ignore her disapproval, which is in truth only concern for me, for us both. I approach the bed.

My sister lies very still, seemingly asleep. Her face is as white as the sheets, her hair loose, spread out across the pillow, lank and damp with sweat. Her arms, equally pale, lie on top of the covers, bound where the leeches were placed. I take her hand. It is limp and hot in mine.

"I am here, Joanna," I whisper.

She opens her eyes. They are dull and listless, and I think that she does not know me until she says, "You should not be here." Her voice is so weak I have to bend low to make out her words.

My eyes fill with tears. "I will not leave you," I tell her.

"You must." She tries to pull her hand away, but I tighten my hold. A fit of coughing takes her.

One of the physicians has stayed with her. He gets up quickly to come to her, but she raises her other hand weakly, stopping him.

"Think of Naples," she tells me, when she can speak again. The effort exhausts her. She lets her head fall back onto the pillow and closes her eyes. This time, when I feel her hand move in mine, I let her pull free.

"She is right," Philippa tells me, wiping Joanna's forehead gently with the cloth. "Go back to Castle Durazzo. Keep yourself safe, and the infant you are carrying. Naples needs a secure bloodline and you cannot help your sister here."

I do not ask how she knows I am with child. Philippa was a mid-wife and my father's wet-nurse before she became Joanna's and my nurse-mother and our royal grandparents' advisor. I have come to simply accept that she knows everything. I watch her tend to my sister a moment before I let her granddaughter Sancia take my arm and lead me from the room.

"Let me know—"

"I will," Sancia promises. "The moment she gets better… or gets worse… I will send someone to tell you." She motions to one of the guards at the outer door to Joanna's rooms. "Have a man saddle Princess Maria's horse and escort her back to Castle Durazzo."

"No, I want to go to Santa Chiara…" I choke on the words and cannot finish.

"Yes," Sancia says gently. "Pray to Holy Mary. That is what you can do to help your sister now."

Charles is furious when I arrive home at dusk, but he is not nearly as angry as I am with him.

"Santa Chiara!" I snap when he demands to know where I have been. I march past without another word, up to my rooms. But no matter how worried I might be for my sister, and how angry I am with my husband and mother-in-law for keeping her illness from me, this baby growing inside me insists we are hungry. When Margherita appears I tell her to order a platter for my dinner—I will not go down to eat with them. Charles enters my chamber as Margherita hurries out.

"You should have told me my sister was ill!" I cry before he can reproach me with what *I* should have done or not done.

"This is precisely why I did not."

"I had a right to know. She is my sister!"

"And you are my wife! Princess or not, you will be governed by me!"

"I will be governed by you," I agree. "If I can trust you. Why did you not tell me the Queen was ill?"

He takes a moment. I am glad to see it. I am glad he does not quickly tell me he wished to spare me worry, or prevent me from exposing myself and our child to her fever. Both of these may be true and I would have heard them happily at one time, but I am no longer the naïve child I was. There is more to it than that and I want to hear him say it.

"Because I knew you would do something foolish if you learned it. And you have!"

"Or is it because I will be Queen if she dies?"

He does not answer.

"And you will be King," I finish for him. "But only if I do not die as well."

"Do you really think that is the only reason I want you to live?"

"No," I admit. I know there is more than that between us. "But it is an important one."

"Next you will ask me if I would have married you if you were not a princess, and heir to the throne. We are not living in a fairy tale, Maria."

"I would not have asked because I do not need to. I know why you married me now, whatever I thought at the time. Whatever you led me to think." I say this in a rush, making it up. I have not thought this before. Our confrontation has not gone at all as I wanted. I expected him to deny my accusation at once. I wait for him to deny it now, to tell me, no, I married you because I love you, Maria…

"Of course I married you because you are the Queen's sister, the only heir to her throne! I wish I had not, for all the good it has done me!"

I stare at him, speechless. And then I turn my head away, so he will not see my eyes tearing. I am fifteen now, I tell myself fiercely. I am much too old for fairy tales.

"I have spent the day praying that my sister will live, and I will pray for it every day until she recovers."

He does not say anything. He cannot tell me he prays for the Queen's recovery, or that he hopes she will live. She is the sovereign he swore allegiance to and he should say it, it should be true; but we are now committed to an honest conversation, and he will not lie. I turn away, but he catches my arm.

"I care about you, Maria," he says. "I do not want you to catch the Queen's fever because I care for you, as well."

I nod without looking up. There are many truths, not just one. But I am tired of truth. I do not want to weigh his motives: this much of one and this much of the other. He might ask me mine, and have me weigh them, too. I realize there is a limit to how much honesty I want between us.

“I am tired, Charles. Margherita is bringing me some dinner, and then I will go to bed.”

“Sleep well, Duchess Maria. Perhaps we will have news tomorrow,” he says with a slight smile that lets me know he understands me better than I am prepared to understand myself.

Chapter 18

God's Will Be Done

Charles insists I do my praying for Joanna in the private chapel at Castle Durazzo. I might as well please him in this, since Philippa, Sancia and my sister are all equally determined I shall not visit Castle Nuovo. The city is becoming more dangerous every day Joanna is ill but no one steps up to impose law and order. I hear of mobs and cutpurses attacking innocent people right outside the gates of the royal castle. Charles insists he is safe going back and forth each day, but he has six of his men-at-arms accompany him, where before he had one or two.

One day he comes home grim-faced and goes straight to his mother in her chamber. I pause at the closed door to my mother-in-law's privy chamber, take a deep breath, then open it and walk in uninvited.

Lady Agnes turns a threatening face to me, but I square my shoulders and push the door closed behind me.

"Let her stay," Charles says, cutting off his mother on the verge of ordering me out. "She would find out soon enough, and she must know."

"Tell me what has happened." I feel a sick clutch at my stomach. He is going to tell me the Queen—my sister, my rival, my closest friend—has died. What else would make him look like this, as though the earth has turned upside down? I sink into a chair, my eyes already tearing up.

"Duke Andrew has taken control. He has ordered the release of the Pipini brothers, and knighted them."

"Released them? Who, Andrew?" I stammer, stupid with surprise. "The Pipini brothers? Those murderers?" I collect myself. "My sister is not dead?"

"The Queen is not dead, but she might as well be. She is next thing to it, neither opening her eyes nor communicating with anyone. It would be better for Naples if she would die, rather than linger, leaving us in this limbo where any fool—" He stops himself; he is talking of the Queen's husband, "—anything might happen."

"Do not say it." But there is no conviction in my voice. I am so relieved to hear Joanna is alive. But can the rest be true? Has Andrew released the most vicious villains in the kingdom? "Andrew has knighted the Pepini brothers? How? On whose authority?"

"On his own! And there is none to stop him. No one is in command, and the only one who could assume it, that pompous fool—" he stops himself again, "—Cardinal Aimeric, will not step in until the proper vows have all been made, and duly recorded, and approved by Pope Clement VI."

"What are the Tarantos doing?" Lady Agnes demands.

"Arming themselves, if they are smart. Calling up their men. Louis has baited and threatened Andrew for years, and Robert scorned him publicly at every opportunity. Now Andrew has the most ruthless killers in the land beside him, and all the might of the Gatti family behind him. No one will be safe."

"Are our men armed?" my mother-in-law asks.

"I gave the order before I came in."

I stare at them in horror. *Wolves. Wolves at each other's throats!*

"I am going to see my sister." As soon as I say it, I start to shake. I want to race to her at once. Joanna will know what to do, she has always been in control of every situation. And Philippa is with her. Philippa always knows what to do!

"You will not!" My mother-in-law says, staring not at me but at my protruding stomach. The infant kicks fiercely as if telling me to listen to her.

"Wait." Charles motions to his mother. "Perhaps she should. Perhaps the true heir should be seen at Castle Nuovo. Let them all see that she is alive and healthy and fertile." He smiles as though this were all his accomplishment.

I glare at them both. I am not going in order to be seen, as though I want my sister to die, as though I am just waiting to leap onto her throne. I will not be part of their scheming. But I do want to see Joanna. What if this is the last time I will ever see her?

"I want to see my sister!"

"And you shall, Princess Maria." Charles smiles. Is he mocking me? "Please tell her for the sake of Naples to live or die, but to choose one of them quickly!"

Charles rides beside my litter, with half a dozen of his men riding ahead and another half-dozen following us. This escort alarms me more than anything he said. It is daytime, and Castle Nuovo is not far, and we are riding through the streets of Naples, not down a lonely country road. Yet Charles believes we need a dozen armed men to keep us safe.

For the first time, I doubt Joanna's ability to rule. How could a well-ordered kingdom sink so low, so quickly? Perhaps Petrarch was right, and my husband also: Joanna is not strong enough to rule Naples, no woman is capable of ruling on her own. It is an affront to God, who made Eve subject to Adam, for a woman to rule over men. This is the result: chaos and barbarity, law and justice mocked. All that I love in Naples—its culture and beauty, its graciousness and sophistication—will be lost, is being lost, as nature is turned upside down and women command while men obey.

I pray my sister will get well, but if she recovers Joanna will never give up the throne. Even if she was willing to share it with Andrew, he is not fit to rule. If there was any doubt of that, he is proving it now.

For the first time, I consider that Charles may be right: Naples would be better off with the two of us on the throne, a strong king who will defend Naples and restore law and order, and a queen by birth who is willing to rule under the guidance of her lord and husband.

If Joanna dies, Charles and I will restore the Kingdom of Naples to all her past glory.

If Joanna dies, no one can say we usurped her crown to do it. Our succession will be natural and peaceful.

I close my eyes and lean forward, the curtains of the litter forming a little confession box around me, but I do not know what to pray for.

If Joanna dies, I will never hold her hand again.

Charles' men wait at the castle gate while he escorts me into Castle Nuovo.

"I am safe here," I tell him. This is my home, I have grown up in this castle. But he escorts me through the rooms, bowing to everyone we meet and asking after their welfare. Of course they must then ask after ours, and Charles replies, with his easy, charming smile, that we—and he gestures to me, or more specifically, toward my belly—are blessed with good health and good fortune indeed, thank you my Lord, my Lady. He will not leave my side until we are at the door to the Queen's presence chamber. Her guard lets me in.

Sancia is there, and her father, Philippa's son, Robert of Cabannis, and Catherine of Taranto with her daughter, Marguerite, looking miserable and frightened beside her. Sancia curtsies to me and Robert bows, but my Lady Aunt Catherine merely dips her head, and glares at her daughter as Marguerite awkwardly stumbles up from the beginning of a curtsy and bows her head also. I pass by them with the barest nod and a rustle of my silk gown against the floor rushes, and enter the Queen's bedchamber.

Philippa is with her, as I knew she would be, and our court physician. I look around for Philippa's husband Raymond, the Royal Seneschal, then remember Charles telling me Raymond caught the summer fever also. Philippa's other daughters must be attending him. Philippa herself looks exhausted, her gray hair falling from its braids, her head drooping… I have never noticed how old she is, as old as our Lady Grandmother, a woman near the end of her life. The thought shocks and pains me. Then I look down at Joanna.

Her fair hair, damp and stringy with sweat, is tangled over the pillow as though it has not been washed or combed for days. Her face is as white as the sheet that covers her, and as still. Her hand, lying over the edge of the sheet, is limp and lifeless. She was always slender, but now she is gaunt, she looks as frail as an old lady herself. I lean forward trying to make out if she is breathing. Philippa motions me back urgently. I am so shaken by my sister's appearance I do not argue but straighten and step back at once.

The look on my face prompts Philippa to murmur wearily, "She is alive still, Duchess Maria."

The physician brings a chair over. I sink down into it. I am going to lose her. She cannot possibly recover. She looks as our grandfather looked at the end, her skin hot, hanging on her bones, nearly translucent, as though her essence were already leaving, slowly seeping out of this world to heaven.

My eyes fill. I blink back the tears. This is no time for weakness. I motion to Philippa. "Let me be alone with her," I say.

She gets up unsteadily from her chair. I am not sure she will make it to the door.

"You need to rest," I tell her. "Go and rest, Philippa. You cannot help her by—" I am about to say, by dying with her, but the words catch in my throat, I cannot speak them. I cannot speak at all, my throat is so tight. A tear slips from my lashes, and another. I cannot hold them back. I bow my head, ashamed to weep before others, and motion again for them to leave. The physician steps forward and helps Philippa from the room.

At last I can permit myself to weep. How can I lose her? How can I bear to lose her?

It must be God's will. He is restoring order to His realm. The Kingdom of Naples needs a strong king; this is why I was led to marry Charles and not travel to France to be Prince Jean's bride. The Holy Father, who gave his permission for our marriage, and even our Grandmother Sancia, must have seen that Joanna would not be able to rule alone, while I was still blind to it out of loyalty to my sister. I have resisted it as though it was temptation, and not my destiny, but I see it now. I see it, but even now I wish with all my heart that Joanna would not die. I do not care if it is God's will, or if it is best for Naples; I do not want to lose my sister. My tears flow faster, blinding me. How will I live without her? How will I learn to be happy without my sister? I will hear the sound of her voice, the music of her laughter, all my life. I will feel her hand in mine—I cover my eyes and close my lips tightly to keep from sobbing, but nothing will stop the flow of tears.

I weep until I am exhausted, until I have no more tears to shed. My face will be red and splotchy, my eyes swollen, everyone will know I have been weeping when they see me leave. Charles will be annoyed. He wants me to look strong, ready to rule a kingdom, but I do not care. Let everyone know I wept for my sister on her deathbed.

I look down at her still, white face and place my hand on my belly. "Before God, on my child's life, I swear to you, my sister, my Queen, that you will not be forgotten. If I am carrying a girl, I will name her Joanna."

I lean forward and take my sisters' pale, limp hand in mine. It is so hot. I feel the heat of her fever, burning away her life. "When I hold her hand, it will be as though you are still with me," I promise her.

She does not move. I do not know if she has even heard me. I am talking of this world, but my sister is already focused on the next. Is she afraid? Is that why she clings to life still, when she is so close to her release?

"Do not fear your rest, Joanna," I whisper. "You go to join our Lord Father and Lady Mother, to dwell with Holy Mary and our Lord the Christ, and all the saints of Christendom. I will follow you in time and we will be reunited." A tear falls onto her pillow. I brush my hand across my eyes.

"I will be a good queen to Naples," I sob. I want her to die reassured that the Angevin line is secure, that her kingdom is in safe hands.

As soon as I say it I realize my error. Joanna expels a small puff of air, which I know to be an insult even in her near-death sleep. Her breathing, which has been shallow and uneven all this while, catches, and slowly begins to lengthen.

"Heaven and the Holy Saints wait to embrace you, sister." I clasp my hands together and close my eyes in prayer. "Take her quietly to Heaven," I implore Holy Mary, the Mother of God.

When I open my eyes again, Joanna's are open also. I feel her forehead. It is no longer as hot to my touch.

But it was God's will, I think, confused.

Joanna blinks. She gives a little moan. As well she should, defying God this way. What kind of woman turns her back on the very gates of Heaven in order to deny her sister a crown?

I rise and walk to the door. I will look like an idiot with my face all splotchy from crying, and Joanna recovered. I hesitate, but there is nothing I can do about it now, so I open the door.

"Fetch a cup of broth," I order Sancia.

I return to Joanna's bedside and stare down at her. "I see you have decided to recover, sister," I say. I do not know if this is God's will or Joanna's, but we would all have been saved a good deal of trouble and false feelings if she had not taken so long to decide.

Joanna's lips part. I bend to hear.

"You would take my kingdom from me also, sister?" Her eyes close again, before I can answer.

Chapter 19

Birth and Rebirth

Summer is nearly over by the time Joanna is well enough to give Cardinal Aimeric her oath of homage. On August 28th, Charles and I stand in Santa Chiara with the entire court to witness the Pope's legate take over the government of Naples.

I glance sideways to where Andrew stands, surrounded by his men and the lords he has drawn to him out of affinity to the Pepinis and the Gatti family. Their alliance with him has changed him from victim back to bully, the natural progression of a coward. He is now publicly uttering threats against anyone who stands in the way of his coronation.

Cardinal Aimeric—"the officious fool" my husband calls him—shivers under Andrew's glare, but he will not be intimidated from doing his duty. In front of everyone he recognizes Joanna as sole heir to the Kingdom of Naples, and then accepts command of her kingdom on behalf of His Holiness Clement VI.

"God help us," Charles whispers to me.

"I believe that is what this is supposed to be," I whisper back. I meet Charles' stare straight-faced for a moment before arching my eyebrow, and then have the pleasure of watching him struggle not to laugh.

"Are you not the least bit sorry for your sister?" he asks, when he has regained control.

"She was offered an honorable alternative," I answer smartly, watching my sister's humiliation clear-eyed. This time my husband's chuckle of amusement is annoying. I should tell him my sister's first words on recovery. See how amusing he would find that. But it is one thing to be annoyed with my sister, and another thing entirely to have my husband angry at her, so I hold my tongue and let him chuckle.

I enter my second confinement less frightened for myself than the first time, but much more afraid for the infant I carry. If this child is weak also—I dare not even think if it might die—Charles will know I am no fit wife for him. If I cannot produce an heir, even my claim to the throne will be in question. A queen who cannot bear strong babies is a threat to the peace and security of her kingdom.

I cannot eat at the feast my mother-in-law and my husband arrange to celebrate my last public dinner before going into confinement. I force myself to smile at the jesters and listen to the musicians as though I am confident and carefree, but I am aware of the Dowager Duchess glancing at me, at my protruding belly, with barely concealed disdain. A dozen times today alone I have let her feel the infant kick. I have made a great deal of wincing to prove the strength of those kicks, only now she has decided that this is proof of my weakness, not of my child's vigor. I tell myself she is nervous, as I am, and it makes her irritable. I would like to be irritable, too, but my anxiety only makes me nauseous and fearful.

I have insisted on a different set of rooms for this confinement—I will not go back into the place where Louis died. Even so, when I stand at the door with Margherita and the midwives beside me, I find I am trembling, unable to enter.

"What is it?" Agnes of Perigord asks impatiently. "Have you forgotten something? Your maid can fetch it. Come in now." With a sweep of her skirts she marches into the room, and I have no choice but to bid my husband farewell. Margherita takes my arm as my farewell lengthens, and draws me into my confinement.

There is one large room where we will sleep and dine and sit together, with only a small, curtained alcove for my personal needs. The cradle has not been moved in yet, or the swaddling board or any little gowns. I do not know if this indicates my mother-in-law's doubt that I will produce a healthy babe, or her sensitivity, but regardless of which it is, I am grateful. I am not ready to see Louis' cradle again.

"Well then, you are set up," my Lady Mother-in-law says. "I imagine you are tired." She is gone before I can respond, or even bid her farewell. I turn as though I would follow her out, but the mid-wife is there, and Margherita, and the door is already closing us inside.

"I will read to you," Margherita offers soothingly. She holds a book already open.

I look at the door, already closed.

The infant kicks, reminding me that there is only one way out of here for both of us.

"Yes, read to me," I say, sinking into my chair. "And I want to hear the news at court. You must tell the Dowager Duchess I insist on being told what is happening." I look at Margherita and try to imagine her telling my mother-in-law anything. "I will give you a note to take to her."

I will not sit in here thinking of the child I carry. It will live or it will not, but I will not love it until its path is clear. I will be read to, I will hear the news, even the gossip—anything to keep my thoughts from another child I may lose.

My mother-in-law gives her word, and she keeps it. She comes in herself every day when she returns from Castle Nuovo and sits with her head close to mine discussing her day at court. I am surprised at her constancy as the weeks go by, although I expect my written threat never to return to court is behind it. She does not ask me about my day, or my health, but she notes, through the layers of my shift and kirtle, every kick the infant makes, and sometimes I catch a small, approving smile on her face. It raises my spirits, that hidden smile, though I do not acknowledge it, neither of us acknowledges my state.

So I learn the Pepini brothers are flaunting their freedom. They appeared at a tournament riding in royal colors, with their family banner raised higher than the Queen's. I learn that Andrew publicly threatened to beat and lock up his wife if she opposed his coronation. I learn that Cardinal Aimeric has dismissed the provincial governors throughout the kingdom and appointed men who know nothing about their new jurisdictions; that the displaced governors are protesting, the provinces are in revolt, and in the resulting chaos dishonest men are resorting to banditry and honest men are withholding their taxes until justice and peaceful trade have been reinstated. Lady Agnes tells me with scorn that the cardinal is helpless to check the increasing lawlessness because his orders are ignored. She tells me with amusement that the Queen has refused to pay Pope Clement the Angevin's annual tribute granting the Angevins the right to rule Naples, since her rule has been transferred to the Pope's legate.

Brilliant, I think, conceding one blow to my sister. While my mother-in-law nods approvingly at Joanna's clever husbandry in keeping the money in our royal treasury, I recognize it as the subtle riposte that it is. My sister may have lost a round, but she has not yet surrendered the field to Elizabeth and Clemente VI.

I do not need to be told how Joanna is enduring Aimeric's blunders. I know my sister. Every blow to the grace and dignity of Naples is a blow to her; every injustice done to her people is an injustice against her. I have watched her hearing petitions at Castle Nuovo. No man is too lowly to bring his grievance to her court, and she deals justly with each one, signing every decision herself. Law and justice, the pursuits for which our university is famous in all of Christendom, are sacred to Joanna, as sacred as her faith in God. Joanna is watching all that she believes in being trampled and destroyed, while she stands by unable to intervene.

Do not give up! I will my sister to hear my prayer. She is our only hope, if Naples is to recover.

I do not talk of this to my mother-in-law. She would neither understand nor sympathize with my sister. To Lady Agnes of Perigord, and indeed to most of the unruly, ambitious and fractious Neapolitan nobles, the throne means power and wealth. They never doubt that they would be more successful, given the chance—and perhaps they would, since their standards are lower.

Which makes me wonder, what kind of queen will I be? Would Charles and I do any better at ruling Naples than Joanna has, in nearly two years on the throne?

When we were children playing in the gardens, Joanna and I used to imagine ourselves as sister queens. We would describe the dresses we would wear, the jewels on our crowns and clasped about our necks, the knights who would carry our favors when they jousted, the entertainments and masques we would organize. That was my favorite part of the game. I became bored when Joanna talked of sending an army to conquer Sicily again, of making every road in the kingdom so safe a lady could ride through the countryside unescorted.

And now a man needs a dozen armed guards to ride on the streets of the city in daylight.

When we were children playing at being queens, we never talked of losing our crowns. We were royal princesses, anointed by God and destined from birth to rule. We never imagined royalty as a game of hazards that one could lose.

I keep these thoughts to myself while I listen to my mother-in-law describe all my sister's failings.

And then I go into labor. Another game that one can lose.

This time I bear a lusty daughter. She howls in outrage when the midwife wipes her clean. She kicks her feet and pummels her hands in resistance when they strap her to the swaddling board. She announces her hunger as though she has to alert the kitchen below us at the other end of the castle, not the wet-nurse sitting beside her cradle. Her little eyebrows pull together into a stubborn frown the minute she awakes, her beautiful bow-shaped lips purse with impatience, and her tiny hands form fists. I laugh every time I see her, with her father's dark brown hair sticking up at all angles and her little face red with passion. The fear that has been gripping my heart all these months falls away before her abundance of life, and I love her with a reckless joy that consumes my every thought. I will not be read to, I no longer care what is happening in Naples, I only want to hold my invincible little daughter, Joanna.

Charles comes the day after she is born. Perhaps he regrets that he never saw his son. I am pleased he has come, whatever the reason. Since I am still in confinement I can only watch through the grill as the mid-wife shows him his daughter. She is strapped to her swaddling board, which usually makes her complain bitterly, but she has just finished feeding, her lips are still milky and soft with contentment. She gazes up at her father solemnly, as though she is deciding his fate, which makes him smile. When the mid-wife returns to lay our daughter in her cradle to sleep, she brings me Charles' gift, a gold bracelet with three large emeralds.

He tells me through the grill that he is pleased, but I know he is not entirely. I have proved that I can bear a strong child, but we need a son. A boy—even better, two boys—will prove our line is stable and secure my inheritance if Joanna dies.

"I will give you a son next time," I promise, as I slip his gift onto my wrist. I look down at the bracelet, admiring it, while I hesitate. I have not told him of my vow to Joanna when I thought she was dying. It will sound foolish now she has recovered, and I had no right to make it without my husband's approval. Finally I simply say, "I would like to name our daughter Joanna." And then, in a rush, because he has to agree, "It will strengthen our bond. Perhaps she will favor the Durazzo family with an appointment." I do not need to mention that she has not done so since my marriage.

"You have reason to think she will be pleased?"

I blush at his perceptiveness. "Yes," I say, although I am not absolutely certain she heard me.

I watch in surprise as a slow smile spreads across his face, and then he chuckles. "By all means we will name her Joanna," he says, grinning. "What better way to show the kingdom that you are the one who must bear her namesake!"

"I did not mean—"

"All the better." He laughs. "Continue not to mean it, my loyal little wife."

My sister visits while I am still in confinement. "Joanna," she repeats when I tell her my daughter's name. She acts surprised, but I am not fooled. I see the trace of humor in her eyes and I know she remembers the promise I made when she lay near to death. The baby sleeps through my sister's visit, looking calm and angelic, her furious ardor temporarily checked. My sister, therefore, considers the name a compliment.

"The legate is being recalled," Joanna informs me, a tone of satisfaction in her voice. "I will soon have complete rule of Naples."

Do I still want to be Queen, I wonder, thinking of all the problems my sister is facing: a husband she cannot trust, lords who want her crown, a royal treasury emptied by the fall of our Florentine bankers and the expenses of the legate, a Pope who has publicly questioned her ability to rule, and subjects who have become accustomed to anarchy. I glance at my sleeping child, the daughter of a duke. I have already chosen, and chosen well.

But you could have both, a little voice inside me whispers. I have a husband I can trust, a man strong enough to deal with those problems.

Who knows what the future holds? I answer that voice. It is enough that I am happy now.

I smile at Joanna. She is exultant, eager to assume the challenge, to mold Naples to her vision. Andrew would have given her a child by now, had she been willing. He might never have taken up with the Pipinis if she had invited him into her circle, been a proper wife and a friend to him. He might have ruled with her. This is a leap, I know that better than anyone. Andrew always showed signs of becoming exactly what he is now: selfish, vain, and cruel. But Joanna gave him no chance to improve. She had already chosen what she wanted.

When we were children, we would hear Philippa whisper at the end of her night-time prayers: *May God hear my prayers, may all that I hope for come true*. No matter how often we asked, she would never tell us what she hoped for. Your good health, was her usual evasion.

"How can I know what I hope for until I have it?" she once said, when we had needled her relentlessly for an answer.

"You will never get it if you do not know what you want," Joanna replied, the only time I ever heard her contradict the woman she considers her adopted mother.

"May God hear our prayers," I say to my sister now. "May all that we hope for come true."

"So be it!" Joanna answers, laughing, as sure of what she wants as she was then.

I look at the daughter I did not know I wanted. "So be it," I agree.

Chapter 20

A Fall From Grace

1345

By the time I return to court in January the tension is so great the air fairly snaps around Joanna and Andrew. Andrew's coronation, previously an annoyance and a liability, has become, with the presence of the Pipinis, a serious threat to Joanna and all who support her. She has received a letter from the Pope returning the rule of Naples to her, and has spent the time since increasing her own alliances within her kingdom, granting promotions, land, and as a last resort, gifts of money, to those already inclined to oppose the Pipinis and the Gatti family. The royal court is made up of her favorites: the house of Taranto, King Robert's illegitimate son Charles of Artois, and Philippa's large family. She holds the Tarantos loyal with gifts and position—and by not favoring their rivals, the Durazzos. I suppose she counts on me to hold the Durazzos loyal.

"Robert of Cabannis," Charles rants in my bedchamber back at Castle Durazzo. "The son of a fish-girl and an African slave has been made Count of Eboli and Grand Seneschal of the Kingdom! Their granddaughter, Sancia, is to be married to the Count of Marcone! While we receive nothing! Nothing!"

I wince to hear him name Philippa's husband, Raymond, 'an African slave.' One should speak well of the recently dead, for they may still be wandering the land and overhear. I make the sign of the cross discreetly behind my back, where Charles will not see. Raymond died while I was in confinement, so I did not have to argue with my husband over attending his funeral.

"She trusts them," I say reasonably. "They have allegiance to no one but her. She has to give them positions that will enable them to help her."

"She should trust us! We have sworn allegiance to her. You are her sister! Are we not better allies than former slaves?"

He knows as well as I that he and his mother nearly caused a war by abducting me. He knows as well as I that he was hoping she would die so we could take her throne. He knows as well as I why she does not trust him.

"She is counting on your brother," I remind him. "Louis is her voice in the papal court. If he can convince Clement VI to rescind the double coronation…" She will trust the Durazzos again, I meant to finish, but I am not certain enough to say it. "She rewards those who serve her," I say instead. "And Duke Andrew and the Pipinis are as much a threat to us as to the Queen. Anything she does to protect herself from them, protects us also."

Charles turns slowly to look at me. "Are they?"

I stare at him. "Of course they are. You know they are. They are ruthless murderers!" I catch my breath. "What are you thinking, my Lord?"

He straightens and smiles. "Nothing," he says carelessly. "You are right, of course."

"You yourself wrote to the Duke of Perigord and your Lady Mother to Cardinal Talleyrand, asking them to advise the Pope against crowning Andrew!"

"I did." He turns to the door.

"Are you leaving?"

He looks back, raising one eyebrow.

I blush crimson. "I only meant—"

"I will stay with you tomorrow night. Tonight I want to think. And you need rest. Today was your first day back at court, you are only a week out of confinement."

Many women pray for a husband as considerate as mine, I tell myself as the door closes behind him. But I would rest better if I knew what he wanted to think about.

Each day at court we are like mummers, pretending everything is fine. Charles and I and the other courtiers and ladies-in-waiting listen to music, and dance, have picnics and archery contests and hunt with our hounds and falcons. We smile and laugh and go to Mass and dine merrily in the great hall of Castle Nuovo. Cardinal Aimeric stays on, waiting for the arrival of the Pope's nuncio, who will 'advise' the Queen. In the meantime, no doubt, he is reporting everything Joanna says and does to the Pope.

Andrew's men spread lies about the Queen, that she is sleeping with Robert of Cabannis, with Charles of Artois' son, Bertrand, with Robert of Taranto and his brother, Louis, both; in short, with every nobleman who receives advancements from her. I am relieved that Louis of Taranto is in such a large company, for his is the only name that gives me pause. But there is no truth to any of them, and no one actually believes them. All they do is make Prince Andrew look like a man so eager to disparage his wife that he will falsely name himself cuckold.

Cardinal Aimeric listens to rumors. Cardinal Aimeric keeps track of the Queen's generosity to her favorites. No doubt he has spies in the royal court reporting to him on every word we say—and there are many words and more than words between Joanna's court and Andrew's. Cardinal Aimeric, waiting for the nuncio who will relieve him, has nothing to do but write his suspicions to the Holy Father.

In February, Pope Clement VI issues a decree based on the cardinal's reports. I am in her presence room when Joanna receives his letter, along with Sancia, newly married, and the other ladies-in-waiting. I watch Joanna's expression freeze as she reads it. Stony-faced, she orders the messenger to send for her advisers. We wait in silence. Even the musician has stopped playing and sits still, afraid to move though he would no doubt love to leave. When the lords she has sent for arrive the Queen leads them into her privy room.

Philippa arrives. I expect her to go into the privy room, but instead she sits beside Sancia. I have never known Joanna to make a decision without Philippa's advice. I stare at her, wondering why she is sitting here. I cannot remember our Grandfather, King Robert, not seeking her input, or our Lady Grandmother, for whom Philippa's granddaughter Sancia is named.

Marguerite of Taranto comes in, her face flushed. She looks around the room, hesitating when she sees Philippa and Sancia. I wave her over impatiently, and withdraw into an alcove. "What do you know?" I ask her.

"The Holy Father has forbidden the Queen from associating with certain persons whom he believes responsible for encouraging the hostility between her and her Lord husband." Marguerite speaks woodenly, as though she is quoting his missive directly. She glances over to where our—Joanna's and my—adopted mother sits with our childhood friend. "Philippa and her entire family are named directly. Charles of Artois and… and the Queen's inner circle of advisors… are mentioned but not named."

"How do you know this?" I want to believe she is lying, or mistaken, but why would she implicate her own family, for they are among Joanna's inner circle?

"The proclamation is posted on the door to Santa Chiara. I went there this morning to pray for one of my cousins, who died of the fever yesterday. I saw it when I came out."

"It has been posted publicly? At the same time as the Queen learned of it?"

Marguerite nods.

I glance up. Several heads immediately turn back to their sewing. "Does Philippa know?"

"I saw her leave ahead of me."

"You might as well tell the others, then, since it is public. But quietly."

Marguerite nods again. I can see she does not want to, since the Pope has implied that her family, also, is a bad influence. Good. Better that the news is given reluctantly, with the distaste it deserves, than by someone who would gloat at the downfall of others.

I walk across the room to sit with Philippa and Sancia.

Hours go by. We hear raised voices from the privy room but cannot make out the words. No one wants to be there, but no one wants to leave without learning what will happen—will there be a major change in the Queen's advisors? Who will survive and who will lose their positions? Will the Queen defy Clement VI as she ignores Cardinal Aimeric's demands?

Servants come up with platters of meat and bread and fruit for the privy chamber, and I tell them to bring a dinner for us. We eat quietly. There is no talking or laughing among the maids and the courtiers; those not high enough in rank to be among the Queen's advisors have relatives who are. All their fortunes are likely to change today. The musician has slipped away; no one is in the mood for a song while we wait to hear the fate of the highest families in the land.

Philippa and Sancia are outcasts. Marguerite is also left alone. She would sit with me, any of them would sit with me—even the Holy Father would not tell the Queen to cast aside her sister, the heir to her throne—but I am sitting with Philippa and Sancia, and no one wants to be seen near them, not even to sit with me.

Joanna will not desert them, I tell myself. They are her mother, her sister. I have always been jealous of Sancia's closeness to Joanna, of the ways in which they are similar and I am not; their humor and clever retorts, their interest in discussing law and literature, their quick grasp of the political implications of a situation. Joanna talks to Sancia; she explains to me. I would have liked to dislike Sancia.

But even when I disdained her for her origins, I could not dislike her. She would not resent my condescension; she was humble, as though she acknowledged the justice of my assessment and accepted my superior position over her. She remained as kind and sweet to me as ever. I am ashamed to think how I disdained her and Philippa, my nursemaid, my adopted mother. I am proud that my sister never stooped to do so.

I do not say any of this to them as we wait for the door to the privy chamber to open. Sancia and I bend over our sewing as if it held some interest for us; Philippa waits in stoic silence.

The longer I sit without speaking, the angrier I become. How stupid can Cardinal Aimeric be, to blame my sister's contempt for her husband on the fact that those around her speak badly of him? Do they think every woman is a fool who cannot think for herself, even an anointed Queen? It cannot be that Andrew is a villain and a coward and a fool! It cannot be that he is short and dark and ugly, and lacking in grace and manners! It cannot be that he is incapable of witty conversation or an appreciation of art and philosophy which so delight Joanna, or that he surrounds himself with criminals and preys cruelly on the vulnerable! No, it must be that those who have Joanna's love because they share her interests, have spoken wrongly against him and turned her heart. No husband could possibly be despised by his wife for his own faults!

If God gave men a greater intellect than women, He certainly balanced it with a greater vanity which turns them back into fools. I stab the needle into the shirt I am sewing for Charles, pricking my finger.

Temper only harms the one who indulges it: how often did Philippa tell me that as I was growing up? I take a deep breath. I will wait as calmly as Philippa and Sancia. This is far worse for them.

Finally the door opens. Robert of Taranto strides out, followed by his brother Louis and their mother, Catherine of Valois, Empress of Constantinople. Marguerite rises quickly to join them. They pay her no attention, crossing the presence chamber with heads held high, their boots striking the floor beneath the rushes as though they were stomping the bodies of their enemies.

Other courtiers emerge, some grim-faced, some smug. Among those who look pleased, I recognize many who have spoken out against Philippa's family in the past, jealous of their rise in fortune and power. My stomach clenches. I drop my sewing into the basket at my feet and reach out to clasp Sancia's hand.

Philippa's sons, Robert of Cabannis, named for my grandfather, and Raymond of Catania, named for his father, emerge last. The look on their faces of beaten curs, of men disgraced, makes me gasp. Philippa rises as one about to hear a sentence.

From inside the room I hear Joanna call them back and I rise also, pulling Sancia up with me, following Philippa even though none of us three have been called. I will watch my sister betray them, this family that has given their lives in service to our family. I will not believe it until I see and hear it myself. I drag Sancia through the open door, my face set. Nothing, not even her refusal to hand over my dowry, has made me so angry, so disgusted, so surprised by my sister.

Joanna looks up when Sancia and I enter the chamber behind Philippa. Her face is as white as when she was ill, but her expression is set. Her eyes look swollen and puffy, as though she has been crying, which I know absolutely she would never do in front of her advisors. When I look closely, I am right: they are as dry as a riverbed in July.

"Very well," she says. "You may as well be here, Duchess Maria." She looks at Philippa. "You know of the papal decree?"

"We know," Philippa says.

"My advisors…" Joanna stops and looks away. Philippa was her adviser, and Raymond, and Robert.

Look her in the face, I want to say. Look at the woman you called Mother when you renounce her. *Love is a changing thing, Princess,* Sancia's words come back to me.

"I cannot disobey the Holy Father. Cardinal Aimeric has not yet officially returned control to me…" she spreads her hands. There is no need to expand on the damage the Cardinal has already inflicted on Naples, and it is no secret that he is watching Joanna, reporting everything to Clement VI. I realize from that slight, defeated gesture, my sister is afraid. What if the Pope changes his mind, and leaves the cardinal in charge? How much more could Naples endure?

Philippa does not move or speak. If Joanna hoped she would interrupt with sympathy or understanding, that hope is disappointed.

Joanna's 'inner circle', the Angevin dukes and lords that make up the rest of her council are not being sent away.

Joanna rests her hands on the table, looking down at them. She sways, so that I almost step forward before she stiffens.

"Do not sacrifice good friends for bad ones," Philippa warns her softly.

"I must ask you to leave my court. Not to see me again, you and every member of your family." Her eyes flick up briefly toward Sancia. "Your husband also. No one …associated with any of you may come anywhere near me." Her voice is low, barely strong enough to carry across the room, but it does not tremble or break. She does not look up from the table where her hands rest on it, as though they are all that holds her upright.

"You are condemning us of a crime we have not committed."

"You are blameless. I do not consent to any of this."

"Your action does. Your lack of objection does. You are agreeing in deed with the Pope's accusation. No one will ever believe us innocent if you do this."

At last she looks up, her face twisted. "I have no choice!" she cries. The sound of it, like a wounded animal, nearly makes me weep. "Every lord who supports me insists I appease Clement VI. They will not risk the possibility that he will change his mind and return the legate to power. Louis of Durazzo and Cardinal Talleyrand are even now in Avignon trying to convince him not to have Andrew crowned with me. Those are the battles I must win!" Joanna stops. Her eyes are desperate, and ashamed. She looks back down at the table, her hands gripping it now.

"Your lords are not advising this in order to appease the cardinal or the pope," Philippa says. "They are doing this for envy of me and my family, because we have been rewarded for our service and our loyalty by your royal grandparents and by you."

"I must have their support."

The room falls silent. Joanna does not look up. At length Philippa curtsies low and murmurs "Farewell, Your Majesty."

Joanna looks up then. "When I am stronger, when I am secure on my throne, I will call you back, all of you." Her voice is so low it is nearly a whisper.

"I hope you do not remember us too late, Your Majesty," Philippa says. She turns and leads her family from the room.

I want to walk out with them. For the sake of my husband I do not; and for the sake of my sister, who hates what she has done as much as I do.

I want to go to her. It hurts me, the way she stands holding fast to the table where all her decisions are made. For the sake of my nursemaid, my *Mother,* the only one I have known, I cannot go to Joanna. I stand still and silent, just inside the room.

There was nothing I could say. Philippa knew it was useless, I saw that in her face before we entered, but she could not let this happen to her family without objecting. And there is nothing I can say now. It is done.

Joanna shuffles some papers on the table in front of her. Her clerk will come in later to take them away. I see her signature, the stamp of her ring—the mark of royalty. This is what she is: the Queen. Where has my sister gone, the girl who slept beside me, who laughed and played with me in the garden and knelt beside me in our grandmother's chapel, praying with such fervor I once thought if I could just tangle my prayers up in hers they would surely ride to heaven on the force of her faith. All our choices then were simple and clear and innocent, even when we chose wrong.

Now she is Queen of Naples and none of her choices are simple, or clear, or innocent, even when she chooses right.

Has she chosen right? Even a strong monarch cannot defy the pope and all her advisors for one family. She has sacrificed those she most loves to keep her crown.

Do I want to be a queen?

And for the good of Naples, I remind myself. For the protection of us all. I walk to her side and hold out my hand, and my sister takes it.

We cannot take back our choices. I said that, or thought it, long ago. I frown, trying to remember. Something about turning love into a wicked thing. Isolde! Isolde and her love potion. We cannot take back our choices, I thought then, with the callous judgment of a child. Joanna will regret this all her life. I open my mouth to warn her, to beg her to reconsider—

Joanna takes a deep breath and raises her head, letting go of my hand. We cannot take back our choices.

I curtsy, low enough to brush the floor with my hand. She fixes a smile on her face and sweeps past me, but at the door she pauses. I do not think she can surprise me further, but I am wrong.

"My advisors have also suggested that I resume… marital relations… with my husband," she says.

The door opens and she is gone.

Chapter 21

The Scales of Justice

I am the first to notice. Perhaps because I am pregnant again myself, I am watching my own rounded belly fill out, wearing looser gowns to hide it, postponing the day I will have to give up riding and come to court in a litter, and then not come at all.

I do not comment on what I have noticed as I slip my sister's shift over her head and pull it down to cover her, but she sees my averted eyes and she knows I have guessed her secret. When we have dressed her and combed and plaited up her hair, she asks me to stay and sends her other ladies-in-waiting out to her presence chamber.

"Has anyone else noticed?"

I shrug. All of those who were closest to us—Marguerita, Margaret, Sancia—are no longer serving the Queen. Still, none of her ladies are blind. "No one has said anything," I tell her.

"Keep this to yourself."

"How can I not tell my husband?"

My sister, who does not speak to her husband unless they are in public and she cannot avoid it, gives me a skeptical look.

"If he finds out by someone other than me…" I leave the rest to my sister's imagination. I have seen Charles' temper, although I have never been the recipient of it. I know he is capable of harsh punishments. One of his serfs failed to come to arms when Louis of Taranto pillaged our lands. Charles had the man's entire family, even a two-year-old babe-in-arms, slaughtered before him. The man himself Charles handed over to his guard, with the instruction that he must be heard screaming for two days as a warning to others of what happens to a man who does not respond to his lord's call. But I do not censure my husband; he does what a lord must do to maintain his authority.

Joanna studies me, her eyes narrowed. She has changed since she sent away Philippa and her family. There is no lightness in her, no more laughter, only a steely determination and a cold aloofness. She has learned to do what a monarch must do to maintain her authority.

And I have learned to do what a wife must do. I sink into a curtsy. "Your Highness, let me tell him before you announce it. Let him hear it first from me. Only that."

"You will wait until I say?"

"Yes, I swear. If only my Lord can hear it first."

"Before my own Lord husband?"

"After," I stammer, feeling my face flush as I stare at the floor. "After, of course, Your Majesty." I take a breath. "But right after."

"From now on you will dress and undress me, you alone."

I look up to see her frowning down at me. Before I can interpret her expression—regret? Anger? Distrust?—she snaps, "You may rise now. I have granted your request."

I rise at once, but keep my head lowered. I want to apologize, but how can I apologize for loyalty to my husband? I would like to regain the closeness we once shared, to remind her we are sisters. I look at her, willing her to see it in my eyes, to understand.

"Come into confinement with me, Maria, if you are out of your own in time."

I smile. "I have missed my courses four months now."

"You must have been got with child the night after you were churched." She shakes her head, smiling. "A little duke this time," she wishes on me.

And I am about to wish her a little prince when it occurs to me, what I should have realized at once. What my Lord husband will realize immediately when he hears. And now I am not at all eager to tell him, and I know why my sister has not announced it.

"When I tell my Lord husband…" There is no way I can ask this without her knowing what I now understand, but I must ask it. I must have her word on this when I speak to Charles. I take a deep breath. "When I tell him, I must also tell him that you have agreed to give him my dowry at last, and in full."

The smile fades from Joanna's face. "I see," she says. "And will it be used to raise an army against me?"

"Never!" I cry. How could she think such a thing? "Never, Your Majesty!" I am so stunned I cannot think what else to say but the truth. "He must have something. The belief that he is in your favor again, that you have accepted… He must be able to hope he will be a court advisor again, that there will be future appointments. That is all."

"That is quite a lot, for the privilege of keeping the Queen's secret."

I hang my head. Then I feel my own temper rising. "I only ask what is mine by rights. What our Grandfather willed to me." With every sentence my resentment rises. "You have had your inheritance these two years, you have no right to continue withholding mine!" I stop before I can say worse.

"You should never have let him take you! Your seduction shames us both."

"I could not prevent it! I fought them! I was not willingly taken."

Joanna stares at me in horror. I clap my hand over my mouth, having told her what I swore she would never know.

"They laid hands on you? A royal princess? They touched you without your permission? And the duke, he ordered them to do so?"

"No! …Yes, of course, he must have." I am hot, flushed with shame. "But you would never have let us marry, you would have broken the engagement. You have the crown of Naples, I had a right to something!"

"You would have had a crown."

"Would I? The second sister? While you were still healthy? At best I would have married a younger son, if there was one who would have me. If Louis of Hungary did not insist I wait to marry Andrew in case something happened to you!" This is all true, and she cannot deny it.

"Have they been executed?"

I blink. "Who?"

"Have they?" she shouts, her face rigid with fury.

"I …I do not know. I did not ask." I look aside, unable to meet her eyes.

"You did not think they should die for touching you against your will? For violating the heir to the throne of Naples with their coarse hands? Our royal blood is holy, we are ordained by God to rule—to touch us is a desecration! And the Duke of Durazzo ordered this?"

"No! I am sure he did not. He… he may not have thought I would resist." Everything I say makes this worse.

"He knew when you arrived at his castle, whether you came willingly or not. And he has allowed them to live. You have made it possible for any man to touch a royal and expect to live! If they can do it to you, they can do it to me! We are both vulnerable now. The Duke of Durazzo has made it acceptable for men to lay hands on those God anoints to rule them!"

"I am certain Lord Charles did not mean that! I am certain he did not intend—"

"What do I care for his intent? He did not object. His lack of action condones it!"

I am struck silent by this. Does she know what she has said? Can she hear Philippa's voice behind her words, as I do? She must, because she turns her head aside, unable to face me.

When she speaks again her voice is low, bitterness replacing anger. "You may tell your Lord husband I will give him your dowry when he has hanged the men who abducted you. The men who laid commoners' hands on you." She says it with such disgust I feel my face redden again. "Every one of them. No matter who they are. No matter how he loves them." She says this last through gritted teeth, but there is a gleam in her eye. A slight rebalance of the scales of justice. She has had to betray those she loved, and they were innocent of any crime, unlike Charles' men.

Her own husband laid hands on me. Will she have him hanged for me? But that is a secret I will never tell.

She waits until I say, "Yes, Your Majesty." I say it quietly, without looking at her.

Charles will be angry when I give him this message. I will have to tell him why Joanna is insisting now, when she did not think of it two years ago. I do not know who they are, I do not want to know, but he will know. They will be men he trusts, men who trust him to stand by them when they follow his orders. He will be teaching his men to question his orders. I do not want to give him this bitter command.

But I cannot deny that a part of me leaps up at the thought. How many times in these past two years have I wondered, in shame, when I stood with Charles before his men, which of them held me while I struggled, which ones knew the feel of my body against theirs. How many times have I wondered if they were thinking of that when they looked at me, and wondered that my Lord husband would allow it, and was humiliated that he did? How many times have I resented Charles for letting them live?

How many times have I subdued such thoughts and refused to allow myself to think them, as I refuse to think of the night Andrew touched me?

"I am protecting you, Maria, better than Duke Charles does," Joanna says. "I am making sure no one else thinks he can lay hands on either of us with impunity."

Does she expect me to thank her? I look at her so that she knows I do not thank her for this. I curtsy, looking her in the eye the whole while.

"You are a fool, Maria. You do not know him at all," she says when I have risen from my sullen curtsy. "But you are my sister. I will keep my promise if you keep yours."

I have already promised, so I am silent.

"You may go now."

I leave her privy chamber and her presence chamber, and find a boy, whom I send to find my husband.

When Charles meets me in the stable I tell him I cannot ride back with him this night. "The Queen wants me to stay in the rooms for the maids-in-waiting."

"You are not a maid." He twists a curl on my cheek that has escaped my braids, and smiles. "I know a better place for you to sleep."

"She wants me near her. All those she was close to have been sent away, because of Cardinal Aimeric's suspicions." The Cardinal will be pleased when he hears the news of her pregnancy, I think. He will believe his interference solved their marital troubles.

Charles' smile broadens. "That could be good for us. Gain her trust, Maria. Encourage her to confide in you, now the others are gone."

"She trusts nobody."

He cups my chin in his hand, turning my face up to his. "Make her trust you."

I pull my head free. "And how shall I do that?"

"Do whatever it takes."

"Remember you told me that, husband."

He laughs. He thinks I am joking. "I will remember, my pretty little duchess," he says.

I do not smile. I will hold him to it.

By late April it is obvious Joanna will not be able to keep her condition secret much longer. In order to keep her promise, she tells me I may tell my husband.

I help her on with her gown and open the door for the rest of her maids, who will assist her with her hair and jewels. Some of them are already wondering, no doubt. I have seen speculative glances aimed at the Queen's belly, and I was beginning to fear that gossip would begin before I could speak to Charles. I leave Joanna's bedchamber and look for Charles among the other courtiers in her presence chamber.

I catch his eye at once and smile, briefly raising my eyebrow. He excuses himself and strolls over to greet me.

"We must talk," I whisper. "As soon as possible." Now that Joanna has allowed me to tell him, I am desperate to do so. One whisper from one of her other maids and everyone will know, and my husband will wonder why that first whisper was not from me to him.

"I have always enjoyed walking in the garden with you," Charles murmurs. I look up to see the smile in his eyes and force myself to smile back. He will not be as pleased to hear what I have to tell him as I was then with what he told me.

On the way to the outside gardens we talk of the new song the troubadour sang at dinner last night and the jousting match that is being planned for next week, and our little daughter Joanna whom I have not seen for two months. Charles tells me she is crawling now whenever she is out of the swaddling board, and that she fights against being put back in.

"She must have straight legs," I tell him. "A girl cannot have bowed legs and dance with any elegance."

"Her legs are straight. Do not worry, Duchess Maria, our Joanna's nursemaid does not give in to her baby tantrums."

"Tantrums?"

"She is strong-willed."

"She is like you, then."

"And my Lady Mother.

"She is nothing like your Lady Mother!"

Charles chuckles. "She is like herself. She is perfect. And soon she will have a brother."

"I want her to visit me in my confinement." Charles does not answer.

"If I must spend all this time at court, I want at least to see my daughter when I am at Castle Durazzo."

"I will suggest it to my Lady Mother."

"I am our Joanna's Lady Mother. I should have a say."

By now we are deep enough into the garden that there is little likelihood we will be overheard. Charles glances around to be sure no one is near. His expression of fond indulgence disappears. “What do you have to tell me?” he asks, stopping on the pathway, too eager to wait until we have reached the bench.

“The Queen has agreed to give you my dowry.”

He laughs, as pleased as a child who has just opened a gift. “Maria, that is excellent news—”

“But she has a condition. You must have the men who abducted me hanged.”

He looks at me, delight shifting to surprise, then to something darker.

“It was not my idea,” I protest. “It is all from her.”

“How does she know? After two years, what made her think—”

“She accused me of going to you myself, of plotting with you against her. I had to tell her I was taken. You yourself told me to gain her trust!”

“By making her distrust me? Does she think I forced you?” His face is red with anger.

“She knows I married you willingly. We swore to that two years ago when she wanted me to leave you. She knows you would never force me.”

We are keeping our voices down but anyone watching us from a window… I glance up. No one can be seen at any of the windows, which does not prove they are not there.

“She would not have given up my dowry otherwise. Now she trusts me. And she will trust you if you do this.”

“How many?” he asks.

“How many?”

“How many of my men?”

“I… I do not know.” He is not even considering refusing, sacrificing my dowry for his men’s lives. He is only calculating who he can save. “Two,” he decides.

I will still have to stand before them and wonder.

“Four. Marguerita was with me.” She was not blindfolded.

“Shall I hang her also?”

I stare at him, horrified. Then I am so angry I do not care who sees us. "You think this is amusing? You think to negotiate the price of my honor?" I whip my hand up to slap him.

He is quicker and grabs my wrist, forcing it down. His face is rigid. He does not speak for a minute, just stares at me, and for that minute I am terrified. Then he says, "In over two years you have never once objected to my method of …attaining you. Your nicety is too late now, Princess Maria, and the Queen's as well. I will do what I must to get your dowry, because it is mine by rights, but this—forcing me to hang my men—do not imagine it is anything other than the Queen's revenge. She will never forgive me, that is what this message of hers means." He drops my hand as though it were dirty. "I will hang two men, and you will assure her that you heard only two voices." He turns to leave.

"Her Majesty is with child."

Charles stops moving. He may not even be breathing, he stands so rigid on the pathway.

This is not at all how I meant to tell him. How can both my husband and my sister make me so angry, and at the same time make me feel guilty for events I had no control over?

"You are certain?" His voice is low, controlled. He turns back slowly, examining my face as though I would lie to him about this.

"Yes. She told me herself. And I could see it when I dressed and undressed her."

"You have known awhile." He studies me coldly. I do not answer. "Who else knows?"

"No one. I know. Now you know. I think she will tell Duke Andrew soon, perhaps today. Her maids will know very soon. She cannot hide it from them much longer."

"And so you tell me now."

"You told me to do whatever it took to win her trust."

He looks at me steadily. "Take care, Maria," he says quietly, "that in winning her trust, you do not lose mine."

I return his look. Right now I am weary of them both, with their demands and their tests.

"I think you had better come back with me today, Duchess Maria of Durazzo. I think you need to remember who your family is now."

I open my mouth to tell him I know full well where my duty lies—and close it again. Where does my duty lie? I have sworn obedience to both my sister and my husband, out of love and duty, and both are convinced I am not steadfast. *Love is a changing thing, Princess; family is a steadfast thing,* Sancia told me, in order to convince me to forget Charles for Joanna's sake. And now Charles uses the same argument to bind me to him instead of Joanna. Family. Love. It would appear they are both changeable things. How can I be constant when everything else is inconstant?

"I will be glad to return to Castle Durazzo," I tell Charles. "I have missed my daughter, and I never wanted to spy for you. I am a royal princess, not a bearer of court gossip."

He puts a hand on my shoulder, stopping me as I turn to leave the garden. "We rise together, Maria," he says. "Or fall together. But I intend to rise, by whatever means necessary."

I look back over my shoulder, considering him and his words, and I understand at last what Sancia tried to tell me about Charles. But she was wrong about love and family.

From now on I must learn to be constant to myself.

Chapter 22

A New Banner

Less than a month after Joanna's condition becomes publicly known, a procession of bishops and lawyers arrive in Naples, sent by Louis of Hungary and accompanied by additional Hungarian men-at-arms for Andrew. The clergy and lawyers sequester themselves in Andrew's rooms, advising him on ways to undermine Joanna's authority and increase his own. We have no doubt a similar group has made its way from Hungary to Avignon to confer with the pope, and are proved right when, in mid-June, the Queen receives a missive from Clement VI reproving her for delaying the double coronation and ordering her to share her administration of the kingdom with her Lord husband, Andrew.

"I cannot compete with their money!" Joanne glares down at the dinner set before her. We are alone in her bedchamber, eating our meal on a little table set before the fireplace. I am in her good graces again, having kept her secret from my husband, in whose good graces I currently am not. I am resigned that there will never be a time when they are both pleased with me.

I commiserate by refraining from eating, even though I am always hungry when I am pregnant, and the smell of the venison has my mouth watering painfully.

"Cardinal Aimeric officially anointed me sole sovereign before he left last month, in accordance with King Robert's will and testament and at the Pope's command. He reverses his mind more often than a woman!" She rises and paces across the room to the window.

It has been a while since I visited our menagerie, I think, trying to distract myself from the rich juices seeping out of the steaming meat.

"He exceeds his authority." Her voice is an angry growl across the room.

Ah. The papal bull Cardinal Aimeric posted just before he left, in which Clement VI revoked all gifts of money and position made by Queen Joanna and Grandmother Sancia since King Robert died. Joanna had it torn down and refuses to speak of it, except in bitter comments like this. I resolutely turn away from the platters of food and give her my attention. Underneath her insult and fury, I know there is injury. Clement's failure to support her reign, after all the devotion and support she and our grandfather, and his father before him, have given the papacy, is a deep wound. My sister's decision to ignore the Pope's edicts—the one concerning her appointments and rewards for loyal service, and this one of a double coronation—have cost her something. A measure of faith. Not in God, but in His church, which is almost as bad for Joanna. There is nothing I can say. She would not want me to know her loss, as if I could help it, understanding her as I do. It is a relief not to have to acknowledge it, though, for I lost the greater measure when my Louis died: it was not the Pope, but God, who failed me then. The one exceeding his power, the other not exercising it.

"He does," I agree, and leave it at that.

"Have you seen my husband the Duke's new banner?"

I take a sip of wine, so that my voice is steady when I answer, "Who has not seen it?" Andrew has had a banner made for his retinue to carry when he rides out, to replace the one bearing his Hungarian coat of arms. This one has an axe and stake emblazoned on it.

"Beheading or burning. That is what he promises everyone loyal to me if he ever comes to power."

"Then he must not *ever* come to power!" I straighten, glad that she is standing at the window where she will not notice my trembling or see the fear in my eyes. Andrew's arrogance and cruelty are well-known now. One of his chamberlains, Tommaso Mambriccio, approached my husband begging for a position at Castle Durazzo. He had a look of desperation about him, as a man condemned. Charles refused him, sent him back to his master. Later I learned Tommaso's wife and son were garroted in an alley.

Everyone I have known, have grown up with, everyone I love, is loyal to Joanna.

The axe or the stake.

Which will it be for Charles? Did he think sending Tommaso back to Andrew would please Andrew?

Which will it be for me? Andrew hates me, ever since that night; I have seen it in his eyes. My costume fooled him—never mind what he did to me—and Andrew hates to look a fool. He had his man killed for witnessing it, and every time he looks at me, he knows there is one witness still alive.

"Your Lord husband says otherwise."

Joanna turns from the window. She is watching me, but I cannot look up. I have heard that Charles now vocally supports Andrew's right to be crowned and rule with Joanna, but I have been hoping the rumors were false. He has not talked to me of it and I am too sick at the thought of it to confront him. "I cannot believe that," I murmur. "He is loyal to you. I know he is."

Do I?

Joanna walks back and sits down. Her arms, resting on the table, tremble. I look up, meeting her eyes. "Naples is in great danger, Maria," she says, leaning toward me. "I am losing control. I have to regain it, and quickly. I have to secure my kingdom before December. I cannot go into my confinement..." Now it is she who looks away, her voice failing.

I have never seen my sister frightened. I reach out, but she moves her hand out of my reach. I am not trusted. I am the wife of a man who supports her enemy. Our enemy.

"Charles will never betray you." I say. "He… he cannot mean what he says." How do I know what Charles means? He has not spoken to me of any of this. "I will talk to him, Joanna. We are loyal. We are loyal to you."

Joanna nods. Her face bears the grim expression of someone who knows she is being lied to, but I am not lying. Am I? "I will do my best, Joanna. I will make him see that Andrew must not rule."

My stomach rumbles, but I am no longer hungry. I put my hand on it to quiet its rumble, and am rewarded with a fierce kick. I will go into confinement soon. How will I keep Charles loyal when I am shut away from him?

That night when I return to Castle Durazzo, I tell Charles I must speak to him privately.

"I will come up to your rooms later," he says.

"It is about the Queen." I say this quietly, only for his ears.

"I will come up when I am ready," he says sharply, not caring who hears him.

I bow my head, a dutiful wife, but my face is hot, my stomach churning. Do you no longer love me? I want to cry. What have I done that has so displeased him? As soon as I think the question, I know the answer. I have not made him king, and now it appears I never will. I have not even done the most common duty of a wife: our nursery has a daughter in it, instead of a son and heir. Pray God, the infant I am carrying will be a healthy boy.

"I await your pleasure," I tell Charles humbly.

It is late when he comes to me. Margherita has already undressed me and let my hair down, and closed the curtains against the night wind. She sat sewing with me until I caught her nodding and sent her to her bed.

Propped up against the pillows I am dozing off when I hear the door to my chamber open. I open my eyes in time to see Charles retreating back through the partially-opened door.

"My Lord," I call softly, so no one will hear me entreating him in.

There is a pause, insignificant really, except that he has never hesitated before on my bedroom threshold. Then he enters. "I have come as promised," he says stiffly. "Have you learned something at court to tell me?"

Is this what we have become? A spy and her master? An untrustworthy spy, by the doubtful tilt of his head. He does not believe I have any information of value, and he is right. I am waiting to petition him, not help him. Not support him, as a wife should.

"If you rise, I rise. But if you fall, I fall with you."

He raises an eyebrow at hearing me repeat his own words back to him. "What have you learned?" he asks, approaching my bed.

"Joanna knows that you have been speaking against her, supporting Duke Andrew's coronation." I have to force myself to say the words.

He stops, aware that I am actually telling him I know it, too. "Supporting the King is not the same as speaking against the Queen. Or do you agree with your sister that a wife should rule over her husband? Perhaps you also agree with her that here in Naples we are above the Church, are free to ignore His Holiness the Pope's directives?"

I am struck dumb. How can I argue against being a dutiful wife and a dutiful Christian? What can I say to convince him? Do I have any influence over him any more? When I regain my voice it is to say, "If you wish me to stay here, at Castle Durazzo, I will do so." I bend my head so he will not see how hard this was to say.

When I look up, his eyes are mocking me. "Why would I want that, little wife?"

"Because Duke Andrew will murder—" I stop myself on the verge of a confession that would ruin me. Charles must never learn my secret. He would not blame Andrew, he would blame me, for wearing that costume, for dressing like a whore in front of everyone. "Everyone! He will kill everyone! He has said so openly!" I am sobbing now. I brush the tears away, hating my weakness, but I cannot stop weeping.

"King Andrew will not execute those who supported him," Charles says. He does not come near to hold me, to comfort me, but stands watching me coolly. "Those who support him will form the new court when he is crowned."

"Is that what this is about? Promotion?"

Now he steps forward, leaning over me, his expression no longer amused. "What else?" he says coldly.

"Then let the Queen promote you. She will reward your loyalty."

He laughs, a sharp bitter sound. "The Queen has promoted everyone except her own sister's husband."

"You have recently been given lands and castles valued at ten thousand florins, and thirty thousand florins, besides!"

"I have *recently* been given what should have been mine these two years past."

I struggle onto my knees, clasping my hands together in front of my burgeoning womb. "Do not trust Duke Andrew, my Lord. He is not to be trusted, and you are coming to his side too late."

"He will need me. I am his cousin, of the same royal house as he is, the only cousin to support him. And I am Neapolitan born, unlike him. I am head of one of the two most powerful families here. King Andrew needs my support: I can trust in that."

"Queen Joanna needs your support. Your voice gives Duke Andrew's cause credibility, hurting hers. You swore allegiance to Joanna!"

"His Holiness the Pope gives King Andrew's cause credibility. I am not breaking my vow. There is no plot against the Queen. I am only obeying our Holy Father."

"How can I convince you not to do this? Joanna needs our support!"

His face hardens. He grabs my arm, holding it so hard I cry out.

"You do not convince your Lord husband of anything," he says, giving my arm a rough shake that draws another whimper from me. I close my lips tightly against the urge to beg him to stop.

He drags me off the bed and across the room, grabbing a lamp from its wall sconce as he passes. It is almost more than I can do not to cry out again as he drags me into the dark hallway in only my nightdress. I pray no one will waken and come out to see us as he pulls me by my arm, now throbbing with pain, through the castle halls. I realize where we are going as we near the nursery. He opens the door and propels me in ahead of him. I stand in the dark nursery, breathing deeply, rubbing my aching arm.

"What do you want for our children?" he asks me, his voice harsh but low, to avoid waking the nursemaid. "Safety and good marriages? Or the axe and the stake?"

"He would never… not even Andrew would…" I stammer, horrified.

"No, of course not, because he has shown himself so tender to the children of his enemies."

I cringe away from him, from the anger and sarcasm in his low voice, and even more from the truth of it.

We stand there in the dark, listening to the quiet breathing of our sleeping daughter. The thin light of the lamp Charles is holding flickers, as fragile as her tiny life. Joanna is eleven months old, already staggering about the room, chattering in her high, sweet baby voice. Charles raises the lamp so I can see her better, the perfect oval of her cheek, the dark fringe of her eyelashes against her pale skin, the little, turned-up nose and rosebud lips.

Joanna, my Joanna!

I give a stifled sob and bury my face in my hands.

Chapter 23

Foolish Young Women

I send a letter to the Queen, begging her leave to absent myself from court that I might tend to my mother-in-law. Agnes of Perigord has been ill for two months and is showing no signs of recovery. This is the excuse I use to avoid my sister's court when she most needs me.

I cannot pretend to be sad as my mother-in-law's condition worsens. She was never my friend, and she has kept my daughter from me as much as she could, claiming one day that my influence will make little Joanna weak like me, and on another that she will learn disobedience from me, for I disobeyed my sovereign to marry Charles. Although it is a sin to think it, I will not be sorry when she dies.

It is not my Lady Aunt who dies, however; it is our grandmother, the Dowager Queen Sancia. Joanna and her court are at Castellamare, one of the royal summer palaces, when we hear of her passing, so I cannot go to my sister. I clothe myself in white to mourn my grandmother. She was a stern, unyielding moral presence in our lives, and I admit it is a little freeing to know she will never again frown at my behavior. But she was also our powerful protector, a wise advisor, and Joanna's strongest ally. My world is shaken by her passing, and more dangerous without her. We are vulnerable now, my sister and I, cast adrift in an increasingly turbulent and treacherous world. There is no one to stand between us and disaster; only the tenuous support of Joanna's favorites and a changeable Pope, while Andrew has the immense wealth of Hungary behind him.

As soon as the Dowager Queen is laid in her tomb behind the altar of Santa Croce, my sister ignores her will, which bequeaths most of her estate to Santa Croce and Santa Chiara, and instead divides her property between Robert of Taranto and my husband, Charles of Durazzo. I understand her desperate bid for allies, but I am shocked she would disregard our Grandmother Sancia's will. Robert has had more than enough bribes and promotions to buy his loyalty, if it could stay bought, and my husband's allegiance is cautiously divided—although he is happy enough to accept the lands. All Joanna does is further annoy Clement VI, who accuses her of stealing the estate from the cathedrals and monasteries it was intended for.

Lady Margherita, married now, keeps me company as I sit in my mother-in-law's chamber. It is August. She has been ill since May. We are losing hope that she will pull through—those who had any, that is. Philippa's granddaughter, Sancia, still banished from Joanna's court like all her family, often joins us. She is a countess now, married to the Count of Marcone.

The room is dark and stifling hot with the curtains drawn to keep out the summer fevers. *It is a little late for that,* I think, cross with the heat and constantly tired by my advanced pregnancy. I stab my needle through the linen shift I am sewing for little Joanna, wishing my contrary mother-in-law would hurry up and die so I could leave this hot, closed room. The needle pricks my finger, drawing a bead of blood onto the fabric. I throw it to the floor with an oath I have heard my husband use. Margherita looks at me, shocked, but Sancia bends her head, biting her lip. I recognize that movement.

"Oh, go ahead," I tell her, which makes her bite her lip harder. I look at my sewing, lying on the floor rushes. Remembering the expression on Margherita's face when I swore, I cannot help giggling. In a minute we are both giggling, Sancia and I, while Margherita sews stanchly in silence. I nudge her foot with mine. She looks up. "Would you like another shift to sew?" I ask, pointing to mine, which sets all three of us off. It is so hot in this room, and so unbearably boring waiting for my Lady Mother-in-law to die, whom none of us like very much and who certainly does not like any of us.

"She would be so angry to hear us," Margherita says between gasps of laughter.

"Vain girls! Vain, silly, frivolous young women!" I scold in my aunt's shrill voice, making us all laugh harder.

"Watch her closely, now. Do not sit gossiping and forget your duty here!" Sancia joins in, mimicking the pompous little doctor, Giovanni da Penne, whom Charles paid to come and examine his mother.

The door opens suddenly. "What is this? What is this I hear? Laughter and foolishness?" Giovanni da Penne struts in, sounding exactly as Sancia represented him. He scowls at us as we choke back our laughter, and marches stiffly to Agnes of Perigord's bedside.

"Look at her! Look at her!" he scolds, pointing to my mother-in-law's sweating forehead and cheeks flushed with heat. He begins to apply leeches to her arms and neck, muttering to himself about humors out of balance and idle young women. Our brief flippancy dies out and we resume our sewing. The heat settles around us again, worse than ever.

How I would enjoy a game of hazards! Or better yet, a picnic in the garden, or an afternoon in the nursery with my little daughter… Instead I sit here day after dreary day while my inconsiderate mother-in-law drags out her death just to spite me. She will, no doubt, keep me shut up in here until it is time to enter my confinement, another dark, closed, hot little room.

The doctor begins removing his leeches. I watch them stick, pulling on her pale, loose skin, leaving a smear of blood when they are finally torn free.

"I must have a sample of her urine," he says, putting the last of his leeches in their bottle. He does not look at us, a man speaking of such things to young women. She is my mother-in-law, so I am the one who must say, "Yes, we will get one for you."

"It must be collected at daybreak," he says. "I will come for it in the early morning."

I nod, but he is not looking at us, so once again I say, "Yes, I will have it done." He gives us another lecture on the irresponsibility of young women before he leaves.

"Irresponsible," I huff when he has gone. "Let him carry and birth a child!"

Sancia smiles. She is pregnant with her first and very pleased about it. "What can he be looking for in your Lady Aunt's urine?"

"Is he too foolish to recognize she is dying? What else does he think could make her sleep day and night?" Margherita says.

"Pregnancy," I say, suppressing a yawn.

"Oh, I would love to see his face if her urine showed that!" Sancia cries, laughing. Margherita and I join in. The more I picture that stuffy little doctor's face, and the image of my stern, righteous old mother-in-law carrying an illegitimate child in her old age, the harder I laugh, until I am gasping. "We could…we could substitute our urine for hers," I choke out through my laughter.

"I could do it," Sancia giggles. "You are too close to your confinement, Lady Maria. I will get up early, when her maid has collected her urine, and tip it out and fill the vial with my own!"

I stop laughing. Agnes of Perigord was one of Joanna's advisers the day she was convinced to send Philippa and her family away from court. Well, why not indulge Sancia's little revenge? I have no love for my mother-in-law. It will be amusing, and no one will know but us three.

"We will do it." I look at Margherita. Before she can voice the objections I see in her face, I say, "What harm can it do? She will never wake. Only the doctor will look foolish, as foolish as he claims we are."

It is worth it the next morning, when we present the false vial of liquid. Giovanni Da Penne stares at it, looks closer, and sniffs it, his eyes nearly popping out of his head. He blushes redder than a young girl. It is all we can do to keep straight faces when I ask, "Does it tell you what is wrong with her, good doctor?"

"S…send for the d...duke," he stammers to a servant.

Send for the duke? I give Sancia and Margherita a startled look. Sancia's eyes are wide, her face suddenly pale. I take a deep breath. Whatever the doctor says now, we are committed to protesting our innocence.

When Charles arrives, the doctor pulls him aside and whispers urgently.

"How dare you?" I hear Charles say in an undertone that does not disguise the rage behind his low voice. "How dare you even suggest it!"

I wince and struggle to stand firm and straight, to look as though I have no idea what is being discussed. Whatever possessed me to do this? I am every bit as foolish, as silly, as irresponsible a young woman as my mother-in-law and the doctor maintained. I have not embarrassed the pompous doctor; I have shamed Agnes of Perigord's reputation and my husband's honor; the whole Durazzo family will be a laughingstock. I cannot breathe for the thought of what I have done.

I dare not look at my accomplices, but I feel Sancia trembling beside me. Margherita and I are part of the Durazzo family, but she is an outsider, and already accused of stirring up trouble between the Queen and King. Margherita and I will be found faultless if Sancia is blamed, but if we confess, she will be accused of inciting us, whatever we say.

It was my idea. Or Margherita's. I do not think it was Sancia's, she only offered to do it for us. She is innocent, or at least no more guilty than we are, and I will not—*will not*—sacrifice her to avoid my husband's anger. I step forward, straightening my knees to stop their shaking.

"What is it, my Lord?" I ask. "Is your Lady Mother failing?" Charles frowns at me. He has barely spoken to me since the hanging of his two henchmen. I have lost his love and his trust for telling Joanna my abduction was forced. I am miserable under his indifference, but I am too proud to beg his forgiveness for I only told the truth, and if the truth is so terrible the shame is his, not mine. I hold my head straight and look at him steadily, waiting for his answer.

"The good doctor," he says, through gritted teeth, "says my Lady Mother is with child."

I do my best to look astonished and outraged. "This is a terrible jest! How dare he?"

"It is no jest, my Lady."

"Then it is incompetence!"

Charles is looking at me, but I dare not look away from the doctor. My husband has never heard me speak this way; in truth, I am pretending to be Agnes of Perigord as hard as I can, acting the part like a common mummer. Will Charles set me aside if he finds out I have shamed his family? Will he have me locked up, and starve me, claiming I died in childbirth? At the least he will beat me, and no one would blame him. I throw myself into the part, glaring at the little doctor. "Who sent you here? Have you been paid to besmirch our family?"

"I can prove it!" he squeaks. The last words I want to hear. I open my mouth to cut him off, but he has already gestured toward his servant and before I can speak he says, "Go at once and fetch the vial." I am left with my mouth open, afraid to protest further.

"I will never believe it," I say. A weak retort, but I raise my chin grandly, as I have seen my mother-in-law do. It always intimidated me, that raised chin. I cannot believe mine will have the same effect. Already I am sorting through my robes and blankets, thinking which ones are warmest. Even in summer the dungeons are cool.

We wait in silence. I hope Charles notices the doctor's nervous fidgeting, for I am holding myself as still as rigor mortis not to do the same. The doctor must be made to look false. It is him or me. He is a man, and I am just a woman, and Charles already distrusts me. But he would rather believe me, for if he believes the doctor, it will shame the Durazzo family.

The servant returns with the vial and Giovanni da Penne begins his explanation of how a pregnant lady's urine differs from normal urine. I can barely follow his words for the pounding in my ears. This is the type of proof a man believes, whether he wants to or not. Can I say Agnes of Perigord has stopped her courses? But that will only prove she is not pregnant; it will not discredit the doctor, it will just point directly to me.

Or to Sancia. Charles will not be able to lock up another man's wife, and a countess at that, in our dungeon. And the Count of Marcone will not risk his first child to have her punished, even to satisfy the Durazzos. Charles will know it was either Sancia or me, for Margherita is not pregnant. I glance at Sancia and find her watching me. She knows what I am thinking. She is expecting the same from me as her family received from my sister.

I raise my chin. This time it feels a little more natural. "How do we know what you are telling us is correct?"

"I am a respected doctor of medicine." The doctor eyes me coldly. He has gained confidence, showing off his knowledge.

I consider several retorts questioning his skill. Agnes of Perigord could have given them, but I dare not. Charles must already wonder why I am defending his mother so fiercely. An old woman, a matriarch, can be arrogant, but a young woman must be clever. The trouble is, I am too frightened to be clever. I draw a silent breath to calm myself, and remind myself to be steadfast. What if this was just Joanna and me, playing a trick on Philippa? We did so, as children, mostly at my instigation. Joanna was the intelligent one, but I could be clever.

"I will provide my urine." I say impulsively. "If it shows the same signs, we will have to believe you." Then, for Charles, I add, "But I will be sad to believe it."

Charles looks at me thoughtfully, but the doctor agrees, pursing his lips complacently. I beckon my maid over to take the vial.

It is a relief to see my maid empty and rinse the accursed vial in the privy room beside my bedchamber. "Lady Margherita will help me," I tell her, taking the vial and sending her outside the curtained alcove to wait with Sancia and the doctor, leaving Margherita and me alone in the tiny space. "Hold up my skirts, if you will, Lady Margherita," I say, loud enough to be heard through the heavy curtain, as I lift Margherita's skirts, deliberately making them rustle. She has already understood my intent, and takes the vial with a grin.

When my maid presents the vial to him, Giovanni da Penne is confounded, for I am clearly pregnant yet this urine shows none of the signs he pointed out earlier.

"Perhaps you got the signs backward?" My voice is light and careless, my smile sweet, but my eyes as they meet his are hard. He looks at me, the Duchess of Durazzo, sister to the Queen of Naples and heir to her throne, and at my husband standing beside me, the son of the woman he has accused of carrying a bastard child.

"Well," he says. "Well… it is possible…" the words nearly strangling him.

That evening Charles comes into my bedchamber as my maid is combing out my hair. He snaps his fingers and sends her scuttling out of the room. "Come here," he orders.

I rise on trembling legs and cross the room to him.

"What have you to say to me?"

"N...nothing my Lord." I raise my chin.

He slaps me across the face so hard I am flung to the floor. I throw out my arms to break my fall, scraping my elbows raw, but at least I do not take the brunt of the fall on my stomach. "My Lord, our child!"

"Get up."

When I am standing in front of him again, he asks, "Whose idea was that?"

For a wild moment I consider denying everything, feigning innocence—

"Do not deceive me," he says. "Tell me now or I will hit you again, much harder, child or not!"

"It was… it was only meant as a joke… a harmless joke on the doctor…" I am crying. I do not want to. I am a royal princess, I should not weep with fear. But I have never seen Charles like this and I cannot stop the flow of tears. "It was not meant to go so far."

"My God, you are even more stupid than I imagined! Who thought to do it? Tell me!"

"I cannot…" He raises his hand. "I do not know, my Lord! We were all laughing at the doctor, someone said… said, what would make your Lady Mother sleep so much? and…"

"It was Lady Sancia. Her family sowed discord between the Queen and King, and now she comes into my castle and stirs up trouble and shame upon my family!"

"It was not! I swear it was not her! We were all—"

"Whose urine was in the vial instead of the Duchess'?"

The *Dowager* Duchess*,* I think, but I am unable to answer. It was not mine, I dare not pretend it was, and there is only one other of us who is pregnant. "We all…" I start, then, "mine!" But he has already seen my hesitation.

"As I thought. Lady Sancia, the granddaughter of that Ethiopian slave. I will remember this. She will be sorry one day to have shamed the Durazzos!"

The look on his face terrifies me. I cannot speak, dare not protest. When did I go from being afraid I would break his heart, to being afraid of him? He leaves without another word between us.

Within a week my Lady Mother-in-law, Agnes of Perigord, succumbs to her illness. I am surprised to find, however much I disliked her, that I am shaken by her death. She was a strong, powerful woman, a formidable opponent, and however much she disliked me, I was securely under her protection. The cornerstones of our kingdom, one by one, are falling away from us. I shiver in the summer heat as she is laid to rest. The winds of chaos are blowing toward us.

The day after the Dowager Duchess of Durazzo is laid to rest, the Pope's nuncio formally announces the latest edict from Clement VI: Joanna and Andrew are to share the rule of Naples. They will have a double coronation on September 20th.

Andrew has his men-at-arms hoist his banner, the axe and the stake, and gallop with him through the narrow streets holding it high and shouting in triumph, trampling anyone not fast enough to dodge his horses' hooves.

Chapter 24

A Foul, Unholy Night

Joanna invites Charles and me to join the royal court as it moves to Aversa, just outside of Naples, in early September. They plan to sojourn there for twelve days, returning to Naples in time for their coronation on the twentieth. I will go into my confinement the day after the coronation. I am pushing my time back by a week, but Charles has allowed it, since he wants us both to be seen at the coronation which he has made no secret of supporting.

The days pass pleasantly away from the city. I walk with the other ladies of the court in the cool, green gardens of the nearby Celestine monastery, while Charles joins Andrew and his men in falconing and archery competitions. After a dinner at which the wine flows freely, they continue carousing at night with those who are drawn to the castle where wealthy young lords are looking to make merry. I retire early, my pregnancy making me weary, and pretend not to notice when Charles returns to our rooms very late, smelling of wine and other women.

I see little of my sister. She works all day and into the night, hearing petitions and signing papers and documents. Delegations from Naples and the surrounding towns and villages bring their requests to her and she turns no one away. She has always worked hard and taken a personal interest in performing the details of governance, but now she works as one driven. When I pass her going to the hall where she sees petitioners, or coming from her morning prayers, her face is drawn and haggard.

"Your Majesty," I call impetuously as she passes without seeing me. "You need not see everyone. Your lords can judge the common people."

She stops and stares a moment, as though she has forgotten I am here. "They ask for me," she says. It is true. No one leaves Joanna's court disgruntled. They may not have received all they hoped for, but they wear the faces of people who have received justice.

"This morning's delegation specifically asked for you?"

She frowns, then remembers the one I am referring to and grins with me. "In fact, I asked for them. The townspeople had their say and I thought it fair to hear both parties. How did you hear of it?"

"The entire court—no, all of Aversa by now—knows that you allowed prostitutes into your court to plead their case!"

"King Robert the Wise believed justice must be impartial."

"He did not carry it so far as you do, sister," I tease her.

"He had our Grandmother Sancia to deal with." We both burst into laughter at the thought of our deeply religious grandmother allowing prostitutes into her castle.

"And what were their arguments?" I ask.

"The townspeople wanted me to ban the independent prostitutes. Bad for business, they argued. Who will go into town to a common house if the business comes to the castle?"

"And the prostitutes?"

Joanna's face turns serious. "They said women must have some means of surviving." She frowns, thoughtful.

"Do not tell me you fed them. Please!"

"They may have stopped by the kitchens on their way out." She smiles at my shocked laughter.

"At least you did ban them. They are no longer to be seen at the castle gates."

"I ordered them not to approach too near the castle. Perhaps if they have to walk farther, the cool night air will bring our lords to their senses and help them resist temptation."

"Or ride into town for it."

"So the townspeople hope."

I shake my head. "After such solemn judgments, you must take some rest. Come and walk in the gardens with me."

I see she is about to refuse, and forestall her. "If you have no time for a walk, at least have dinner with me. This grueling workload is not good for your child. I am sure you are not eating enough."

I have taken a chance, speaking with such liberty, but she smiles. I recognize in her expression that she, too, has been missing the comfort of being guided by those we have lost, however chafing that guidance may have felt at the time.

"Set up a table in the shade by the fountain," I order a servant. "And have our dinner sent there. A good dinner, mind, not a paltry bit of cheese and some olives. Have you any quince preserves?" Joanna laughs as I ask this. I grin at her, an expression straight from our childhood, and tell the boy watching us, perplexed, "Well, bring what you have, and be quick. Do not keep your Queen waiting!" He bobs into a hurried bow and races off to alert the kitchen.

"I do not have time for all this," Joanna murmurs, but she lets me lead her outside. I notice her glance behind to make sure her guards are following us, but do not comment on it as we wait for the servants to set up our table and chairs. A man hurries over with a platter of meat and a girl, sweating from the ovens, brings us bread and preserves. It is not quince, Joanna's favorite, but it is orange spice, almost as good. A man from the cellars follows them with a bottle of cool wine and two cups. One of Joanna's guards steps forward and samples everything on our food platters, even the orange spice preserve. He nods and steps back beside the other guard.

"What are you afraid of?" I ask her when we are finally alone, save for her guards, who stand in sight but outside hearing distance of our conversation.

"What every ruler fears."

"No one in Naples would harm you. Your people love you, even the prostitutes. Everyone here with us supports you. Even Andrew, now that he will soon have joint power, has no cause to harm you." I reach for her hands and clasp them in mine. They are cold, even on such a warm day.

She pulls her hands back gently and takes a chunk of the meat. "My advisors tell me they uncovered a plot against Duke Andrew. A hunting accident, it was going to be."

I stop eating and look at her in alarm. Charles goes hunting with Andrew. "You caught them?" I say. "It is finished?"

She nods, spearing another piece of venison on her knife. "I am glad it came up, in fact. Andrew will be more cautious now, his guards more alert. As are mine." She glances at her guards, watching us. Watching me.

"They do not think *I*—"

"They suspect everyone, Maria. They are not pleased at having to stand so far from me." She smiles at me, lifting her wine cup.

"Stop!" I grab the cup. "Let them taste it!" I wave the guards over. "Are there guards in your kitchen? In the wine cellar? Standing by the roast pit?"

"My guards are everywhere." She sighs, but she lets one of her guards taste her wine.

I do not sleep well that night. It is near the end of my time, I cannot get comfortable, and have to rise often to use the privy room. Even when I go to sleep, I am disturbed by dreams. I wake imagining I hear footsteps in the hall, and hushed voices. I tell myself I am imagining it, and slowly, like a beached sea creature, roll onto my side, close my eyes and sleep again.

Suddenly, the night is rent with screams. I wake in a terror, my heart pounding, ready to scream myself. I shake my head, dispelling the nightmare image of someone creeping up behind me, but the screaming continues.

"Andrew!" someone is screaming, "Prince Andrew!" and other voices, male ones, take up the cry, "The Duke of Calabria!"

I jump out of bed and stand at my door, shaking. Is it safe to go out, to see what is happening? Are there others coming for us? For Charles because he has spoken for the duke? For me, the heir to the throne? For Joanna?

Joanna! I pull the door open and run barefoot down the dark hall toward her rooms. I can think of nothing else but that I must get to my sister, get to her now!

The closer I get the louder the voices become, men and women shouting, screaming, weeping! The thudding of my heart fills my ears as I run, propelled faster by the cacophony of voices. I am panting with terror, heavy with child, but all I can think as I race toward the rooms at the end of the hallway is Joanna! Joanna! My sister!

I run through the open door into the sitting room Joanna and Andrew shared between their bedchambers. It is crowded with people—guards and servants, courtiers and ladies, dukes and nobles, Neapolitans and Hungarians. Across the room I see my sister as stiff as a statue at the door to her bed chamber, unmoved by the clamor around her. She is clad only in her nightdress, her face as white as a ghost!

"Joanna!" I scream. Is she dead? She is dead, and this her ghostly presence, haunting us because we did not value her enough in life, did not protect her—

"Joanna!"

—And I am Queen! In my nightgown, barefoot, with my hair down!

She turns her head, and sees me, and lifts a hand, as though reaching for support—

Alive! Alive and unharmed.

"Joanna!" I throw myself into the crowd of people, pushing my way through them, desperate to reach her, until at last I can touch her, catch her outstretched hand, pull myself into her arms and feel hers holding me.

"Andrew," she chokes against my hair. "They have murdered him. They have murdered the duke! What will I do? Merciful Lord, whatever will I do to appease his family when they learn of it?"

"Hush," I whisper. "Hush. You are alive. You and your child are safe. You will know what to do." I close my eyes. I am shaking with shock. Murdered! A royal prince, an Angevin, murdered in our own castle! Thank God I am not Queen!

Joanna lets me hold her for a moment, and be held by her. Then she straightens and moves into the room, calling her guards to report what they have found. I listen, clutching the wall for support, as they describe the shocking state of the body. His body. Andrew's body. The next King of Naples' murdered and mutilated body.

He was found lying in the garden beneath their balcony, half-undressed, his face and bare arms bruised from a violent struggle with his assailants. A rope was tied around his neck, sawed off a few feet above the noose, as though he had been hanged from the balcony and was later cut down from above.

"I heard him fall! The awful sound! The awful sound of it!" his nurse, Isabelle the Hungarian, wails at this point, her hands covering her face.

"It was she who raised the alarm," a servant beside me whispers. "She chased the murderers away with her screams. Woke us all, she did, a wonder she didn't wake the dead duke, as well."

I shudder, looking at Andrew's blood-crusted body, laid out on a table for washing as soon as it has been examined to learn as much as it can tell us, now that his voice is silenced forever.

He can never tell our secret now. We have been bound together by that secret, each of us humiliated that night and terrified the other would tell. One of us had to die, to free the other, and I am glad it is him. His was the greater offense, though mine would have been the greater shame. I look at his still, bruised body and I can feel no pity, I can only think, I need never fear him again!

A sheet has been laid on the table beneath him, a stiff cloth of some sort… With a start of horror I recognize his banner. His mutilated corpse has been laid out on the axe and stake, a gory offering upon the platter he threatened to serve up to others! I cover my mouth to stop myself screaming, but it is so awful I am beyond screaming.

Joanna seems oblivious to what I have seen. While others are still wringing their hands and weeping, she has taken command of the situation as she always does, sending the courtiers and the few court ladies who have dared come to see what has happened back to their rooms, ordering servants to bring water to wash Andrew's body, and others to bring the duke's best clothes to dress him in. She sends two of her men to Naples to prepare the clergy at the Cathedral of Naples for Andrew's interment there the following day, and another to arrange his eventual burial in the chapel of Saint Louis, next to his grandfather Charles Martel, our grandfather King Robert's older brother.

I look around for Louis of Taranto. He will help Joanna, he has always supported her. But I cannot see him, or either of his brothers. Can they still be sleeping? Did they make so merry that all this outcry has not wakened them? I saw them yesterday, I am sure of it, walking with Charles of Artois and his son Bertrand, and the Count of Terlizzi. None of them has gathered about Joanna now, though they are her closest councilors at court.

I am about to step forward, to circle the room to see if I can find them, there are so many people here, when Charles appears beside me. Shock has made him suddenly sober, despite the stink of drink on his breath and clothes. I expect him to chastise me for coming out of my room in my nightdress and bare feet, but he does not seem to notice, any more than anyone appears to notice that the Queen of Naples is standing in public in only her nightdress.

"A gruesome deed, a foul, unholy night's work," Charles mutters in a toneless voice, staring at Andrew's corpse.

I cannot look at my husband. *He has made us vulnerable. He has made it possible for men to lay hands on those God anoints to rule them,* Joanna told me. Is Charles pretending to be horrified, or does he truly not see laying hands on a royal female as being in any way equivalent to raising one's hand against a male one? I thought he was caught up in passion when he had me abducted, I thought we were lovers in a troubadour's song, in a fairy tale where anything is possible and everything is permitted. Why did I not see before where we were all headed with that first act to control a throne guarded only by two girls and an aging dowager queen?

Charles stares gloomily at the prince nobody loved, the prince he has recently aligned himself with, a cause now lost.

"Your plans have been thwarted once again," I observe dryly. I leave before he can point out a worse truth: that I, too, agreed by omission to align myself to this most unfit prince, in order to keep my children out of the path of his vengeance.

None of us need fear him now. At last I feel pity, remembering the dark-haired, frightened boy left here at six years old, a lost and lonely little misfit in our glittering, sophisticated court.

Chapter 25

Rumors and Veils

Joanna retreats to her privy chamber with her advisors, her lawyers, her court seneschal, and fights for her crown in the only way she knows how: an army of letters marches forth to Clement VI, to Dowager Queen Elisabeth and King Louis of Hungary, to all the allied governments and influential figures whose support she needs. Letters informing them of her grief and horror at the crime, letters arranging daily masses to be said for Prince Andrew, letters assuring her kingdom's partners in trade and commerce that Naples is secure and stable and the situation is under control, letters ordering an investigation to find the murderers. This last is tricky. Someone must be blamed and punished, but the most likely culprits are Joanna's closest allies.

However quickly these letters sally forth, proclaiming the Queen's shock and sorrow, they cannot keep up with the rumors of the Queen's dry-eyed indifference—and, it is hinted, her shame—when confronted with the murder. Vile rumors of her culpability in the crime.

Two days after Andrew's death, while we are still at Aversa, Charles comes into our sitting room. "They have captured one of the murderers," he announces.

I drop my sewing. While I stare at him, unable to speak, the other ladies-in-waiting in the room exclaim and beg Charles to tell what he knows. I do not want to know. I am sick with fear, dreading to learn who it is, afraid to even think the names of those I could not find in Joanna's sitting chamber two nights ago.

"Tommaso Mambriccio," Charles says.

Tommaso? Who is Tommaso Mambriccio? Then I draw my breath in sharply. Tommaso, who came to Charles asking for a position.

"But who is he?" one of the ladies asks.

What if Charles had said yes? What if the man had worked for Charles? What if he had murdered *my* husband in the night?

"He was the duke's chamberlain," Marguerite of Taranto answers. "He is the son of a nobleman ruined by the Florentine bankers."

"But why would he murder the duke?"

"Has he confessed, my Lord?" I ask quickly, before Marguerite can answer. I send her a sharp look, hoping she will heed the warning in my eyes. I do not want anyone to wonder why Marguerite of Taranto knows so much about one of the murderers.

"He has," Charles answers. "He said the duke threatened to execute him when he was crowned."

There is an embarrassed silence in the room. Now that he is dead, no one wants to remember that Andrew was hated in life, and with reason. No one wants to acknowledge how relieved they are that the Pipini brothers have lost their royal protector.

"The duke must have perceived the evil in Tommaso's nature. His life might have been saved if he had acted sooner," Charles continues, easing the awkwardness with an image of Andrew's misplaced leniency.

I think of Tommaso's wife and infant son.

"The duke, our would-be king, was always too trusting," Charles continues. "Many took advantage of that, as did this false servant, a sinner hateful in the sight of God and men." The ladies lean forward in their seats, hanging on his words as though he was a troubadour entertaining them with a story. The lords nod sagely as though this twist he is giving to Andrew's character is just what they have always thought.

I feel a little nauseous, but then I am late in my pregnancy.

Charles takes out a letter. "Here is an account of what occurred, gathered from the scoundrel's confession under questioning." He opens the letter and begins to read it to us: "The duke and his men had dined gaily that night, anticipating the joy of his coronation, and he arrived late back at the royal residence. Her Majesty, our beloved queen, a pious woman wearied by her condition, retired early and fell asleep before he returned. The good duke, mindful of her need for sleep at this time, did not awaken her but went quietly to his bedchamber. As he prepared for bed, his chamberlain, this most deceitful servant Tommaso, came to him and told him a courier had arrived bearing papers that needed his immediate attention, concerning his coronation. In his youth and trustfulness, he followed the man out."

The room is silent. Not so much as the rustle of a silk gown or crackle of the floor rushes mars the stillness. I wonder if anyone is breathing, so intent are they all upon this story of trust and treachery. I am fascinated myself; only the memory of Tomasso's desperate eyes when he begged my husband's help keeps me from falling completely under the spell of this written account given to my husband. I do not doubt the facts, only their interpretation.

"No sooner had the young duke left his bedchamber than he saw a group of armed men waiting for him. He would have fled, but his faithless servant leaped to close and bolt the door, barring his escape. The traitors seized him, overpowering the duke by their numbers. They covered his mouth to prevent him summoning help and tore his hair, his clothes and beat him savagely, leaving the bruises we all witnessed. They dragged him to his balcony, and hung him from it with the rope they had brought, while others, waiting below, leaped to grab his legs and pull him as he hung there, hastening his death."

When Charles has finished, no one speaks. I raise my hand to my neck, half-expecting to find a noose, so real and immediate do these events seem, only two days after the terrible deed.

"Who…" Marguerite clears her throat as though she too, feels the noose there. As well she might if she is not more cautious.

"Who has he named as his accomplices?" I ask before she can, because everyone knows my husband spoke up for Andrew, we had nothing to gain by his death.

Charles turns from Marguerite back to me. "He would not name them," he says. "But he will be tortured again, publicly, tomorrow. God willing we will learn the names of all those involved in this horrible crime." He looks again at Marguerite, who averts her eyes, picking up her sewing again with hands that tremble.

"Who is questioning him, my Lord Duke?" one of the young nobles asks.

I hold my breath. The question hangs in the air, strangling me. *Not one of Andrew's court!* If there were time to pray between the question and the answer I would fall to my knees and press my cross to my lips, but I can only think, Dear Lord, dear Holy Mother Mary and all the saints and angels, not the Hungarians who hate us…

"Lord Charles of Artois and the Count of Terlizzi."

I let out my breath in a gasp. So great is my relief that I am dizzy. I sway in my chair, lean forward quickly, and vomit onto the rushes.

I hear them before I see them. The yells and jeering of the crowd lining the narrow streets rise in an oncoming wave as the cart approaches the wider main road where Charles has brought me. We are all—the lords and ladies of the court—crowded onto the balconies of the dwellings that line this road, their owners mingling with the crowd so that we may watch from above.

I stand away from the balcony edge. Charles leans over it to see the cart as soon as it turns onto our road. I had hoped to be excused from this after my embarrassing deportment yesterday, but Charles insists we be seen. The cloud of suspicion that has fallen over everyone at court here in Aversa is so great that I do not argue. Anyone might be dragged off for questioning. I would be eager to go into my confinement where no one will think of me if it were not that I am as desperate as I am terrified to know who will be proclaimed guilty of the foul act. I hear the nervous whinny of a horse, the rumble of wagon wheels, the roar of the crowd below me. The cart turns onto our street. I cannot help myself, I push forward, grabbing the railing of the balcony so tightly it hurts, and strain to see.

The horse tosses its head, throwing foam from its lips as it fights the bit. The excited crowd of townsfolk pressing around it, yelling and throwing rotted fruit at the prisoner inside the cart, has terrified it and the driver strains to hold it from bolting. Inside the iron cage behind the driver a man is standing with his back and head bent, his legs and arms chained to opposite ends of the cage so that he is spread-eagled, standing as upright as the ceiling of the cage makes possible. Behind the cage, at the end of the wagon bed, a torturer dressed in black leggings and tunic holds a pair of iron pincers. Charles of Artois rides beside the wagon on his massive black stallion, shouting questions to the prisoner concerning the details of the plot.

The man in the cage—Tommaso—neither answers nor looks up in response to Charles' questions. I watch the torturer dip his pincers into a cauldron of hot coals beside him, and thrust the sizzling end through the bars of the cage to seize Tommaso's flesh. An inhuman, gurgling cry which makes my flesh crawl comes from Tommaso.

I would not recognize him as the man I saw only weeks ago. His hair is no longer fair, but filthy and wet—I realize the red tint is his blood, which covers his limbs and the tattered loin cloth over his maleness. His arms, legs and torso are scorched and bleeding from the burning pincers. I look away, feeling my gorge rise, but cannot help looking back when Charles of Artois shouts another question: "Who were your accomplices? Speak up and your death will be merciful and swift."

I cannot imagine how he dares ask, unless my suspicions are wrong? Let it be someone else, I pray, my hands gripping the balcony rail and my eyes fixed on Tommaso's bent head. Slowly he raises his head, until he is staring at Charles of Artois with a look so full of hatred and—loathing? betrayal?—No, I must be wrong, it is only suffering, his agony has eclipsed all other emotions, he is not even trying to answer the questions.

"You refuse to speak? You will not tell us their names?" Charles of Artois roars. The crowd bellows its outrage in response as the torturer applies the pincers. Tommaso opens his mouth and the terrible, eerie noise pours forth again. There is something wrong, but I am too occupied in swallowing the gorge that rises in my throat, to know what it is…

"It is all a show," my husband says, his voice low for my ears only. "He has his tongue cut out. He cannot confess anyone's name, even if he wants to. It is a spectacle to appease the people, to give them a villain to blame and a pretense of justice. The Queen will never yield up those who are truly guilty, nor let men like this confess their names."

"Stop!" My voice, a fierce whisper, surprises him. I am gripping the railing so tightly my hands are white, but I raise my head and look him in the eye. "Say no more, my Lord. You speak treason."

A look comes over Charles' face, an expression both proud and fierce, as I imagine he must look in battle before he kills a man. I never thought such a look would be turned on me, but I do not look away, or lower my eyes. I am speaking as a royal princess, to a duke. He looks at me a moment longer, then turns his head. He is silent, but I have not won. I have lost a great deal. I fear we will never get back what I have lost, but at least he is silent, watching the wagon pass down the street below us and around the next corner with its cruel parody of justice.

Despite my sister's army of letters, another army of words moves faster: rumor. Andrew's nursemaid, Isabelle the Hungarian, sent her son Nicholas, on the very day of Andrew's murder, to inform the Dowager Queen of Hungary of her son's death. We have barely returned to Castle Durazzo in Naples when Margherita comes to my room, pale-faced and trembling, to tell me she has heard people talking of Queen Joanna as blushing and averting her dry eyes in shame when she was told of the murder, of her hiding away from her people out of guilt.

"Who says so?" I cry, and before she can answer, "They lie! The Queen is innocent. I was there!" *Not when he died*, a little voice inside me whispers.

"Domenico da Gravina and Giovanni Villani, the most respected chroniclers in Florence, are saying these things."

"It is not true," I insist, but I am shaken. I remember my sister, frozen in the doorway of her room, as pale as a ghost. Surprise and shock? Or guilt at being caught?

"What will you do?" I asked her, the night our grandfather died. "Whatever I must," she said. "I will keep the oath I made this night, whatever it requires of me. Before God, I will be sole ruler of my kingdom!"

Is it possible?

No, it is not. Joanna would never condone murder. She is ambitious, but not ruthless. I have seen ruthless, in my cousins, in my own husband. But never in my sister. She prays with the same devotion our grandmother had, she washes the feet of the poor at Easter, she is devoted to God and to His Church. I know she would never do such a thing, or allow it to happen if she had known. But who else knows her as I do?

I think of her shut in her chamber in Aversa, writing her letters, instead of returning to Naples with her husband's body. Instead of being there when he was interred at the Cathedral of Naples, as we were there when our grandfather was interred at Santa Chiara. She has treated this as a political calamity instead of a personal one, and no one is blind to that.

Margherita is looking at me, no doubt wondering at my silence. "How do they know in Florence what happened here?" I demand.

"Nicholas the Hungarian stopped in Florence on his way to Hungary. Apparently, they are spreading the story he told."

His story. Because he was here. And that is the version he will take to the Hungarian court. "Does Her Majesty know? Has anyone told her what he is saying?"

Margherita lowers her eyes. “I am sure I do not know what Her Majesty the Queen knows.” I snap my fingers, impatient with her bitterness at still being excluded from court. “But everyone else knows it,” she adds. “I do not see how she could not.”

“It is a lie.”

She does not look at me.

“Margherita, it is a lie. I was there, that night. And you know Her Majesty, you grew up with her. Do you think she would do this?”

“No…” Margherita says. She sighs, as though reluctant to give up the titillating story.

“Be certain to say so if anyone else whispers these lies to you! They are not only false, but treasonous.” I almost add, remember the axe and the stake: that is what we have all escaped by his death. But I stop myself, for words can be repeated, and anyone can be accused of doing what needed doing.

I have to hope Joanna’s army of missives will prevail. There is nothing more I can do. I have already delayed going into my confinement as long as I can. I must do nothing to endanger the life of the son I pray I am carrying, for if Joanna has a girl, my son may still be the next King of Naples.

Chapter 26

Wolves at the Gate

A girl. I look down at my daughter sleeping in her cradle, and wonder if my mother felt this way about me, a second daughter when a son was needed. Charles has been notified but has sent no word. As the days pass, I realize there will be none: no congratulations, no message of relief and joy that I and our daughter are safely through childbirth, not even any instructions as to her name. I am ill with regret. My husband's silence, the silence of all the Durazzos—except loyal Margherita who has left her own family to come into confinement with me—is physically painful to me. I almost miss my critical mother-in-law, who would most certainly have come to see the baby, complaining about her all the while and my inadequacy in producing boys. She would have insisted on naming her over my objections. Even that would have been better than silence, as though it is not worth the Durazzo family's time to choose a name for this unwanted girl.

When Margherita arrives to take her to be baptized in the castle chapel—no public ceremony followed by a feast for this baby—she tells me my daughter is to be named Agnes, for her grandmother. This is unwelcome news, but as I lift her from her cradle to hand to Margherita, my daughter looks at me and purses her mouth, as though she is sharing a private joke with me. I cannot help but smile. She is a pretty little thing, and contented with her lot regardless of the lack of festivity over her arrival. She rarely cries, but eats well and sleeps soundly and entertains herself when she is awake with watching everything in her small world. She will make a good, obedient wife, I think a little sadly. It is a virtue I seem unable to master.

When they return, I ask to have little Joanna brought to my confinement room to see her sister. The nurse arrives, sour-faced, and sets her down reluctantly. I hold out my arms and experience the joy of having my daughter stagger eagerly into them. I lift her onto my lap and present her sister, sleeping in the cradle. Joanna examines Agnes critically. For a moment I think she, too, is disappointed by a girl, but Joanna is too young to know her sex is a detriment. She smiles and says with satisfaction, "I am much bigger."

"Yes, you are. You will have to take care of little Agnes, and protect her, because you are the oldest." And all that comes with that, I think, feeling for the first time a tender sympathy for my new daughter, who will always be the second girl.

In mid-November I am churched and leave my confinement.

"The Tarantos have won," are Charles' first, curt words to me as we sit together at dinner. No time wasted asking after his new daughter, or my well-being. His expression is cold and he looks away from me. For him, I was a gamble—one that has not paid off, I think with a heavy heart.

"What have they won?" My calm response belies the fear I always feel when Charles is displeased with me.

"The crown of Naples!"

For a moment I cannot speak. Have they killed my sister as they killed Andrew? And stolen my crown for themselves?

I catch my breath. Even in confinement I would have heard of an armed attack on Naples—and it would have required an armed rebellion to put my Taranto cousins in power. My husband would have done battle to keep my inheritance, and the people of Naples would have risen up—they love Queen Joanna. Even if the idea of a woman driven to have her husband killed fascinates them, even if it makes them shiver and cross themselves, they know it is only a story. They know what Andrew was, they know they would have suffered under him, and they know Joanna loves her subjects as much as Andrew despised them.

My relief is short-lived. There is only one way the Tarantos can have secured the crown without a battle; only one possibility that would make Charles look at me as though I am an obstacle in his way.

"Who?" I ask, but I already know the answer. "Louis." She has always favored him. Charles would never have had a chance, even if he had waited instead of marrying me. Now Joanna has everything: a husband she loves, the Kingdom of Naples, and an heir in her belly. And I, what do I have? A nursery of girls and a husband who will never make me a queen. I look up at Charles, wondering whether I still have a husband who loves me, and realize he is talking.

"…Robert of Taranto is boasting all over Naples that the Queen has asked Clement VI for a dispensation to marry again."

"Robert of Taranto?" Why would Robert be boasting? I could tell him how little it means to be the sibling of the monarch.

"Robert." Charles nods, as though I have confirmed his very thoughts. "This proves his complicity in King Andrew's murder."

"You think Lord Robert killed the duke in order to further his brother's ambition?" I stare at Charles stupidly. Surely he knows our cousin Robert better than that. Robert would not stir himself to save his own mother, let alone to help a younger brother. I remember a time when we were all young, and Louis beat Robert in an archery tournament. Robert immediately turned his bow upon his younger brother. If my grandfather, King Robert, had not roared at young Robert of Taranto to disarm himself, Louis would never have seen his thirteenth birthday.

"Brother? What brother? Are your wits addled from your women's time? I am speaking of Robert, not his brothers. Robert of Taranto has written to Clement VI for a dispensation to marry Queen Joanna, and she has also petitioned the Pope to marry him!"

"Marry Robert? She cannot marry Robert! He is an arrogant, ruthless… monster!"

"Well, we are agreed on that, at least."

"You must be mistaken, my Lord. It is impossible. Joanna would never agree—"

"There is no mistake. The situation is plain and simple. Lord Robert has moved into Castle Nuovo with a large number of his men—the rest are to be seen everywhere, in the city, outside the castle—"

"Moved in? On who's authority? Not Joanna's, never by her invitation. She has been coerced, forced to—" I cannot finish, I am choking on my own words.

"Are you still so naïve, Maria? Men do not await a woman's invitation. You should know that from our own marriage." He laughs.

Joanna's warning echoes again in my head: *He has made us vulnerable. He has made it possible for men to lay hands on those God anoints to rule them.* What have I done? A single thoughtless action, the giddy consent of a young girl who imagined herself in love… And what has it led to? Where will it end?

I was just a child, I could not have foreseen this, a desperate voice in my head pleads.

Joanna would have, the answer comes. Joanna would have understood the consequences at any age; Joanna has always thought like a queen.

And now, if I would help her, I must think like one also. Why would the Queen of Naples allow Robert to move into Castle Nuovo with his men?

It is not thinking like a queen that helps me, but thinking like a new mother. How helpless we are, praying for our life and the life of the child we carry, as we enter those rooms. And if the Hungarians should come to claim Andrew's throne while she is shut away? Robert is the wealthiest duke in the kingdom, he can summon an army among his vassals large enough to defend Naples until Joanna is churched and able to order up her own army once again.

But Robert's army is loyal to Robert. What if the real enemy is within? Robert has always frightened me. How much worse must it be for Joanna, locked in her confinement where her guards cannot reach her, with no protector?

"Who has gone into confinement with her?"

"Isabelle the Hungarian."

I am stunned to silence. Andrew's nurse. She despises Joanna. Her son is responsible for half the rumors of Joanna's culpability in Andrew's death. What is my sister thinking, to put herself in the hands of her enemy when she is most vulnerable?

The answer comes to me at once. It is because of Robert. She is afraid he might harm the babe, making way for his own offspring to inherit the throne when he has forced her to wed him. I imagine my sister torn between these two devils, surrounded by those who despise her and whom she despises as she awaits the most dangerous hours of childbirth.

I jump up from my chair. "I must go to her at once."

Charles smiles slowly. I am disgusted to see it. Another wolf laying plots to trap my sister. But Joanna is no lamb for their taking, she is a queen in every way; they will all learn that.

"I will stay with her for the rest of her confinement." I do not wait for Charles' permission. I am afraid if I hesitate at all, I will change my mind. I am walking into a den of wolves, they will not hesitate to attack me if I get in their way. But Joanna is my sister: a bond that can never be broken. I call for my maid to pack my things and prepare herself to come with me.

"If you think it best," Charles says, looking smug, as though my decision was all his idea. And perhaps it was. Perhaps he led me to it. I have never been the cleverest one among the Angevins. But it does not matter. Joanna needs me. Isabelle the Hungarian and Robert of Taranto! Circling her like hawks assessing their prey. But I will be there soon. If anything should happen to my sister or her child, it will be God's doing and no one else's, I will make certain of that.

Charles smiles at me. I know what he is thinking: if it is God's will to take her, I will be right there, beside her, to catch my crown as it falls from her head, before another can steal it. Just as Charles intended I should be.

Robert will try to kill me before he will let Charles take the throne, if it comes to that. Has my husband thought of that?

"But will they let you go in to her?" Charles muses.

I snort. Robert most likely fears Isabelle the Hungarian will kill Joanna before she will let Robert of Taranto marry her, and Isabelle no doubt fears Robert will try to kill Andrew's child, especially if it is a boy. I cannot imagine Joanna trusts either one. I am the balance that each of them will count on to hold the other in check. And if God should weigh in, I will be the proof that He did not have human hands helping Him.

"They will let me," I say. "Joanna will insist upon it. In a way that will be remembered should I be refused and anything happen."

"Go to your sister, with my blessing," Charles says grandly. I study his face. He smiles blandly at me. Yes, he is aware of the risk to me, and worse, he thinks I have not realized it. I turn away with a heavy heart. Once again he is gambling, and I am his pawn. Nevertheless, I am going not at Charles' bidding, but on my own. But his smirk is annoying, so I snap, "See that little Agnes is well-cared for, while I am seeing to the Crown of Naples."

He deliberately misunderstands me; I see it at once in his broad smile.

I should have said, the Queen of Naples, not the crown. He knows well enough that is what I meant, that they are the same thing. And yet he smiles that complicit smile, and any denial I offer now will only make him laugh.

Chapter 27

A Royal Heir

Robert himself comes to greet me when I am announced at the door to Castle Nuovo. No doubt he wishes to make certain my husband's escort returns to Castle Durazzo and I enter alone with my maid. My legs shake as I curtsy to him, the smallest bend possible. He bows his head as though he is Lord of the castle. I walk straight and proud past him, but he sees through the act and smiles tauntingly at me before he leaves.

Isabelle the Hungarian peers at me suspiciously from behind the confessional grate when I arrive at the entrance to Joanna's birthing rooms. No doubt she enjoys the power she has had over Joanna's confinement until now. She frowns at me, but she, too, allows me in.

Joanna turns to see who has come. Her face lights up. She opens her arms and I run into them.

"I have only just been churched," I apologize. "Else I would have come sooner."

Joanna smiles though her eyes are moist, with a look I have never seen on her face. I have no more than a quick glimpse of her vulnerability before she straightens and forces the weakness away. "Yes, I have heard. Congratulations. What have you named her?"

"Agnes. She is healthy and thriving. And very pretty," I add defensively.

"I am certain she is. The Duke of Durazzo is handsome and you are beautiful. My beautiful sister, I am so happy you have come." She says this quietly enough, but I have never heard Joanna speak so effusively. Then she laughs shakily and calls for a servant to bring us food and drink.

That night I sleep with my sister as we have not done since our childhood; her lady-in-waiting must sleep with Isabelle the Hungarian and my maid in the outer room. When we are alone together I ask her, quietly, "I have heard you are to marry Lord Robert, Duke of Taranto?"

"I will never marry him!" Her voice is low and fierce. I do not answer, but wait for whatever she wishes to tell me. Under the covers, she touches my hand, and I impulsively grasp hers. We lie there holding hands as though we were children again, alone together in a frightening new place.

"I am helpless in here," she whispers in the darkness for only my ears. "I cannot meet with my councilors or pass laws or even order the palace guards to close the gates and man the walls if it should become necessary. I am dependent on others' eyes and ears to know what is happening in my kingdom. Louis of Hungary is threatening war if Andrew's murderers are not caught and publicly executed. What if they come while I am in here? They would eagerly take Naples from me, and this is their chance."

"They would not break the treaty!"

"They accuse me of sheltering Andrew's murderers."

This is so close to my own suspicions I hesitate before I answer. "Have the two cardinals appointed by Clement VI made any progress in their investigation?"

"They have not even arrived!" Her low, harsh whisper is laced with frustration. "I believed an investigation by the Curia would prove the result impartial and satisfy King Louis and his mother, but this delay just makes me look worse. They claim I am the one putting off the rightful punishment of my husband's murderers. The war between England and France has distracted the Holy Father from our troubles, but Louis of Hungary is not distracted!"

"Lord Robert is defending your kingdom while you are in confinement. But what will you do when your child is born and he expects an engagement? What will you do when His Holiness sends you permission to marry Lord Robert?"

"He will not."

"He gave Lord Charles permission to marry me."

"Not because we are cousins. Because…" she hesitates. I am stung by her distrust, but I know I have earned it. I am about to release her hand, and tell her she need not confide in me, when she says, "…because I have sent a secret emissary instructing him… asking him not to permit it."

I feel her shift in the bed beside me. More to it than that, I tell myself, but this time she remains silent.

"Well," I force myself to speak lightly, "your enemies will not get through Lord Robert's men—I have seen them guarding the castle. So let us sleep soundly under his protection and toast his ignorance at every meal."

"His ignorance or his arrogance?"

"Both, for each is the cause of the other." We laugh softly in the darkness together. Her hand releases mine gently under the cover, and she rolls over laboriously. In a few moments her breathing lengthens into sleep.

Why did she not call on Charles, her brother-in-law, to protect her instead of Robert? I wonder in the darkness. But I am relieved. If Robert is here at Joanna's invitation, to protect her during her confinement, he will have to leave when she is churched and able to take command again. And he will willingly do so if he expects a future engagement. The delay will not alert him. If the Pope takes three months—or more—to send his cardinals to investigate the shocking murder of a prince, one can hardly expect him to give permission for a marriage in less time. And they must wait the proper period of mourning, in order not to insult the Hungarians. I close my eyes, reassured enough to sleep.

Joanna rises early as she always does. I hear her murmuring at the prayer station in the corner of the room. I crack open one eye. She is kneeling on her prayer pillow. But it is still dark—or at least not fully light yet—so I lie a while longer with my eyes closed...

When I wake again Joanna is sitting at her desk, composing a letter. I watch her for a moment. One would not know her as the same pale woman who greeted me last night. Her eyes are bright and determined, her back straight, her head held high as she writes her message.

"Good morning," she says, although I have not moved or spoken to indicate that I am awake. "I have had an excellent idea. I am writing to ask Clement VI to be my child's godfather." She looks across the room at me, in command once more. "Whatever happens, no one will harm the godchild of His Holiness the Pope."

I sit up at once. I had expected we would be the child's godparents. Joanna is my little Joanna's godmother. "God will not allow anyone to harm your child, the rightful heir to a Christian throne."

She gives me a twisted smile, as if to say we both know by now that God allows many things we would not have imagined He would.

Still, she is strong and confident, her natural self again. How it must have weighed on her, for her to be so changed at the thought of finding a strong ally. "It is a fine idea, but you need not look so far afield for support, sister," I tell her. "I am here to make sure no harm befalls you or the child. And Duke Charles has sworn to protect your child, as well."

"I know why you are here, Maria. And words cannot express how much comfort I take in your presence. But you will have to go home to your husband when this is over, and that is as it should be." She returns to her letter, leaving me to wonder whether I have been thanked or put in my place. Both, I decide, as I climb out of bed and call for my maid to help me wash and dress. Joanna finishes her letter and entrusts it to one of her own palace guards.

I miss my daughters and my husband, but other than that our days are easier than I dared hope. We live in our little cocoon almost able to forget that we are surrounded by armed guards keeping us in as much as they keep our enemies out. Minstrels sing carols outside the Queen's confinement rooms, and the palace jesters dance and juggle sticks and balls for our entertainment as December progresses. I read for Joanna and sew a fine shirt for Charles, and a little gown for each of my daughters. With every stitch I miss them more. Agnes will be unaware of all the Yuletide preparations, but Joanna is old enough to notice, this year. I wish I could be there to see the wonder in her face. What if Charles forgets to send some little treats to the nursery when there is a feast, or to let her watch the mummers just a short while? He may not think of it.

Well, she will see them next year, I console myself with a sigh, and I will be there with her. I close my eyes and say a quick prayer, for spirits are tempted to interfere when humans imagine they control their future.

When they bring us the Yule log, I cannot help but think of my first confinement and my son. How he stared at the Yule fire! As though he must absorb as much delight as possible in the few days that he had.

I shake my head and try not to think of him. It will call bad luck down on Joanna's child to bring memories of my poor lost babe into her birthing rooms. I pray for Virgin Mary, a mother herself, to strengthen the soul of my sister's child that it should not be tempted to follow the path of my son.

In fact, I pray much of the time. Underneath our false Christmas cheer there is a growing tension. No one knows what will happen when Joanna's child is born. The Hungarians, for now, appear to be waiting, as is our cousin Robert. All the Angevins wait, watching, ready for… what? Like a dry woods in summer, all of Naples waits in hope that this birth will redeem us, and in fear that it may be the spark of lightning that destroys us. What if Joanna dies? Will Taranto step aside for Durazzo? Will Robert try to murder me and take the throne? What if the child dies? What will King Louis of Hungary do then?

I pray for my husband, for my little girls, and all my family. Secretly, I pray Joanna will have a girl. After all, I may have a boy myself next year, and it would be disloyal to him to pray for my sister to have an heir ahead of him. But most fervently, I pray for my sister's safe passage through childbirth, and her infant's healthy birth. For no spark of lightning to strike our kingdom. Day and night I pray that we may all come through this, while I am sewing and listening to the musicians, while I am eating, even in my sleep I wake up dreaming a prayer for our safety. There are those who are praying for the opposite, praying for a lightning opportunity, perhaps my husband among them. I pray constantly, hoping God and all the saints will hear my prayers above theirs.

Joanna receives Pope Clement's answer in a letter brought to us by the same loyal guard. She breaks the seal with trembling hands and reads it quickly. I watch her face and see the emotions she tries to control, but I do not know whether the tears that gather in her eyes are from relief or disappointment, until she looks up and says: "He will be godfather to my child!" She crumples the letter and throws it onto the fire.

I express my delight, we all do, smiling at her joyous relief, our eyes on her as she laughs with happiness. Not one of us allows herself to glance at the burning parchment. Clement VI will make the announcement himself when the child is born.

On Christmas Eve, Joanna goes into labor. The midwife and her assistant bustle around her, ordering rosewater to moisten her brow and arms, helping her walk between contractions. When the sky begins to lighten, the midwife sends a maid to alert Joanna's court that the time is near. Joanna's councilors and officers, led by Robert, come to the outer receiving room, followed by the ladies of the court, who stand at the entrance to the birthing room as witnesses. We are all awed by the timing; the Queen's child will share the birth day of Our Holy Savior. Surely God is blessing this birth.

Joanna bites on the leather they have given her, and holds my hand so tightly I fear she will crush it as I stand beside her bed murmuring reassurance, but she does not scream.

As Christmas morning breaks, the royal infant emerges into the midwife's hands. The silence is so heavy I am certain every breath is being held as the midwife's assistant cuts the cord and the midwife runs her finger around the inside of the child's mouth to clear it, and holds the naked babe high for all to see. With a lusty wail, the heir to the throne greets the most powerful nobles of his kingdom.

"A healthy prince," the midwife calls for those who are not close enough to see him and note his little manhood. The succession to the throne of the Kingdom of Naples is assured.

"He will be baptized tomorrow," Joanna says to me as the midwife hands her son to the wet nurse. "Tell them to begin making the arrangements. The Bishop of Cavaillon, chancellor of the realm, will perform the ceremony. Tell the Bishop Pope Clement VI is to be his godfather."

When I return, the infant has finished suckling and lies in Joanna's arms in his little gown and a clean clout. I look down at him, my sister's son, so tiny in her arms. Not so long ago we were children too, his mother and I. Joanna is nineteen now, and I am seventeen. We have survived more than we could ever have imagined when we were children together in this castle, and we are not safe yet. How long it seems since we were children together.

"Charles Martel," Joanna murmurs.

I start at hearing the name she has given her son, his great-grandfather's name, King Robert's oldest brother. It is a tribute to his father's line, and a reminder to his uncle, King Louis of Hungary, that we have kept the terms of the contract made by his father and our grandfather when Joanna married Andrew. When this Charles Martel takes the throne of Naples—the throne his grandfather King Carobert should have had according to our Hungarian cousins—our two kingdoms will be joined and we will have peace at last.

That is, if Joanna can maintain the delicate balance between our arrogant, ambitious Angevin cousins, Hungarian and Neapolitan alike, long enough for Charles Martel to grow up.

"Sleep well," I whisper to the drowsy prince, his lips pursed and soft with his nurse's milk. His brows pucker into a little frown, as if he knows his childhood, like ours, will end too soon.

Author's Note

The people and main events in this story are historically accurate. I have invented their conversations and a few minor entertainments, such as the masque and Maria's dance with Charles, although all the feasts, including their engagement feast, did occur. Occasionally, I have placed people where they might not have been, most notably Maria being present at Joanna's court when major events took place. She may have been there or not, but she was in Naples, and it is very likely she was part of Joanna's court, so I consider it a small liberty. I have tried to portray Naples in the 14th century as accurately as I can, through extensive research and personally visiting Castle Nuovo and the churches in Naples that Joanna would have gone to. However, it is still likely I have made some errors, for which I beg my readers' indulgence. The 15th Century picture of Naples on the back cover shows Castle Nuovo (the large white one) where Joanna and Maria lived, and Castle del'Ovo (the round tower built out onto the water), which served as an impregnable retreat in times of war.

Enjoy the continuation of the story of Queen Joanna's reign in my novels, The Girl Who Tempted Fortune and The Queen Who Sold Her Crown, books 2 and 3 of The Kingdom of Naples series.

Acknowledgements

I'm grateful for the help and support I've had from so many people for my writing and for this book specifically. Thanks to my husband, Ian, for taking me to Naples to do my research, to my family and my early readers, Amanda, Linda, Lori, and Barbara –your comments made this book much better. Also thanks to agent Carrie Pestritto for her sage suggestions, and to my cover artist Heather and interior designer Chris Morgan

About the Author

Jane Ann McLachlan was born in Toronto, Canada, and currently lives with her husband, author Ian Darling, in Waterloo, Ontario. They spend most days sitting in their separate dens typing on their laptops, each working on their next book. When they get out it's usually to do research.

Between books, Jane Ann enjoys gardening, quilting, travel, spending time with family, and getting away from the cold Canadian winters. She is addicted to story, and reads just about any kind of book, but she writes mostly historical fiction set in the Middle Ages and young adult science fiction and fantasy.

You can learn more about her novels and joining her launch team on her author website: www.janeannmclachlan.com

Find resources for creative writing on her website for writers: www.downriverwriting.com